The Late Greats

Nick Quantrill

Nick
Quantrill

Having been convinced by their manager, Kane Major, to put their acrimonious break-up behind them and launch a comeback, 'New Holland' Hull's most successful band of the 1990s is reforming. Allowing one privileged journalist to document the process...

Joe Geraghty is employed to act as a liaison between the different camps. What appears to be a straightforward assignment sees him neck deep in trouble when singer, Greg Tasker, disappears leaving behind a trail of people who wanted him out of their lives. Having to choose sides, the investigation penetrates deeper into the city, and as the rich and famous rub shoulders with the poor and vulnerable, the stakes increase. Forced to keep his friends close but his enemies closer still, the case could see Geraghty lose everything.

The Late
Greats

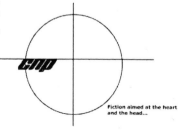

Fiction aimed at the heart
and the head...

Published by Caffeine Nights Publishing 2012

Copyright © Nick Quantrill 2012

Nick Quantrill has asserted his right under the Copyright, Designs and Patents Act 1998 to be identified as the author of this work

CONDITIONS OF SALE

Published in Great Britain by Caffeine Nights Publishing

www.cnpublishing.co.uk

British Library Cataloguing in Publication Data.
A CIP catalogue record for this book is available from the British Library

ISBN: 978-1-907565-18-2

Cover design by
Mark (Wills) Williams

Photography of the Humber Bridge
Courtesy of
Nick Triplow

Everything else by
Default, Luck and Accident

The Late Greats............... Nick Quantrill

Also by Nick Quantrill

Broken Dreams

Rotherham MBC	
B54 014 153 3	
Askews & Holts	19-Sep-2016
AF	£8.99
BSU	

Dedication:

For Cathy and Alice

Acknowledgments:

As ever, writing this has not been a one man show. I owe a debt of gratitude to many people.

Darren Laws, Mark Williams and Julie Lewthwaite at Caffeine Nights for all their help which often goes beyond the call of duty.

My Mum for all her support and help. And that to come.

Mac for his continued willingness to read early drafts and help me improve the book with his eye for detail.

Stephany NJC for her unstinting support.

Richard Sutherland for all his organisational help at Hull Truck and pretty much anywhere else I've pitched up over the last two years.

Jason Goodwin for continuously coming to my rescue when I make a mess of updating my website.

Ian Ayris, Paul Brazill, Col Bury, Andy Rivers and all the other writers behind the many excellent crime websites who've interviewed me, plugged me and offered the hand of friendship. It's appreciated.

Drop me a line here:
www.hullcrimefiction.co.uk

The Late Greats

You flush the toilet. You've been sick. Nerves. All the hours in the rehearsal room haven't prepared you for this moment. How could they? The Adelphi is like being in someone's front room. It's so small. Maybe thirty people in, but it's enough to make it look busy. You're the first band on tonight. The other two bands look like men compared to you. You see them laughing and joking with each other. They're relaxed. You know they're far better than you are. You find the rest of the band. You smile, but you still feel sick in the pit of your stomach. You can tell Priestley is every bit as nervous as you are. You met a few months ago at university, answering his advert for a vocalist and songwriter. He's a couple of years younger than you, but despite your reservations, you believe in him. You've bonded with him. It's maybe ten paces from the bar to the stage, but every one of them feels like a mile. You're on stage. It's lit up, but you can't see any of the faces in the crowd. You don't want to see any of the faces in the crowd. You mumble into the microphone, announce that you're New Holland. Your voice sounds quiet. You assume the microphone is working. You glance at Priestley. He's ready. You count the band in. Your first gig.

CHAPTER ONE

Kane Major did nothing quietly. His entrance attracted a buzz of attention at the bar. People knew who he was. Arrogance and false sincerity dripped off the man. Like family, it's a fact you can't pick your clients. He made his way to where we were standing. Even during the afternoon, the Princes Avenue cafe-bars were busy. Still the place to be seen.

'Julia, always nice to see you' he said. I watched him kiss her on both cheeks. It wasn't the way we did things here. 'I trust PI's being a good boy and giving you all the help you need?' He held out a £20 note to me. 'Be a love and get the drinks in.'

I didn't care for his tone, but I was glad to get away. I called myself a Private Investigator, and although this job was a little unusual, I would be earning every penny. Major was reforming New Holland, the band he'd managed during the 1990s. Hull's not had many musical success stories to boast of, but fronted by Greg Tasker, these had been the exception. He'd invited Julia Gowans to document the process for her newspaper. She was going to be there from the early rehearsals right through to the comeback tour. It was important coverage. My role was to act as a buffer between her and the band.

'I was just telling Julia how well the rehearsal went' he said to me when I returned. 'They sounded fucking great, didn't they?'

I nodded. I'd spent most of the morning sat in the rehearsal room, bored, waiting for something to do. Seemingly, I was the odd-job man.

'I can't wait to hear them again' Julia said before turning to Major. 'But Joe was telling me you've employed him to keep an eye on me.'

'It's not like that' he said.

I said nothing. I was keeping out of it.

Julia let it go. 'I thought Greg was joining us' she said.

'He's not feeling too good' said Major.

'I need to talk to him again. A bit more for the article I'm working on.'

Major shrugged. 'I'll sort it.'

I felt like a gooseberry. They lapsed into talk about their lives in London, discussing mutual friends and swapping gossip. I zoned them out and we finished our drinks. Major told me to take Julia to her hotel, so she could check in. I bit my lip. I'd do as I was told for now. He allowed her to head for the exit first. Once she was out of sight, he pulled me back. 'Have you heard from Tasker yet?'

I said I hadn't. There'd been no sign of him at the morning's rehearsal. He passed me a piece of paper. It had addresses for Tasker's studio and his girlfriend's boutique on it.

'You best find him, PI' he said to me. 'And find him quickly.'

We hurried back to my car and followed the one way system back onto Princes Avenue.

'Why does it always rain when I'm back in Hull?' Julia said.

I shrugged and concentrated on the road. We were heading for her hotel. I turned left off Princes Avenue and onto Spring Bank, towards the city centre. The afternoon drinkers sat under canopies gave way to young men huddled around shop doorways. Signs I couldn't read. Some were Arabic, some were Eastern European. Julia was a little younger than me, mid-thirties, attractive, with a glint in her eye which drew you in. It was dangerous, seeing as she was a journalist.

'It's just nice to get out of London for a while' she said.

'Catch up with some old friends?'

'Not exactly' she said, before going quiet on me. I concentrated on the road until I pulled into the hotel car park and switched the engine off.

'Does Kane think he's being funny calling you PI all of the time?'

'He's paying. He can call me what he likes.'

She turned the conversation back to New Holland and asked me what my job title was.

'I'm just another pair of eyes and ears for the band, that's all; make sure things run smoothly.'

'Keep me at arm's length, you mean.'

'Not at all.' I hoped I sounded convincing. 'You've got a decent story, haven't you?'

'Definitely. Bands reform all the time, but New Holland are different. If I can go behind the scenes and get the real story, from the first rehearsals to the comeback gig, it'll be really interesting.' She smiled at me. 'I just have to make sure you don't stop me.'

I smiled back. 'I'm here to help.'

'Good, because I'm not here to play Kane's childish games.' She paused. 'Want to tell me about your position within his little empire?'

'I'm just the hired help' I repeated.

'You're a hard man to get anything out of' she said, laughing. 'I understand. You're obviously not allowed to tell me.'

Daring me to say something. 'You'll have to do better than that. Oldest trick in the book.'

'So what makes you suitable for working on this job?'

'I said I'd do it. Simple as that.'

'Keeping your cards close to your chest, I like that.'

'I knew Tasker when he was a kid.'

'Really?'

I nodded. 'My dad knew his dad. Rugby team-mates back in the day.'

'You're older than him, though?'

'We weren't really mates. He was just a kid who'd appear every now and again.'

'Does Kane know?'

I nodded and concentrated on the road. That was the sum of it. I'm a few years older than Tasker, and that kind of thing is important when you're a child. Kane had laughed when I'd told him, but he seemed to think it was a good thing.

Julia changed the subject. 'You don't look like a rugby player to me.'

She'd done her homework on me and knew my background. I was impressed. 'Retired. I'm too old now.'

She laughed again. 'You know what I mean.'

'We come in all shapes and sizes.'

'I'll take your word for it.' She got out of the car. 'I'll be in touch very soon.'

I looked at the address Major had given me for Tasker's girlfriend. I hoped she'd know where he was. The boutique was out to the west of the city, on the corner of Willerby Square, hidden away amongst a plethora of estate agents and banks. I found a parking space and walked in. I don't like regular clothes shops, so this place was well out of my comfort zone. It was small, with mirrors strategically placed to suggest it was bigger than it was. The sparse rails only contained a handful of items, emphasising the place's exclusivity. I walked across to the sales assistant and asked to speak to Siobhan. When she appeared, I told her who I was. She walked me over to the door, looking for a quiet corner. She looked to be in her mid-twenties, which made her about fifteen years younger than her boyfriend. A decent age gap. She was pretty, with that highly styled look which was meant to make me think she'd made no effort at all.

'How can I help you?' she asked.

'I'm looking for Greg.'

'Aren't we all?'

'It's important.'

She looked me up and down, like she was deciding whether or not to take me seriously. 'What do you want him for?'

I told her I was working for Major.

'Haven't seen him for a couple of days' she said eventually.

'Where did you last see him?'

'At his flat. I stayed over.'

'You don't live together?'

'Never have done. Greg likes his own space.' She shrugged. 'That's way it is. I live above the shop.'

'Right.' It seemed a bit odd to me, but I let it go. 'Did he say when he'd be in touch?'

'No.'

'Care to hazard a guess?'

'No.'

I looked around the shop again before turning to her. 'Nice place you've got here.'

'It's not bad.'

I glanced at a price tag. 'No offence, but I'm surprised there's a call for it here.'

'You'd be surprised. There's plenty of money around.'

She was right. Some wealthy people lived in the city's suburbs. 'You don't sound like you're from around here' I said.

'I can see why you're a Private Investigator.'

I laughed. 'Fair point.'

It softened her. 'I'm from London. I met Greg down there when I was a fashion student. I moved up here when he decided he wanted to go back home.'

'He set you up here?'

She nodded. 'It made sense. Greg put the money up for the lease and paid for the first run of dresses.' She turned away from me and busied herself tidying the nearest rail. 'It's a bit quiet at the moment.'

I thought about the band. Tasker was very much a jeans and T-shirt kind of man. The kind of everyman touch which helped boost his popularity. I couldn't see this place being to his taste.

'I've really no idea where he is' she said again.

'Anywhere you recommend I try?'

'I really don't know.'

'What about his studio?'

'He hates the place. Look, this isn't the first time he's gone missing like this. He's done it before. He just takes off without telling anyone and then reappears a couple of days later, like nothing's happened. He always has done. It's his way of coping.'

'What about his friends?'

She turned to face me. Angry. 'You should try that slag, Lorraine.'

Siobhan had nothing further to tell me, so I headed to Tasker's recording studio. It was a small unit on an industrial park, hidden away around the back of Hessle Road on a small industrial estate. It was sandwiched between a light engineering firm and a printing company. The fishing industry may be long gone, but the area had found new uses for itself. Time never stands still. I headed straight in. The reception area was bare, more an area for dumping equipment. I shouted out, but nobody answered. The place was unlocked and silent. I didn't like the combination. To my left was a door. I walked into the main recording area. A man was slumped over the mixing desk, headphones on. I could hear music leaking out of them. I put a hand on his shoulder.

He shouted at me, sitting up. 'What are you doing?'

It wasn't Greg Tasker. 'Looking for the boss.' I sat down on a chair next to him. The mixing desk in front of me was huge, a bewildering array of switches and buttons.

'Why don't you knock like everyone else?' the man said.

I pointed to the headphones and smiled. 'You must have been in the zone.'

He took them off. 'What do you want?'

'I need to speak to Greg.'

'He's not here.'

'Know where I'll find him?'

He looked at me properly for the first time. 'Who are you? I don't talk to the press, alright?'

'I'm not the press.' I passed him a business card. 'What's your name?'

'Why?'

I held my hands up. 'Only asking.'

'Michael Rusting' he eventually said. 'Greg been a naughty boy, has he?' He smiled. 'Jealous husband, is it?' He stopped and turned away from me, like he knew he'd said too much.

I waited a few moments, but he didn't offer any more. 'I'm not interested in that stuff' I lied. 'Nothing to do with me. When did you last see him?'

'Who do you work for?' he asked.

'Kane Major.'

He considered the information. 'What does he want to speak to Greg about?'

I shrugged and played dumb. I didn't know who knew about the reunion. 'I don't ask too many questions' I said, before repeating myself. 'When did you last see him?'

'Sometime last week. He doesn't spend too much time around here. Don't see him much at all, really.'

'Got his mobile number?' I wondered if it'd match the number Major had given me.

He shook his head. 'I'm not giving you it.'

It was worth a try. 'Any idea where I might find him?'

'Have you tried his girlfriend?'

I nodded. 'Spoke to her earlier.'

'Surprised. She's usually down in London, supposedly meeting designers and buying stock. Must cost him a packet.'

'She mentioned a woman called Lorraine.'

He laughed. 'I'm not surprised. She hates her. Lorraine runs a New Holland website. Obsessed with the band.'

CHAPTER TWO

As soon as I was back at the office, I switched my laptop on. Sarah sat at her desk, hard at work. Don was on the phone. Father and daughter working in harmony.

I spoke to Sarah. 'I need to find a woman called Lorraine. She runs a New Holland website.'

'Why?'

I explained about Tasker's disappearance.

'Who is she?'

'Someone who might know where he is. His girlfriend thinks they were having an affair.'

Don had finished his call. 'This isn't the job we signed up for' he said.

'It's the job we've got now' I replied. He hadn't been keen on me taking the contract. If it went well, the work would go on for several months. And steady work wasn't to be turned down. There weren't many jobs coming in. Although Don was the senior partner, I'd made a judgment call. I knew Sarah would side with her father, but my decision was for the best. Don was old-school. I could see the bigger picture. The bank account was running on empty.

Sarah worked quickly, searching Google, until she found the website. I walked across to her desk.

She pointed at the screen. 'There you go.'

I asked Sarah to email me the link and went back to my desk. The website was basic, but up to date, the news page hinting that the band was considering reforming. Lorraine had some level of inside information. I clicked onto the contact page. Just an email address. It would have been too easy any other way. I typed out a message, asking her to contact me. It was the best I could do for now.

'You reckon he's with her?' Sarah asked me.

'Best lead I've got so far' I replied.

'Maybe he's lying low?'

'Maybe.'

We both looked up as Julia Gowans knocked on the door and walked in. Don must have left it unlocked. She was wearing jeans and a casual top, but she was carrying her laptop. She was here on business.

I smiled and said hello. 'Wasn't expecting to see you.'

Don picked his coat up and said he needed to be somewhere. I said I'd speak to him later. I turned to Sarah and shrugged. She turned away from me.

Julia spoke. 'The area hasn't changed much since I left. I must have staggered down the cobbles a fair few times when I was younger.'

Our office was in the Old Town of Hull. It sat on the edge of the city centre, nuzzled quietly up against the River Hull. In the past, warehouses lined High Street, now it was small offices and the museum quarter. The area boasted some of the city's oldest drinking places only yards from our office, but the increase in apartments and student accommodation meant the loud chain pubs were moving in. It wasn't change for the better in my eyes.

'What have you been doing?' I asked Julia.

'I've been working from the hotel. Keeping busy.'

Sarah stood up and left the room.

'What are you working on?' she asked me, taking a seat.

'This and that' I said, closing down the New Holland website.

'Heard from Kane?'

'Not since earlier.'

She leaned closer to me. 'I was hoping you might know if Greg was feeling any better.'

I smiled. 'Can't help, I'm afraid.'

'I was hoping to get to their next rehearsal' she said.

'I'm sure Kane will let you know when they're ready for you.'

'Maybe we could drop by the rehearsal room, see how they're getting on?'

'I'll see what I can do for you.'

She sat back in her chair. 'Are you a fan of the band?' she asked me.

'That would be telling' I said.

'You're a diplomat. That's good, but you don't have to worry, I won't mention it in my reports.'

'They're not my favourite band in the world' I admitted.

'Not even the early stuff?'

'The first album's not bad. They had something then.'

'You should have seen them before they were famous.'

'Big fan, were you?'

'I went to a lot of their early gigs when I was a student. The Adelphi. The Blue Lamp. Good times. Once word got out about them and they started to attract a crowd, it changed.' She paused. 'You were probably a bit too old given that you'd been Greg's babysitter.'

She was playing with me again. I smiled. 'I'm not that much older than you.'

'I've still got their debut single somewhere' she said. 'Limited edition vinyl. Yellow, I think. Might be worth something now. I think I've still got a demo tape they sold at gigs somewhere, too.'

'Hardcore fan' I said.

She stood up and headed to the door. 'I'd love to continue chatting, but tell Kane this wasn't what we agreed. He said I'd have full access to the band whenever I wanted it. I haven't got time to be sat doing nothing. If he's got a problem, any kind of problem, you should tell him to give me a call.' She turned back to face me. 'And don't forget he told me you're at my disposal.'

I watched the door close. I was sure she knew something was wrong.

I called Major. Early evening and I'd made no progress. If I was going to have Julia on my back, he was going to have to be more helpful.

'What's the score?' he said after he'd eventually answered my call.

'Still looking.' I could hear noise in the background. 'Where are you?'

'I'm going outside.' He told me to wait a minute. It was quieter when he came back on the line.

'I'm at the fucking Guildhall. A Civic Reception.'

'Why?' I didn't understand. I knew the place, but I'd never been invited in. Not even when I had been playing rugby.

'Do you think I want to be here, PI?' Major said. 'There's a lot riding on this reunion. Not just for me. It makes the city look good, too. PR. Everyone wants a piece of good news, especially the freeloading arts cunts who invited me here.'

I stopped his rant and updated him on what I'd been doing and my lack of a breakthrough.

'Fuck's sake. You keep looking, alright?' he said.

'It's like looking for a needle in a haystack.'

'No it's not. That's why I'm paying you. You're supposed to be a professional. We're in Hull, not London. This place is like a fucking village by comparison.'

'It's not my job' I told him.

'Your job is whatever I say it is.'

'My job is to keep an eye on the band and Julia Gowans.'

'Don't you think that includes keeping an eye on the singularly most important member of the band?'

I was tempted to hang up. I took a moment. Made my decision. 'My invoice will be in the post.'

'What?'

'We're done. It's not the job I signed up for. You should go to the police. They can help you. I can't.'

'Hold on, PI. Without Tasker, there's no band' he said. 'And with no band, there's no reunion. With no reunion, there's no story. And with no story, there's nothing. We're all wasting our time.' He paused. 'I'll double your money, alright?'

It was as close to an apology as I was going to get. And the money would be useful. Not that I'd seen any yet.

'Start again. What have you got for me?' he said.

I told him who I'd spoken to and how I hadn't turned up any concrete leads on where Tasker might be.

'The studio's a waste of time' he said.

'His engineer said he wasn't there too often.'

'Sounds about right. It's a shithole. It isn't hi-tech enough to attract decent bands, but it's too expensive for your local bands.' He shrugged. 'Pointless. No good to anybody.'

'I've spoken to Greg's girlfriend' I said. 'She thinks he was having an affair with a woman called Lorraine. She runs a New Holland website.'

'I know who you mean. She's been hanging around the band like a bad smell from day one. She's fucking weird.'

'Weird?'

'Too interested, wants to get too close. The kind who's probably got a shrine dedicated to the band in her back bedroom. Might stick a knife in your back one day, you know the sort.'

'Do you know where I'll find her?'

'No idea, PI. I'm not in touch with her, other than the odd email. She's been sniffing around, wanting to know if there was going to be a reunion. I wouldn't be surprised if Greg's been opening his mouth to her.'

'Are they sleeping together?' I asked.

'How would I know?'

'I need more' I said.

'All I know is he's been with Siobhan for a while. Dragged her up from London. The works. If he's been a naughty boy, I wouldn't know about it.'

I changed the subject. 'We might have a problem with Julia' I said.

'What kind of problem?'

'She was sniffing around earlier, wanting me to sort her some time out with the band. I think she knows he's missing.'

'She knows nothing. She's rattling your cage, trying to see if you'll let anything slip. I know people like her. They're parasites. She'll use you to get what she wants and then she'll spit you back out again. You tell her nothing and I'll keep her in line if she gets out of hand.'

I didn't like the suggestion I couldn't handle her, but I didn't push it any further. 'Do you think Greg's alright?'

Major went quiet. I could hear the party going on behind him in the background. 'I know where you're going with that thought, PI. But I'll tell you this; you're wrong. Greg played me a CD full of new songs recently. He's going to be massive again and I'm going to make sure it happens. What happened before was a mistake. It was a long time ago. Greg said it had been a cry for help, nothing more. It's not relevant. Are we clear on that? He's coming back.'

I ended the call.

I left the office and headed to Sarah's house.

'Any luck?' she asked me.

I shook my head and slumped into her settee. She'd invited me to her house once I was finished for the day. I was beginning to wish now I'd never taken the job from Major. Maybe she was right. It was going to involve a lot of late nights and already it was clear dealing with him and Julia Gowans was going to be my worst nightmare. 'There's no business like show-business' I said.

'And you don't even like the band.'

'I don't mind their early stuff.' It was becoming my stock answer.

'That's because you're a music snob.'

I'd inherited my older brother's record collection when he'd left home, so I was brought up on ska and punk. The Specials and The Clash in particular. Now my taste ran more to acoustic singer-songwriters. I asked if there was anything I could eat. Sarah went into the kitchen and came back out with lasagne and salad. I thanked her. There weren't many friends prepared to cook for me.

'You don't think he's done something stupid, do you?' she asked me.

'I don't know.' I was beginning to worry and Major hadn't eased my fears any.

She told me about a couple of small jobs which had come in throughout the day. With me working exclusively for New Holland and Don slowly reducing his role within the partnership, Sarah was taking on more of the day to day jobs. She'd always been good at the work, but I suspected she'd got a real taste for it now. 'I don't think your dad is best pleased with me' I said.

'He thought it was going to be a straightforward job. No messing about' she said.

I'd hoped so, too. 'But it is what it is.'

She seemed to accept what I was saying. 'What else have you got on your showbiz agenda?' she asked me. 'Entertaining Ms Gowans?'

I ignored her. Sarah put New Holland's debut album on the stereo. She turned the volume down. Opening track, 'Welcome to Hell' had been their biggest hit, making the top three. I looked at the CD cover. It had been released in 1995, so the band had been lumped in with the burgeoning Britpop scene. To be fair, they were better than that. Five years later and a further two albums, it was all over for the band.

'Have you looked through the press clippings I printed off for you?' Sarah asked me.

She'd given me a full ring-binder of stuff to read. 'Only briefly.' I'd read the earlier ones, amazed at how arrogant Tasker had sounded in those days. The tone of the articles was patronising, like a band from Hull shouldn't be expected to succeed, but he hadn't done himself any favours, writing off almost every band that had gone before New Holland. I wondered how far his words had been twisted. Flicking through more printouts, I suspected not too much. Despite myself, I couldn't help smiling at his words. He'd claimed that what good music there had been had come from the North. The South didn't do anything for him. Not that it had stopped him moving down to London.

'Have you read the more recent articles?' Sarah said to me.

'Not yet.'

'There's some stuff about the opening of his studio, basically saying how much he was looking forward to coming home, leading a quieter life and making the business a success. You know the kind of thing.'

I found the article. I quickly scanned it, but didn't find anything else of interest. I turned back to the coverage of Tasker's suicide attempt. It had happened just over five years ago, shortly after his solo comeback album flopped. I held the page up for Sarah. 'Do you remember this at the time?'

'Vaguely. I wasn't that interested, to be honest.'

The BBC report said Tasker had taken an overdose of pills and made an emergency call for an ambulance.

'Skip a few pages' Sarah said, 'there's a couple of bits about the aftermath.'

I found them. Tasker had gone into rehab and received treatment for depression. Seemingly, he couldn't come to terms with things.

I turned back to the more recent articles in the file. The photographs of Tasker showed he hadn't aged well, but that he was still just about clinging to his rock star looks and haircut. I'd been thinking about things. I put the file to one side and called Major.

'Any news?' he asked me.

'No.' It hadn't been that long since I'd spoken to him. 'I need to talk to the band properly' I said. 'Steve Priestley in particular.'

'Why?'

'He might know something. Something he didn't want to tell you.' Priestley had been Tasker's long-standing co-songwriter in the band. They'd been friends back then.

'I'll sort it. First thing tomorrow' he said.

'Good.' I terminated the call and turned to Sarah. 'Gut feeling?'

She sat down next to me. 'If the band's about to reform, why would he kill himself? It doesn't make sense.'

That was the way I saw things, too. Unless something came to light to suggest otherwise, I was treating Greg Tasker as missing, but nothing more than that.

'They should go to the police' she said.

I shrugged. 'It's Major's call.' I'd been thinking it over. Sarah was right, but it wasn't a situation I could force. There was no guarantee the situation would be taken seriously.

That said, crossing your fingers and hoping for the best wasn't the way it should be handled.

Sarah yawned and looked at her watch. I took the hint and stood up. Looked for my coat.

'Your brother called the office earlier' she said.

'Niall?'

'Have you got another?'

'What did he want?'

'Said to just give him a call sometime, you know, like families sometimes do.'

'Ok.' I started to make a move, but I didn't want to go back to my flat yet. I could make last orders at Queens if I was quick. It was where I always retreated to when I needed to think.

CHAPTER THREE

Major called me at lunch time to tell me Priestley would be expecting me at the rehearsal room on Bankside. Music is a nocturnal business, so I'd spent the morning in the office, trying to get a handle on where Tasker might be. I'd read articles, looking for any clue or hint of a favourite place. I called a handful of associates who can usually help with missing persons, but they hadn't called back yet. The reality is that it's easy enough to disappear if you really want to. I was frustrated and getting nowhere. I shut my laptop down and headed out to meet Priestley. If you walked in a line from my office, out of the Old Town and along the River Hull, you'd find the area. It was nice to know some of the buildings still had a purpose, even if they weren't the important warehouses where goods were once docked. The building I was looking for backed directly onto the water. It was nondescript from the outside, but that had probably been the attraction for the band. If you weren't looking, you wouldn't notice the place. I found the door around the side of the building and walked in. No one there. The instruments were neatly set up on the stage, untouched and quiet.

'Joe?'

I turned around and nodded. Steve Priestley. 'Nice to see you again.' He was about forty years old, like Tasker, but time had been kinder to him. He'd probably looked after himself better over the years.

'I'm the first here' he said, pointing me towards a pair of plastic chairs. 'Any luck in finding him?'

'Not yet.'

'Right.' Priestley nodded. 'Kane said you wanted to talk to me.'

I sat down and asked him if he was looking forward to the reunion.

'Of course.'

'Honestly?'

He smiled. 'I want us to record some new stuff, but that's a way off yet. I can't say I'm looking forward to the media side of things. No offence, but having people like you and Julia tagging along isn't my idea of what it's all about.'

It was understandable. I knew he lived on a farm, well away from the city. A rural retreat. I turned to business. 'Did Greg say anything about going away? Drop any hints?'

Priestley shook his head. 'I'd have told Kane if he had.'

'Was he troubled in any way?'

He thought about my question. 'I wouldn't have said so. But maybe he was putting an act on, so he didn't look weak in front of us, I don't know. It still feels like we're circling each other, finding our feet, if you know what I mean? It's been a long time since we played together. Maybe he was actually full of confidence.' He picked up his mug of tea. 'I can't read him that well. I don't know how he thinks.'

'What's your relationship like?'

'We don't really have one. Those days are gone. Until Kane contacted us about the possibility of a reunion, I don't think I've spoken to Greg for six or seven years. I always knew what he was doing through the Internet and stuff, but we never actually made contact. It's what this business does to you. It builds you up, tells you you're the best thing in the world and then it demolishes you. And some things don't survive it.' He swallowed the last of his tea. 'Our friendship was one of them.'

I wasn't surprised by what he said. It fitted with what I'd read in the pack Sarah had given me. After I'd left Queens, I'd stayed up late flicking through it. The music industry was littered with such stories. I hesitated, then asked the question that needed asking. 'Do you think he's done anything silly?'

'Because he's tried to kill himself before?'

'Maybe the pressure was too much?'

'I really wouldn't know. He was my best friend a long time ago, but too much has happened since. We didn't split on good terms. His problems were too much for us. We couldn't continue. I'm sorry he took it so hard, but there wasn't anything I could do.'

I understood what he was saying. I'd played professional rugby league before injury finished me, just as I was getting started in the game. The margins of error were so small, there was always the chance that however well you did your own job, your team-mates could let you down. You need them to be strong.

'So you wouldn't have any idea where he might have disappeared to?' I asked.

'Assuming he hasn't changed that much, he's probably sleeping a binge off, or holed up somewhere recording some new songs on his own. That's the way he used to work. He'd disappear for a few days and then turn up like nothing was wrong, like we were all supposed to just deal with it. Used to drive me mad.'

That was what Siobhan had told me. I asked him if he'd met Tasker's girlfriend.

'He told us about her when we first rehearsed a couple of weeks ago, but I've not met her.'

I asked Priestley about Lorraine and her website.

He told me he knew her. 'She was a fan from the start. Coming to the early gigs and supporting us. She even used to jump in the van with us and sell demo tapes and T-shirts at gigs.'

'Kane said she was a bit weird, that she can't let the past go.'

'We were happy enough to use her when we needed a hand, but once we became more professional, we got rid of her without a second thought. I still feel bad about that. She did nothing wrong.'

'Do you think she's still in touch with Greg?'

'I wouldn't really know. Maybe they've rekindled their relationship? I know they stayed in touch, even when he moved down to London.'

I was surprised. 'Rekindled their relationship?'

Priestley picked up his guitar. Started to tune up. 'They were an item before we left Hull. Kane used to hate it.'

I went back to the office and looked over the paperwork Sarah had left out for me. She'd also left me a sandwich. As I ate, I wondered how a famous man simply disappears. Clearly, there was plenty about Tasker I still didn't know, not least his private life. My mobile vibrated on the table. I looked at the display – Sarah.

'I've got an email for you from Lorraine Harrison, the woman who runs the New Holland website' she said. I listened as Sarah summarised it for me before finding a pen in my pocket to take the details down. I didn't know if Lorraine would lead me directly to Tasker, but she was the best lead I had. I must have been lost in thought, as I didn't hear Julia Gowans walk into the office.

She sat down opposite me and smiled. 'What's new?'

'Nothing.'

'No need to be so defensive. It really doesn't suit you, Joe. We're all friends here.'

She had that glint in her eye again. I couldn't decide whether she was flirting with me or not. I was out of practice on that front.

'I'm not being defensive.' It was the best I could manage.

'Have you spoken to Kane?'

'Not since this morning.'

'Did he tell you Greg is missing, nobody knows where he is?'

I tried not to show my surprise. There was nothing I could say. I stalled for time, taking another bite of my sandwich, hoping she would go away. It wasn't the best of plans.

She continued. 'Are you telling me you've not been running around trying to find him?'

What kind of investigator was I? She knew at least as much as me. 'What makes you think he's missing?' I said.

She smiled at me. 'Cut the shit, Joe. You've got two choices here. We can either work together or I can file the story right now. Kane will no doubt tell you there's no story yet, but don't believe him. There's always a story. You need to choose the first option. You need to find Greg and it looks like you need all the help you can get.'

We headed out of the office to my car. Major wasn't going to be happy, but I'd weighed the situation up. There was no choice: I'd told Julia she was in. A story now about Tasker's disappearance would be damaging. I was trying to control the situation. Major would surely see that. As we drove, I asked her how she knew Tasker was missing. She said she'd spoken to Michael Rusting, the man at Greg Tasker's studio. He'd happily told her about our conversation the previous day.

'What do you think?' I asked. She knew what was going on, so there was no avoiding the big question. I kept my eyes on the road.

She said she had no idea. 'Until the interviews I did with him last week, I hadn't spoken to him for years. Certainly not since the New Holland days.'

I was surprised. 'I thought you were closer than that.'

'We go back, but it's not the same thing. He was off touring the world with the band. I was trying to make a go of things with my job. It was good enough for my paper, though. They think I'm in some sort of inner circle, so I got the job.'

Sounded familiar. 'Do you think Kane approves of you being involved?'

'I know them. Maybe he trusts me? I've not asked him. I don't really care.'

I pulled up outside Lorraine Harrison's house at the bottom of a quiet cul-de-sac. It was on a 1970s housing estate out to the east of the city. The area itself was quiet and nondescript. The house looked like it needed a lick of paint and new windows. I nodded to Julia that I was ready. I made her promise to behave; no recording, no photographs. I'd be doing the talking.

The inside of the house was similarly dated, only the TV and Nintendo Wii looked like recent purchases. The two women stared at each other.

'Nice to see you, Lorraine' Julia said. 'It's been a long time.'

Lorraine nodded and told us to sit down before disappearing to put the kettle on.

'You know her?' I said to Julia. I don't know why I was surprised. If they were both friends with New Holland, there was every chance they'd have met at some point.

'We go back' she said.

I wondered if this was a good idea still. Lorraine came back in with drinks.

'So what brings you here?' she asked. 'Your email was very intriguing.'

'I work for New Holland' I explained, trying to avoid using Kane Major's name directly, given that I now knew he hadn't approved of her and Greg's relationship in the past. 'I'm sure we can talk to you in confidence, though I suspect you already know. The band are considering making a comeback.' I paused, tried to make light of the situation. 'The problem is we've mislaid Greg. I'm sure it's nothing to worry about. He's more than likely gone away somewhere for a few days without telling anyone. You know how he is.'

'Why is she here?' Lorraine said, pointing at Julia.

I was about to answer, but Julia took over. 'I'm documenting the reunion for my newspaper and Joe's employed by the band's management to make sure things run smoothly. I'm just helping him out.'

'When did you last hear from Greg?' I asked Lorraine.

'He rang me about a week ago' she said eventually.

'About the reunion?'

'What else?'

'Did he mention anything about going away?'

'No.' She looked up at me. 'Why would he?'

'Did he ever give you any reason to think he might be unhappy?' I asked.

'No.'

'I spoke to Siobhan and she didn't know much, either.' I wanted to mention her, see what response it got. Not a flicker. Nothing. I was about to go for it and ask the question we'd been skirting around, but was stopped by a man and a teenager walking into the room. She introduced us to her husband, Jason, and their son, Jay. He looked at us and told Lorraine to go check on their tea. Jason Harrison was a bear of a man. His hands had the ingrained dirtiness manual workers never quite manage to wash away.

'Tough day at work?' I asked him, hoping to break the ice.

'Could say that.'

'What do you do?'

'I repair classic cars. My mate has his own garage.'

I nodded and told him why we were speaking to his wife.

'I don't want her upset.'

'We're not here to upset her' I said. 'We're looking for Greg Tasker.'

He thought about it for a moment before answering. 'She needs to let it go.'

'Let what go?' Julia asked.

'New Holland, Greg Tasker, the website, everything. Nobody cares anymore. She needs to be concentrating on our son. Not that shit.'

'It's only a website' Julia said. 'A bit of harmless fun.'

She was baiting him. She must have known that Greg and Lorraine had history. I was beginning to wish I hadn't brought her along.

'I don't like the man, alright?' Harrison said. 'I'm an ordinary bloke who goes out to work each day. I work hard and I bring home a fair day's pay, and that's me. It's what I do. His fame means nothing to me.' He pointed at me, angry. 'If you do find him, you can tell him from me I want him to stay away from me and my family. He doesn't come near us again. Is that clear?'

I stood up, ready to leave. We were finished. 'Crystal clear' I said.

You love the stage now. The nerves you suffered from at the early gigs are almost under control. You can channel them positively into your performance. The band has been making strides forward. You now headline gigs around the city and have a demo tape to sell to fans. Things are beginning to move. You meet Kane Major after a gig. His confidence, both in himself and the band, blows you away. You're in awe of him. You know your judgment is right. You decide you want him to manage the band. Priestley is reluctant, but you convince him. You tell him it's the way forward. You know it's a watershed moment for New Holland. He falls in line. Kane puts the money up for a limited edition vinyl single. Your first proper record. When you get a copy, you can't stop looking at it. It has your name on it. It's the proudest moment of your life. You tell anyone who'll listen about the record. Even your parents are proud of you. Things move fast. The record is played on Radio One. The music press love you. Kane brokers a deal for you with a major label. You tell Priestley you were right. You knew it all
  along. You're on your way to becoming stars.

CHAPTER FOUR

We drove away from Lorraine Harrison's house. Julia was hungry. We headed for a quiet Italian restaurant I knew off the main drag of Newland Avenue, well away from the loud bars which continued to spring up. It was on Julia's expenses. It was going to be the only perk I got from this job. We sat down and she ordered drinks. I asked her if she had been friends with Lorraine Harrison.

'Not really.' She poured herself a glass of wine before offering me one.

I shook my head and waited for my soft drink. I wasn't drinking. I didn't want to leave my car on the street for the night.

'More like acquaintances' she said. 'I went to a few of the gigs when the band first started, usually when some friends of mine were also playing. I knew her more by sight at gigs and we got talking once or twice in nightclubs. Sisters together in a male environment, if you like.'

'I got the feeling she didn't like you very much.'

Julia sipped at her wine. Asked to see a menu before turning back to me. 'She never did. We both wrote for a local music magazine, but she never pushed it any further. I became friendly with Greg and the band.' She shrugged. 'Maybe she read more into it than she should have.'

I thought about it. Maybe life had ground Lorraine down, I didn't know, but she was far from being unattractive. Maybe she'd hoped life would have turned out differently for her. Maybe having such close access to people who had become famous had led her to think about what might have been. I was regretting not asking her more directly about her involvement with Tasker. I picked my drink up and changed the subject. 'What did you think of her husband?'

'I've met nicer people.'

I couldn't disagree. Julia ordered our food.

'Who does he think he is' she said when she returned to our table. 'Laying the law down to his wife like that? If she wants to run a website, it's none of his business. I didn't get a good feeling off him.'

'Me neither.' I bet being compared to a rock star, whether his wife ever said it or not, wasn't good for his ego, but it was no excuse.

'Do you think Greg wants this reunion?' I asked. The pressure was going to build up. I wondered if he'd realised what he'd got himself into and changed his mind.

'I know he struggled with the failure of his solo album. The press were savage towards him around that time. I think a few people in the media had scores to settle with him. The reunion's certainly a brave move for him.'

I could understand that. Professional failure cuts deep, especially when you do it in the public eye, but there had to be more to it. 'Have you had a word with Kane today?' I asked her.

'Not yet.'

'Best let me talk to him first.' I wasn't looking forward to telling him Julia knew Tasker was missing, even if I had been backed into a corner. He wouldn't see it that way, but if anything, I should ask him for a bonus, as I'd at least stopped the situation escalating. 'Are you going to file the story?' I asked her.

She shook her head. 'Not yet.'

I was relieved. The food arrived, saving me from any further discussion.

'You never got around to telling me about yourself' she said, biting into a slice of pizza.

'Not much to tell.'

She shook her head. 'You don't get away with it that easily.'

'It's the truth.'

'Let's start with the basics. Tell me about your wife.'

I put my pizza down. 'I don't have one.' She hadn't done that much research into me.

'Girlfriend, then.'

'I don't have one of them, either.'

'What about Sarah?'

I hesitated before I answered. 'She's a good friend who I work well with.' There'd almost been a moment, but it hadn't gone any further. It had been a possibility for a short while, but we were friends first and foremost. Good friends.

Julia smiled and shook her head. 'There must be someone.'

'There isn't.'

'Are you really a monk?'

'Widower.'

Julia put her food down. 'I'm sorry.'

I waved away her apology. 'You weren't to know.' It'd been a couple of years now. I wasn't ready to buy into the theory that time heals, but day by day it was getting a little easier.

'How did she die?' She put her head down and apologised. 'Sorry, it's the journalist in me. You don't have to tell me if you don't want to.'

'House fire. She was babysitting for her sister and didn't get out in time.'

'That's awful.'

I nodded. I was able to talk about it a bit more these days. 'The police never got to the bottom of it. It was down to me.' I told her a bit about a previous case and how it had brought me a measure of closure. 'At least I got the truth in the end.'

'It must have been awful.'

'At least I had Don and Sarah to lean on.'

'How did you meet them?'

'I used to work for a firm of solicitors as a freelance investigator, but I'd been looking for something steadier, something with prospects, and Don had been looking for some help. It worked for both of us. Just good timing.' I changed the subject. 'How about you?' I said. 'Married?'

She shook her head. 'Not even close. I'm your classic case. Career first and never met the right man. You know the drill.'

'Boyfriend?'

'Nothing serious. Work doesn't leave much time for anything else.'

'There must have been someone?'

She picked her pizza back up. 'Not really. There was a guy in Hull, but I was too young and stupid. I needed to get away from him because he wasn't good news. There's been a few in London, but in the main, they were arseholes.'

I smiled. 'What about family? Are they still in Hull?'

'None worth coming back for.'

It explained why the change in the city fascinated her. She didn't have a reason to visit regularly. My mobile vibrated in my pocket. It was Kane Major. I excused myself and took the call. He wanted me to go with him to Tasker's parent's house. They wanted to speak to me.

I went back inside. 'I've got to go' I said to Julia. I picked up a slice of pizza. Food on the move. 'I'll call you later.'

The Taskers lived in a modest semi-detached house, out in the suburbs to the west of the city. Only a short distance away from Siobhan's boutique. The area was convenient for quick access to the M62 and the bigger Yorkshire cities of Leeds and Sheffield. There was a social pecking order - east to west Hull and then out to the outlying villages. They'd nearly made it. I lived just outside of the city centre, which put me in no man's land. On the way there, Major had told me Keith Tasker was mid-management at Smith and Nephews, one of Hull's most prestigious employers. My dad had opened a pub like many ex-sportsmen, but Keith Tasker had taken a different and more prosperous route. His wife, Kath, had stayed at home once Greg had been born.

I parked up as closely as possible to the house. It looked just like any other in the area. The front garden was neat and tidy, the furniture in the house modern and recently purchased. They were doing ok for themselves, a model of good order. I didn't know what to expect, but it was a distinct contrast to their son's life as a famous musician.

The Taskers greeted me like an old friend, even though we hadn't seen each other in decades. It was the nature of the city. It might be sprawling, but the static population meant you were never far away from people you knew. You couldn't hide. They fussed around, offering tea. I waved the offers away, wanting to get down to business. It was late and I didn't like the situation I was getting myself into. Looking around the room, there were no photographs of Greg or the band.

'Thank you for agreeing to help us, Joe' Kath said to me.

I turned to Major, who was looking at the floor. He wasn't going to be much help. 'With all due respect, I don't really know what I'm doing here' I said to her.

'I'd assumed Kane had told you all the details' she said.

'Not really.'

'Kane said you can find Greg' Keith said. 'We trust him. We know how close he is to Greg. If he says you can help find him, we have to believe him.'

'You should think about talking to the police' I said. 'I'm just one man. I don't have the back-up they have.'

'Do you remember when your brother went missing?'

I nodded. I vaguely remembered something, but not the details.

'You were only little, five or six, which would have made your Niall about nine. You'd been playing football on the local field with some other kids, but you wandered off with your mates. Your parents thought you were still with Niall, so when only you returned home, they were frantic. Me and your dad got some other blokes together and we searched the area for him. We stayed out for hours, then I found Niall on the drain, just sat there, throwing stones into the water. He was too scared to go home in case he was in trouble.' Keith shrugged. 'It happens, but sometimes all you need is a bit of help.'

I got the point, but said nothing.

He continued. 'It's been a difficult decision to make, but it could do more harm than good at the moment. It would cause a lot of trouble for the band and Greg wouldn't want that. We know what he's like. We're sure he's just taken off for a few days, but we need to know he's safe. That's all. When he comes back, the band can get on with things. If the press find out, they'll be talking about him for all the wrong reasons. It'd ruin things before they've even started. I know he wouldn't want that.'

I understood what he was saying, but I wasn't convinced. 'The police have ways of dealing with these things. They'll be discreet' I said.

He glanced at Major before shaking his head. 'We're not prepared to take the chance.'

It was crazy. 'The police have got more chance than I have of finding Greg' I said. 'He could be anywhere.'

They were adamant. This was why Major had dragged me away from my meal with Julia. He wanted me to hear it from them.

We left the house and went back to my car. I'd said I'd do my best for them. I stared out of the window towards the house. Keith Tasker hadn't been too subtle in reminding me of a debt my family owed.

Major stared straight ahead. 'We can't go to the police. Once you're famous, you have no privacy. Everything's fair game and you can't control it. You can't stop your family being caught in the crossfire and they don't need the media on their doorstep. We can take care of it for them. We're not going to the police, PI. It complicates things.' He knew I wasn't buying it. He turned to face me. 'Look, if we go to the police now, it could ruin the whole plan, and you heard his parents, nobody wants to do that.'

'Julia knows Greg is missing.' I explained what she knew and how she'd found it out.

'Fuck's sake, PI, I thought you were a professional?'

He looked like he was going to say something more, but stopped himself. I ignored his comment. I knew there was nothing I could have done differently.

He passed me a note. 'I need to go there.'

I read the address. City centre. I knew the area. 'Why?'

'Just do as you're told, PI.'

He was beginning to annoy me. I wasn't his lapdog. 'Why?'

'It's Greg's flat' he said.

'Did they give you a key?' I hadn't seen them do so.

'They haven't got one.'

I knew where this was heading. 'How are you going to get in?' I asked him.

'Just drive, alright?'

I repeated the question.

'Look, if Greg was doing anything stupid, I need to know.'

'And what might that include?'

'Stop being a cunt, PI. We both know what we're talking about. If the police were to find anything in there, it'd destroy his parents. We're doing this for them. Now, you either drive me there or you walk away from the job and your payday.'

I glanced back at the house again and made my decision. They were worried for their son and I could help them. Everything else was secondary. I drove.

Tasker lived in a new build flat close to the New Theatre, right in the heart of the city centre. The area was quiet. We'd argued during the course of the drive. Breaking in was a bad idea. I made my position clear to Major: I wanted to help, but I wasn't going in the flat. I wouldn't cross that line. If we were caught, I wouldn't be able to work again. And nor would Sarah and Don. I parked up and switched the engine off. Settled in to wait whilst Major did whatever he needed to do. If there was one aspect of my job I'd happily change, it was the sitting around in a car, watching and waiting. I sat for twenty minutes and only saw one lonely drunk stagger past. Nobody else passed until Major walked back towards the car. He opened the passenger door and eased back in.

I turned towards him. 'Well?'

'Nothing.'

'Nothing?'

'It's clean. The police can look around it if they want.' He laughed. 'Feels good to break the law, doesn't it, PI?'

I started the car up and pulled away. I was ready to call it a night.

CHAPTER FIVE

'**You** did what?' Don said to me.

It was too early in the day to be arguing and I was tired. Unable to sleep, I'd sat in my front room and watched the sunrise. The walls were thin, so I'd put my headphones on and listened to music until it was time for work. I walked back to my desk with my drink. 'I shouldn't have done it' I said. It was the best I could offer.

'You should have gone to the police and put a stop to it. You've done your best, but you can't do it all by yourself. This isn't what we do here.'

I shook my head. 'They don't want the police involved. They've made their decision. It's not what Greg would want, so I think we've got to respect their wishes on this.' I felt for them. I could see both sides of the argument, but I wanted to help them to the best of my ability. I'd been thinking about what Keith Tasker had said to me the previous night. He'd helped my family when asked. I had to repay the favour. It was that simple.

Don picked up the morning's post and rifled through the pile, throwing my letters onto my desk. 'It doesn't mean you can go around breaking into people's flats' he said. 'It's against the law. We'll be shut down and then we'll all have nothing. Everything we've worked for would be gone.'

I understood that, but at least I was getting paid for my troubles. 'The main thing is we find him' I said. I passed him one of the bills I'd found in the pile. 'And then we might be able to pay this.'

I glanced at my mobile, but there had been no calls so far this morning. I called Major again. Straight to voicemail.

Don looked at his watch and stood up. 'I'm going out. I'll be on my mobile.'

I watched him leave. Don had every right to be angry. I wasn't comfortable with the way Major had forced this upon me, either. He had expected me to go along with things without so much as a murmur of dissent. He might be paying for my services but it didn't mean he owned me and I'd blindly follow his instructions. I had to decide how far I was willing to go with this.

The buzzer to the office went. I looked into the camera and saw Julia. I realised I'd not spoken to her since I'd left her in the restaurant. Shit. I met her at the door.

'You were supposed to call me' she said, walking straight past me.

I said I was sorry.

She walked right up to me, inches away from my face. 'You're been very naughty, Joe, and to make it up to me, you best have a very, very good story for me.'

I smiled and took a step back, tried to think.

She followed me across the room. 'I know you're holding out on me.'

'Of course I'm not.'

'Good. Because that's not what we agreed, is it?'

'No.'

'Is Kane cool with the situation?'

'Not really.'

Julia shrugged. 'He'll deal with it. Has Greg turned up yet?'

'I've not heard from Kane today.'

She laughed. 'I bet you've been ringing him all morning.'

'Not at all.'

'Liar.'

I walked back to my desk, wanting her questions to stop.

'I need a story' she said to me. 'Have you told him I know Greg is missing?'

I nodded. 'It didn't go down well.'

'He'll have to deal with it.'

'He's got a lot on his plate.' I wasn't sure why I was defending him.

'He needs to have a think about his priorities.'

I understood. She was probably stretching her brief as far as possible. If another paper got the story first, she'd be in serious trouble.

'Where is he, Joe?'

'I don't know' I said. 'If I knew, I'd tell you. In fact, if I knew, he'd be back here by now.'

'Not good enough.'

'I thought you weren't going to file the story?'

Julia leaned in close to me. 'Don't be so naive, Joe.'

'How am I naive?' I felt like a parrot. It seemed whenever she invaded my personal space, I had nothing sensible to say.

She walked away from me, towards the window. 'Tell me why Sarah doesn't like me.'

'She does like you.' It sounded ridiculous as soon as I said it. 'She didn't want us taking this job on, that's all.' And neither did her father, I thought.

Julia shook her head. 'It doesn't matter, but don't forget you're relying on my goodwill here, Joe, and it can't last forever. Whatever's going on, you're in the loop, so I suggest you talk to Kane and sort it out. Otherwise I'll have to speak to him on the record, and I can't imagine he'll like that very much.'

With Julia's words of warning still ringing in my ears, I tried Major's mobile again. Straight to voicemail. Enough was enough. I grabbed my coat and headed across the city centre to his office. His temporary base in Hull was a ten minute walk away in The World Trade Centre, a high class office block overlooking the city's marina. I'd had clients in the past who were based in the building. Bad memories.

The receptionist tried to block my entry, but I wasn't going to be stopped. I walked straight into his office. Major was on the telephone. The office was a mess; empty mugs weighed down piles of paperwork, leaving little of the desk visible. I couldn't believe he'd only just arrived in town. I walked across the room and opened the blinds. He finished his call. 'I said I wasn't seeing anyone today, PI. You can't just barge in here when you feel like it. I employ you. You might want to remember that.'

I took a deep breath and sat down opposite him.

He looked up at me. 'There's no word.'

'Nothing?'

'No.'

Major yawned and rang through for more coffee. 'It'll be fine. Don't worry; we'll find him.'

I didn't share his enthusiasm. Things don't just work out. You have to make them happen and we didn't possess the tools to do that. Tasker hadn't made contact and he wasn't answering his mobile. We had nothing. And that was being positive. I didn't want to think how fragile his mental state might be. 'I've spoken to Don. It's time to call the police' I said.

'Fuck Don. Can't you make your own decisions? You saw his parents. We've agreed, we don't want the police involved.'

'The reunion's not worth that much, surely?'

'You were there. You spoke to them. They know how important it is and they don't want to spoil it for Greg. Keep looking for him. He'll turn up and then we put this behind us and move on. Alright, PI?'

This was getting out of hand. I'd seen the state Tasker's parents were in and I wanted to help them, but this wasn't the way. As well as talking to people, I'd been on the Internet trying to track him down, but nothing. He might be famous, but it seemed if you were determined enough, you could hide away. All you needed was cash, so you didn't leave an electronic trail, and somewhere to lie low. He walked me over to the window and we looked out across the marina. When the weather's good and the yachts are on the move, it's a beautiful sight. It makes a nonsense of the city's reputation. Today wasn't one of those days.

'What's the score with Julia?' he asked me.

'I'm keeping her at bay.' I didn't offer any more than that.

'Good. I don't need her making the situation worse.'

'She's all over the story and starting to run out of patience.'

Major didn't seem bothered by this. 'Is she flirting with you?' he asked me.

'Why would she do that?'

'Come on, PI. We're both men of the world.'

'I'm just trying to do my job.'

'Of course you are.' Major smiled at me. 'She's an attractive woman, though. I wouldn't blame you, but don't let her get too close.' He tapped his head. 'She's got issues. Just be careful, that's my advice. Fuck her and then get rid. And make sure you don't go in for any pillow talk.'

Thirty minutes later and I was back at my desk in the empty office. I hadn't liked the way Major had spoken about me and Julia. Truth was, I liked her more than I was comfortable admitting. She was attractive, intelligent and good company; what wasn't to like? My thinking was interrupted by Lorraine Harrison appearing at the door. I invited her in.

'Do you mind?' she asked.

'Of course not.' I told her to sit down. Her appearance wasn't a huge surprise to me. As soon as her husband had returned home, she'd stopped talking. I asked if there was something I could do for her.

'I need to speak to you' she said. 'Away from Julia and everyone else. I don't trust her. And nor should you.'

I waited for her to continue.

'Can we speak in confidence?' she asked me.

I told her we could.

'Have you found Greg yet?'

'Not yet.'

'He's just gone away for a few days, I'm sure.'

'Does he have any favourite places? Anywhere I could check?'

She shook her head. 'Not really. It doesn't make sense. I know he was nervous about the band's comeback, but he was also really excited about it all. He had all kinds of plans for what he was going to do once the band had finished their tour. He wanted to get out of his studio and do things, make his own music again.' She paused and took a deep breath. 'He hasn't killed himself. I know he hasn't.'

'I'm sorry to be blunt, but he's tried it before.'

'That was years ago. He's changed since then.'

I asked her the question I wanted to ask back at her house. 'Are you having an affair with Greg?'

She started to cry.

I rummaged in my drawer for some tissues. Sarah usually kept us stocked up. She was good with the small details. Finding them, I passed them over to her and let her clean herself up. Admitting the affair seemed to lift a weight from her shoulders.

'I know it's hard for you' I said, 'but I need to ask you some questions about Greg, ok? When did you last see him?'

'I haven't seen Greg for a few weeks' she said. 'He was getting himself ready for the rehearsals. We'd speak on the phone regularly, but that was all.'

'When did you last speak to him?'

'About a week ago.'

I nodded. It didn't tell me anything new about his movements over the last couple of days. 'Has he mentioned any problems he might be having?'

'No.'

'Any problems with his family?'

'No.'

I was getting nowhere. 'I'm sorry to be so brutal, Lorraine, but does your husband know about your relationship with Greg?'

She shook her head. 'He mustn't know. Please don't tell him.'

I told her I had no reason to speak to him. Not at the moment. If they didn't speak it was their business. Sometimes it's easier to say nothing. But I know how it eats you up and eventually it boils over. 'Have you considered telling him about you and Greg?' I said.

'If he knew he'd throw me out. He wouldn't be able to forgive me, however much he loves Jay. Neither of us can afford to divorce. He doesn't earn much from his job and neither do I.' she shrugged. 'We just muddle along the best we can.'

I wasn't sure what to say.

Lorraine continued. 'Greg doesn't love Siobhan, you know. He deserves better than her. Most people don't know him, but I do. He's not the wild rock star people think he is. He's made a huge effort to sort himself out.'

'I understand' I said. I wasn't entirely convinced, but I thought I got it.

I called Major to find out if there had been any progress. Voicemail, again. I looked up as Sarah walked into the office. She offered to make me a drink.

'Don't be thinking this gets you off the hook. Dad called me earlier.'

I'd expected as much. I followed her into the kitchen area and told her why I'd gone along with Major's plan, trying to justify what I'd done. She passed me my drink and we sat back down.

'I take it there's no news on Tasker?' she said.

I shook my head. Changed the subject. 'Julia knows Tasker is missing' I said.

'You told her?'

'She found out.'

'How?'

'She's spoken to a man at Tasker's studio. He told her I'd been asking questions.' I explained Julia wasn't filing a story on Tasker's disappearance just yet.

'She's not to be trusted, Joe.'

'She's keeping to her part of the bargain.'

'She'll use you, Joe. All she wants is a story.'

I shut my eyes. 'I'm not stupid.'

Sarah turned away from me. 'I sometimes wonder.'

I opened them again. 'What's that supposed to mean?'

'You're not thinking straight.'

'Of course I'm thinking straight.' I was getting sick of being told how I should deal with things. I thought she was a bit more pragmatic than her father, less black and white. I thought she understood.

'We should never have taken the job' she said.

'Don't be ridiculous.'

'I'm not being ridiculous. You can't see how you're behaving and how it's affecting others.'

'How am I behaving?' My head was starting to hurt. I didn't want an argument, but I couldn't let it go, either.

'You're being reckless' Sarah said. 'Helping Major to break into places? It's stupid and dangerous.'

The venom in her voice surprised me. 'There's a man missing. I don't see how trying to find him is stupid.'

'It's not a job for you.'

I shrugged. 'It's not my place to make the call. I've been asked to help, so that's what I'm trying to do.'

'You've been asked to help by Kane Major, a man who's so far removed from the real world, he probably doesn't know what day it is anymore.'

'It's his call.' It wasn't just that. I'd explained to both Sarah and Don that I had ties to the Tasker family. I hadn't expected it to cause such an issue, but nor had I expected to find out that I owed them like I did.

'You've got to take some responsibility, Joe.' She was pointing at me. 'You've got to call a halt to this carry on. You're not going to find him. You're only one man.'

I knew she was talking sense and I wasn't arrogant enough to think I could resolve the case by myself. But I was prepared to try. 'It's not just Major's decision. Tasker's parents agree with him.'

'What about Julia?'

'What about her?'

'If she blows the whistle on this, Major's plan is in tatters.'

'She won't.'

'Don't be so naive, Joe.'

I was getting sick of being called naive. 'You don't like Julia, do you?' I said. 'And neither does your dad.'

Sarah sat upright. 'What's that got to do with anything?'

'Julia's trying to help us, but you've not given her a chance. You're not being much of a help.'

'I see.'

I apologised. It was a stupid thing to say. 'I didn't mean that.'

'If you give her an inch, she'll take a mile.'

'That's not fair.'

'Call it women's intuition if it makes you feel better. She'll use you, Joe, and when she's done, it'll be me you'll want to come crying back to.' She put her empty mug down. 'And I'm not going to let that happen.'

'That's out of order. You don't know her.'

'And you do know her?'

Sarah's words stopped me in my tracks. Kane Major and Lorraine had warned me about Julia, too. We were both standing, facing each other, eyeball to eyeball. Trying to find Tasker was a difficult enough task and I needed Sarah's help and support. I thought I could count on her. Breaking away from her stare, I headed for the door.

CHAPTER SIX

'Cheers.'

I toasted my brother. 'Good to see you.'

'It's been too long' Niall said, setting his glass back down on the table.

Queens wasn't busy, probably wouldn't be for a couple of hours yet, so we found a table in a quiet corner. I needed a drink after my argument with Sarah. It was good of him to join me at short notice on his way home from work.

'How are Ruth and Connor doing?' I asked.

'Ruth's great.' He laughed. 'But Connor is another matter. You should come and see them.'

I smiled. My nephew was eighteen years old. I hadn't seen him for a couple of months. 'Soon. I'll try' I said.

'Try harder.'

'I will.' I wanted to make the effort.

'You know what Dad would say, don't you?'

I did. 'Family first and don't neglect it.' I was looking at what I had left of my family.

'Maybe the weekend, then?'

'Maybe.' I took a mouthful of diet coke. I hated the taste, but I still had work to do. I thought about my father. He'd also played professional rugby for Hull KR. He'd lasted longer than me, though. He'd been a legend and I'd always felt like I was in his shadow, even when I made the first team. People always wanted to talk about him. I remembered the hundreds of people who'd turned out for his funeral, lining the streets of east Hull. Not many people get that treatment. I chased the thought away for now. 'How's work?' I asked my brother.

'Shit. Don't think I'll have a job in a few months.' He shrugged. 'At least I'll get the redundancy money. Start over, maybe.'

Niall worked in the caravan industry. I wasn't surprised by his news. After a few minutes silence, he asked how I was doing.

'Don't ask.' I didn't give him details, but I gave him a general outline.

'Used to love New Holland' he said. 'Saw them in Sheffield, at the Arena. Great night. They were the best band around at the time. And they were from Hull. Who said if you're from Hull you can't do something? I should dig the CDs out again.'

'You'll only feel old.'

My brother laughed. 'Can't beat it. Do you remember when I went to Paris to see them?'

'You couldn't really avoid them, could you?'

'I guess not.'

'Never really cracked it in America.'

'That's true.' When we were younger, we'd agreed a band had really made it when they'd had a hit there, like The Clash had done. I'd read more of Sarah's file earlier in the day. New Holland had been constantly on the road from the moment they released their first single. The UK gigs had quickly increased in size, from the clubs Julia saw them in to the large arenas my brother had. But in America it had been a different story. They'd never got beyond the small club circuit in a never ending stream of towns and cities. They weren't the first band to fail in the world's largest market and they certainly wouldn't be the last. I told him about my argument with Sarah.

'She doesn't approve of the job?'

'Neither does Don.'

'You should listen to them. They know what they're doing. And be careful. That place is the best thing that happened to you.'

'It's not so much the job, it's this journalist we've got on the scene.' I told him about Julia. 'They don't get on.'

My brother was smiling at me.

'What?' I said.

He put his glass down and smiled. 'You like this journalist, don't you?'

'She's ok.'

'You're allowed to like her. It's not illegal.'

I relented. 'I'm sure she's flirting with me.'

'She either is or she isn't' my brother said, laughing.

'I'm out of practice.' I picked my drink up, hoping we could change the subject, but he wasn't going to let me off that easily.

'Debbie would want you to get on with living, you know.'

I stared at my glass. I knew what he was saying was right. If I had been the one who died, I'd have wanted her to be happy again. But there'd been no one since. I was talking about a step into the unknown.

My brother shrugged. 'How do you feel about it?'

'I've no idea.' It was the truth, but I didn't know what to do about it, whether it was really happening or whether it was just in my mind.

'But it's a not a definite no?' he said.

'I suppose not.'

'It's only natural.'

I felt I was being horribly egotistical talking like this, like it was just a matter of me making a decision.

'Tell me about her' Niall said.

I thought about how Major, Sarah and Lorraine had warned me off her. Tried to weigh up the good and the bad. 'There's something about her' was the best I could offer. 'You know what I mean?'

'I take it she doesn't live in Hull?'

'No.'

'So she's not going to be looking for anything serious, is she?'

'Probably not.'

'There you go. It's not going to be a problem, is it? But there's something you've forgotten.'

'What's that?'

He stood up, ready to refill our glasses. 'If you like someone, you've got to do something about it.'

I walked back to my flat. I stood at the window and looked out. The scene was quiet. People were returning home, closing their front doors behind them for the night. I headed into the kitchen, poured myself a glass of water and sat down in my front room. I put a lamp on and switched the stereo on low. Gram Parsons drifted quietly around the room. I sat down and mulled over what my brother had said. We'd left the pub making promises to meet up again as soon as possible, and I wanted to keep my promise to him. It was time to move forward and look to the future.

I looked over the paperwork I had. I was nowhere near finding Tasker and all I'd done was upset people. I knew I should apologise to Sarah, but looking at my watch it was too late to call. It would have to wait until tomorrow. I'd drop into the office first thing in the morning and get it over with. It would be a start. Maybe Don would be there, too. I thought about calling Julia, but realised it would be a stupid thing to do. I had nothing to tell her, and I had Major's warning to think about. First and foremost, she was a journalist. I warmed up a frozen lasagne and promised myself yet again I'd start to eat more healthily. It was supposed to be part of the new me. I had too much to think about. Eating wasn't helping. Night was beginning to draw in. A thought struck me. If I was Tasker, I'd wait for darkness before attempting to return. I found my car keys and left.

There was no light on in Tasker's flat. I remembered which one it was from my visit with Major. I drove past and parked up about a hundred yards away, just in case anyone recognised my car. I walked back to the flats. The area was quiet, but the show at the New Theatre would be emptying soon. I pressed the buzzer to Tasker's flat. No answer. I took a step back and looked up. Lights were on, so plenty of people were in. I pressed the buzzer again and waited. Nothing. I thought about trying his neighbours, but decided against. I saw someone walking down the stairs towards the door. I walked quickly back to my car.

The studio was next on my list. Again, I parked well away and walked. As I got closer, I could see the door was open, the wind gently moving it backwards and forwards. Probably a late night session for the engineer. I walked in, remembering the lay-out from my last visit. There was no noise. I was on my guard in case I ran into a burglar. I slowly walked into the main room. It was too dark to see anything. I fumbled for the light switch, believing I was ready for whatever I was going to see. But I hadn't expected to see Greg Tasker's body lying on the floor.

I waited outside for the police. It didn't take long for them to arrive. I watched a man in his early fifties, tall with grey hair and the unmistakable air of authority, walk across to me.

'Mr Geraghty, I assume?' He flashed his identification card at me. 'DI Robinson – Major Incident Team, Humberside Police.'

'Call me Joe' I said.

'I only call my friends by their first name.'

I smiled. I'd heard the routine before.

'I'll get to the point for you, Mr Geraghty. This is a police matter now and what I won't be needing is a Private Investigator running around thinking he's Philip Marlowe.'

'I'm more of a Sam Spade man myself.' He wasn't laughing. 'Just doing my job' I said.

'Where have I heard that before?' Robinson stood up and walked a couple of yards away from me. He stopped and turned back. 'I want to know everything you know.'

'About?' I wasn't feeling particularly helpful.

'About how long you've known Tasker was missing would be a start.'

I hesitated before telling Robinson what I knew.

'You didn't think of giving us a call?' Robinson said. 'Given the circumstances? We have people who deal with this sort of thing. Specialists.'

I explained about Kane Major. 'We thought we could handle it' I said.

'You thought you could handle it, Mr Geraghty?' Robinson laughed and moved closer. 'I'd hardly say you've handled it.'

It was like being back at school. There was nothing to say. He was right.

'And it's people like me, the professionals, who have to sweep the mess up' he continued, pointing at the studio. 'It's people like me who have to tell people like the Taskers their son is dead.'

'There were wider considerations' I said. 'We had a lot to weigh up and think about. Greg often disappeared. We didn't think it was a problem.'

Robinson turned to face him. 'Wider considerations? Surprise me, Mr Geraghty.'

'We agreed it was best for the band if his disappearance was kept low-key.'

'Who agreed?'

'Me, Major, the family.'

'Bad publicity?'

'Something like that.'

'I've just been hearing about the band's reunion, and although I don't really know anything about them at the moment, I'll be looking into it. Your reputation precedes you, however, and I'll tell you this for nothing: I don't think we're going to get along.'

Robinson was now standing directly in front of me, ensuring I had to look up at him. 'What's going to happen now is you're going to go to the station and give a statement to my little helpers. And you're not going to leave a single detail out. If you do, I'll be coming back for you. I promise I'll make your life a misery. I know you work for Don Ridley, and I've got a lot of time for the man, but when I've finished with you, you'll wish you were a Charted Accountant rather than a Private Investigator.'

DI Robinson's team took their time taking a statement from me. I'd been kept waiting before being sat in a sterile interview room, despite being told they were thankful for my co-operation. Half an hour after leaving the station, a taxi dropped me back at Tasker's studio. The Scene of Crime Team was at work. I was told in no uncertain terms that I should collect my car and go. I drove to Tasker's parents' house.

Major was already there, stood outside the front door, cigarette in his mouth, mobile to his ear. He finished his call. 'What's going on, PI?'

There wasn't much I could say. 'He was attacked. Looked like a single punch and his head caught the sharp edge of the mixing desk.' I'd seen and heard enough to put that much together. That was it for the moment.

He turned towards me. 'I was sure he was just going to turn up.'

'Me too.' Meaningless platitudes. I hadn't taken his disappearance seriously enough. I should have been more insistent that the police were informed. It was too late now. Looking at the house, the only light on was in the front room. The police would still need his parents to formally confirm it was their son. It would be a grim job for them. Identifying my wife's body was the hardest thing I'd ever done.

'How are they doing?' I asked.

Major shook his head and lit another cigarette. The shock was hitting him, too. 'Not particularly good.'

'As you'd expect.'

'His mother's not too good.'

'Are the police in there with them?'

Major nodded. 'They asked me to leave.'

'It's procedure.'

He offered me a cigarette. 'I need you to sort this for me, PI.'

'There's nothing we can do at the moment' I said. I'd already decided I had to help. I was partly responsible. I could have put a stop to this and insisted they call the police. But I hadn't. Someone had killed him and I couldn't let it lie. I thought back to my wife's death. You couldn't rely on the police. I wasn't going to let them suffer like I had.

'How about enemies? Had Greg said anything to you? Now's the time to say.'

'Not so far as I know.'

'How about in London?'

'Nothing.'

'Right.' The press would soon be on their doorstep, and if the press was interested, it meant the police would make extra resources available to ensure they got a result. The situation would feed on itself and snowball with Tasker's parents stuck in the middle of it. I remembered there weren't any photographs of New Holland in the front room. If they hadn't enjoyed the associated fame their son brought them, being in the public eye was about to get a whole lot worse for them.

I walked into the front room. Kath Tasker was being consoled by her husband. He told me to take a seat. 'We should have told the police from the start. We should have listened to you.'

I waved his words away. 'They needed to know.'

'We don't blame you, Joe' he said. 'Chances are, the police wouldn't have been able to find him, either. We understand how it works.'

'How are you doing?' I said. Trite, but what else was there to say?

'He was our only child, and you're not supposed to outlive your children, are you? Especially not under these circumstances.' Keith stood up and walked across to the windowsill where there was a box of tissues. He passed them to his wife. 'We've got a lot to do and so much to organise. I haven't even started to ring the family yet.'

He looked like he'd pulled himself together, but grief acts in funny ways. Once the initial shock was over with, I hoped he would have people to turn to. People who would help him.

'Is there anything I can do?' I asked. 'Anybody I could call for you?'

He shook his head. 'Thanks for the offer.'

'We've made a terrible mistake' said his wife.

We both turned to listen to her.

'It's important to us that you know we were doing this for the right reasons.' She felt for her husband's hand, gripped it tight. 'We need your help to put it right. We let our son down, so the least we can do is to make sure we get justice for him. The more people who are trying to do that, the better.'

I didn't know what to say. I'd sat outside and thought it through. I hadn't done enough for them. I knew I was at least partly culpable. I was the outsider. I should have seen things more clearly.

'We can pay you' she said.

I told her it wasn't necessary. Major was already paying me. 'What did the police say?' I asked.

Keith Tasker took over. 'They didn't tell us much. They've asked us to formally identify him tomorrow. Maybe they'll tell us more then. I assume they'll have to do their forensic work first and work out exactly what happened. They'll want to do a thorough job.'

I looked him in the eye. I could see his pain. I knew I was already in. 'I'll do what I can for you' I said.

Kath started crying again and thanked me through her tears. 'He was our son. He was just our Greg.'

I thought back to the story Keith Tasker had told me about how he'd helped my family. I made the promise again. 'I'll do what I can.'

I drove back to the city centre. I'd phoned Julia as soon as I was clear of the house. It was nearly two in the morning, but news of Tasker's death would break quickly. I said I'd go to her hotel. I stared at Don's number in my mobile. I decided I wasn't going to give him the satisfaction of him telling me I'd been wrong. Not yet. I sent Sarah a text message and said I'd speak to her first thing in the morning. I felt like a coward. Julia was waiting for me as I walked down the corridor towards her room. I sat down on the bed and told her what I knew. She hadn't been as upset as I thought she would be. Maybe it was the shock of the situation. He might not have been a very close friend, but she'd still lost a friend. I supposed, in a way, I had too. It wasn't a pleasant situation.

She stood up and looked around the room. Her laptop was in the corner. 'I need to write this up' she said.

I reached for her hand. 'Not yet.'

She sat back down.

'There's plenty of time for that.'

She relented. 'I'm sorry, Joe. It must have been horrible for you.'

I nodded. I had nothing to say, but I pulled myself together. I had to.

'What are you going to do?'

'Whatever I can' I said.

'What about the police?'

I shrugged. They were better resourced and connected than I was, but I'd been asked to assist. 'I'm going to need your help' I said. 'His parents are in pieces. As well as having to bury their only child, there's going to be a media shitstorm heading their way. They're going to need all the help they can get. I need some help, too. You know as much about Greg as anyone. If we work together, I'll feel happier that they'll get the answers they want.' I dangled the carrot. 'And you'll get the exclusive.' She had my story, too, but I left it unsaid.

'The police won't like you sticking your nose in' she said.

'I don't care.'

She held her hand out. 'I want to know everything. You don't keep anything back from me.'

I shook it. 'Deal.'

We took a break whilst she made coffee. I needed it to keep going.

'What do we need to do?' she asked.

'We have to build a picture, find out more about Greg's life' I said. 'It's where the answer will be. We need to know how he spent his days, what he did and who he did it with. All that kind of stuff. We need to know his habits and routines. We need to know everything about him.

'If he had secrets?'

'Everyone has secrets' I said. I'd promised to hold nothing back. 'He was having an affair with Lorraine.'

She considered the information. 'I'm not surprised.'

I asked her how she knew.

'It's obvious, really.' She smiled. 'The engineer guy said as much.'

'Right.'

'I can't believe we're talking about Greg like he's a piece of meat' Julia said.

We sat in silence for a moment until I broke it. 'We've got to do the best we can for his family.'

Julia moved closer to me. 'He didn't deserve this.' She snuggled up against me and kissed me on the cheek before turning her head to kiss me on my lips.

CHAPTER SEVEN

I woke early, and seeing Julia sleeping next to me, I got out of the bed and headed into the shower. I turned the hot water up as far as I could bear it and closed my eyes. The previous night had been clumsy and awkward, like being a teenager again. Part of me felt it was wrong, but part of me knew it was a necessary step. I had to start living again. Stepping out of the shower, I towelled myself dry and put yesterday's clothes back on. The shower had woken Julia. She was sitting upright in bed with a T-shirt on when I walked back into the room.

'Morning' she said.

'Morning.' I smiled, aware I was fully dressed and ready to be on my way. 'Busy day' I said, hoping it explained why I was leaving so early. What I didn't say was that I didn't know how to behave or what to do. I headed for the door. 'Speak to you later.'

An hour later, and following a detour to my flat to change into clean clothes, I was stood on the doorstep of Steve Priestley's farmhouse. I knocked and waited for an answer. They lived on what I assumed used to be a working farm halfway between the small villages of Mappleton and

Aldbrough. It was out towards the North Sea coast, about fifteen miles away from Hull. It stood by itself, no other houses in view. It certainly offered isolation. A woman answered the door. She was in her late thirties. She looked washed out and tired. 'If you're a reporter, I'm not interested' she said, trying to shut the door on me. I got a foot in the doorframe and stopped her. She relented. 'Steve's not here.'

'Can I talk to you?' I asked. I told her who I was and who I was working for.

She hesitated before letting me in. She told me she was Priestley's wife, Carly. I followed her through the house and into the conservatory. We sat down.

'He's out walking, getting some fresh air' she said.

'How's he doing?'

'He's not said a word to me.' She lit a cigarette. 'What are the police saying?'

'Not a lot at the moment.'

I told her I was working for Tasker's parents.

'How are they doing?'

'Not too good.'

'It must be terrible for them.' She took a long drag.

'They're struggling' I said. 'I'm trying to make it a bit easier for them.'

She stood up and turned away from me. Opened the conservatory door. 'I knew this reunion was a bad idea' she said. 'Steve hated the idea right from the start, but he let himself be talked into it.'

'Major?'

'Who else.' She shook her head. 'This isn't my Steve. He's better off out of it, but he never could say no. I met Steve as the band broke up and he was a total mess' she said. 'Once Greg became incapable of functioning normally, it was Steve who carried them all. He was the one writing the songs and keeping things together, yet Major carried on treating him like something he'd scraped off his shoe. Major's first concern was always for Greg and it never changed.' She took a long, angry drag on the cigarette.

'You won't be having him around for dinner any time soon' I said, trying to lighten the mood.

'I don't want the man anywhere near me. I've lost count of the number of times I've told Steve to stand up for himself. He shouldn't let Major walk all over him. He should be treated with more respect.' She paused and shook her head. 'The music business nearly broke my husband the first time around. I'm not going to let it happen again.'

'When I spoke to him, he told me he was looking forward to being in a band again.'

'He would do, wouldn't he? But I'm telling you, the idea of a reunion terrified him. He wasn't sleeping properly at night. The worry of it was making him ill.'

'Why do it, then?'

'Because he's an idiot. He thinks it's all about the music. He's closed his mind off to the money side of things. I think he finds it easier to cope if he pretends the others are in it for the same reasons as him.'

It didn't tally with the way Priestley had presented himself in the rehearsal room.

'He was with me all night' she said, staring at me, as she put her cigarette out. She closed the conservatory door and headed into the kitchen.

I nodded. 'Right.' I hadn't asked her to offer an alibi. I stood up and followed her.

'My husband always went with the flow in the band and he never caused any trouble.' She turned away from me. 'Just leave us alone, please.'

Returning to my car, I checked my mobile for messages. Clicking onto my address book, I flicked through the numbers until I found Julia's. I stared at it for a moment, unable to decide whether or not I should call her. She might have misinterpreted the way I'd left her hotel this morning. I shouldn't have left as quickly as I had, but it was too late to undo it. I continued to look at the number knowing leaving it wasn't going to help the situation. I put it back in my pocket. She hadn't called me, either.

I took a deep breath and walked into the office. Sarah sat in the far corner, working on her laptop. Don stopped what he was doing and stared at me.

'Couldn't be bothered to ring me, Joe?' he said.

I apologised. 'I should have called' I said.

'Too right you should have' Don said. 'What the fuck have you got us involved in here?'

Don rarely swore. Not that I needed a clue as to his anger. There was nothing I could say. I sat down and opened my laptop, connected to the Internet and went straight to the BBC homepage. News of Greg Tasker's death had broken. Details were limited, but the information was out there. The fact the band were rehearsing for a reunion tour was now being widely reported. I wondered how much malice was behind the blow that killed him. It indicated an argument, but not excessive violence. Who hadn't thrown a punch in anger or frustration? Usually the outcome was some minor damage. But not this time.

Don shook his head, stood up. 'We're finished with the job.' He stood up and left the office.

Sarah and I sat in silence for a few moments until she spoke. 'Long night?'

'I was going to ring, but I didn't want to disturb you.' I told her what I knew about Tasker's death. She'd read the media reports. She knew as much as I did. I wanted to speak to the engineer at Tasker's studio again, hear his story firsthand. There was no mention of him on the studio's website, and he wasn't going to be there for the foreseeable future, certainly not until the police had finished their investigations there. Finding him could be a problem.

'So that's it for us? We're finished with the job?' Sarah asked.

I shook my head. 'Not yet. I said I'd help.' I explained why I'd involved Julia in the case. Sarah looked like she was going to object, but changed her mind. I shut my laptop down. 'She has the contacts we don't have' I said. It probably sounded weak to her. 'She can help us' I said.

We lapsed back into silence. Neither of us had the inclination to push the matter any further. Maybe I was wrong, but it was too late to turn back now. I'd made promises to people. Sarah went back to her work. I knew the last big case we'd undertaken had almost been the final straw for Don. I'd brought trouble to his family's door. Add to that a general lack of work, and he'd decided it was time to take a step back from the business. Being a former detective, he also had his police pension to fall back on, so he was comfortable. He didn't need the bother. And I wasn't his son, despite the sign above the door saying, 'Ridley and Son Private Investigators'. He didn't really owe me anything at all.

Whilst we'd been talking, I'd received a text message from Lorraine Harrison. She was in a cafe, a ten minute walk away. I decided the fresh air would do me good. I left Sarah with a list of people I wanted background checks done on and headed out of the office. Walking in, I spotted her slumped in the far corner, staring into space. I was surprised to see she was dressed for work.

'I take it you've heard the news?' I said, sitting down.

'On the television this morning.'

I felt bad for not telling her myself. The smell of food reminded me I hadn't eaten yet, so I ordered a bacon sandwich and coffee. She said she wasn't hungry, her drink remained untouched. The cafe was hidden away down an old fashioned shopping arcade, just off the main shopping area. It came complete with Formica tables and sauces in plastic containers. A throwback to the days before the trendy cafe bars of Princes Avenue. I think I prefer things this way.

'Are you on your way to work?' I asked her.

'I don't think I can ask for a day off, do you?'

'Fair enough.' I asked her where she worked. She was a receptionist for a firm of solicitors.

'I can't let Jason know how upset I am about Greg's death' she said. 'We had a massive row about him the other night. He won't understand or care. In fact, he'll no doubt be having a right good laugh about it all at the moment.'

'It must be tough.'

'I didn't want to leave Jay all upset, either, but I needed to speak to you.' She blew her nose and took a deep breath.

'I'm glad you called me' I said. 'Greg's parents have asked me to help out. Just to make sure the police don't miss anything.' I waited until I was sure I had her attention. 'I need your help to do that. I need to know if Greg had any enemies. You're probably the person who knew him best in this city. Did he ever mention anything to you?'

She shook her head. 'He didn't have any enemies.'

The waitress brought me my food and drink. It gave Lorraine time to rethink her answer.

'Obviously he had at least one enemy, but why would anyone want to kill him?' she said. 'I know he had his problems with Priestley in the past' she added.

There it was. I bit into my sandwich and told her to carry on. Priestley's wife's behaviour had intrigued me. Lorraine was reluctant, but I told her she wasn't pointing the finger at him. The more background she could give me, the better picture of Greg's life I could form.

'When I met them, they were the best of friends. It was the time of my life, to be honest with you. I used to love listening to Greg talk about how they were going to be bigger than The Beatles. We'd go to Spiders every weekend and then on to a house party. I felt like I was on top of the world. It felt like they ruled the city. It's hard to describe, but it was just inevitable. I knew they were going to make it. They were just too good not to.'

'Did you see him when he moved away?'

'Not really. He was always busy. It was relentless. I can't deny it hurt when they left, but we always stayed in touch. We'd write to each other every week. He never forgot. Sometimes I'd get pages and pages from him, sometimes it was just a postcard, but we made the effort. It was only really when the band split up that the letters stopped.'

I let her reminisce for a short while before asking why Tasker had fallen out with Priestley.

'The pressure. Major was always pushing them to do more. Despite what you think, Greg wasn't cut out for that world and there was always more expected from him. He was the one doing the real hard work. Deep down, I don't think he particularly enjoyed it. I think all of the living out of a suitcase, moving on from one city to another, took the fun out of it. It was just too much, but Major expected him to keep producing new songs. I can't imagine many people thrive under those circumstances.'

'But things changed?'

She nodded. 'It all got too much for Greg in the end. He ran out of steam. He had writer's block and couldn't produce anything. Priestley didn't need asking twice; he was straight in there with his own songs, taking over things.'

'Greg didn't like it?'

'Of course he didn't. It was his band, not Priestley's.'

'What did he do about it?'

'He went into a downward spiral of drink and drugs. He had no confidence in himself. Although he eventually got his act back together, Priestley wanted to be the one calling the shots and Greg never felt comfortable trying to take the lead again. Part of me thinks it was just boys being boys, that they both wanted to be top dog, but Greg told me he was really freaked out by how much Priestley wanted control of things.'

'What about Major?' I asked. 'I thought he was Greg's mate?'

'It was always about the money for him. He needed the band on the road and making records.'

'But they stayed in touch after the band split up?'

'So far as I know.'

'They weren't as close to Priestley?'

'Definitely not' she said.

'Priestley's wife said he was looking to the reunion as being a chance to right some wrongs, say a proper goodbye?'

'I wouldn't know about that.'

'What did Greg want out of the reunion?'

She thought about my question. 'I think he saw it as a chance to put the past behind him. He'd recorded a new solo album, which he was really proud of. It was a chance to start over.'

I could see that re-launching his solo career on the back of New Holland's tour made sense. Especially if his previous work hadn't been well received. It seems that there was plenty at stake for everyone.

The cafe was emptying. A few stragglers remained, making hot drinks last as long as possible.

'You won't tell his parents about me and Greg?' she asked.

'I won't tell them' I said. More secrets and lies.

You're in a whirlwind of recording and touring. You move down to London. It's the place to be. You're sharing a flat in Camden with Kane. Only Priestley has decided to stay in Hull, preferring to travel down when he has to. You don't understand his attitude. You want to make a great album, but you want to enjoy yourself as you do it. There's alcohol, drugs and women on tap for you all. Kane joins in, encourages your behaviour. Even though the music press love you, you veer from outrageous self-confidence to crushing self-doubt. You push the thoughts to one side. There's always another party to go to. You indulge in more alcohol, drugs and women. You play your first gigs in America. New York City. Your dream has come true, but this is like starting again. No one knows you, but you don't care. You stand in front of the microphone like a giant. You feel like Manhattan is yours. The bright lights of Times Square are all for you. You return to the UK. Your single, 'Welcome to Hell', makes the top ten. You're a star. There's no place for you to hide now.

CHAPTER EIGHT

Lorraine left the cafe and headed to work, leaving me to finish my breakfast. I wasn't sure what my next move was going to be, so I headed back to the office for another look through the printouts Sarah had prepared for me. There were no messages and my mobile was quiet. I searched around until I found the CD of New Holland's third and final album. Glancing through the song writing credits, this was the one that saw Priestley take charge, contributing eight out of the eleven tracks. I only needed to hear the first two tracks to know the band was all but finished by then. Tasker was a spent force with a drug problem. I wasn't surprised this was New Holland's final album.

Next, I logged onto the Internet and made another attempt to track down Tasker's studio engineer. This time I Googled the studio and trawled the message-boards until I found a mention of the man I wanted. Michael Rusting. I wrote his name down. I'd ask Sarah to work her magic.

I flicked through the folder of interviews and articles, which had been filed in chronological order for me. The lead interview to accompany the third and last album had been carried by a more highbrow music magazine. It was a million miles away from their early days as NME darlings. It didn't make pleasant reading. Tasker and Priestley were jostling for position; the bickering embarrassing.

I put the printout down, switched off the music and put my head down on my desk. I was tired. I wondered what Debbie would make of Julia. More importantly, I wondered what she would make of my behaviour. I'd stopped wearing my wedding ring quite so regularly. At first it was only the occasional day without it, more to see how it felt. Now it was more like second nature not to wear it. It was another step in the never ending process of moving on. It'd be nice if I could pick up the phone and talk to somebody about it. I was still in contact with Debbie's sister, but her husband had never been a friend, more someone who was just there. I'd had good friends when I'd played rugby, but following my injury, I'd not kept in touch with them. I glanced at the photograph I had on my desk of myself diving over for a match-winning try in a mid-1980s local derby. I wondered what the rest of the players had amounted to. It was professional sport, but it certainly wasn't Premiership football; they'd all be out there somewhere in the city, working day jobs to pay the bills, just like Keith Tasker. Sarah shook me awake. I'd fallen asleep.

'You can't leave it alone, can you?' she said, taking in the information on my desk.

I quickly came around. I conceded she was right, hoped she was more willing to help me now. I had to get to the truth. I explained about Lorraine's affair with Tasker.

'It's not normal, is it?' she said.

I had no answer. It was weird. 'Love moves in strange ways' I said. 'They've known each other for years' I offered by way of explanation before telling her I'd spoken to Priestley's wife earlier in the day.

'Not the man himself?'

'He was out walking somewhere.'

'Must be hitting him hard.'

'His wife was quick enough to tell me he had an alibi for last night.'

'Did you ask for one?'

'No.'

She didn't look impressed, but at least she was interested. 'You think he was involved in Tasker's death?'

I stood up and stretched. 'Why not?'

She paused, like she was trying to justify an argument. I stopped her before she had chance to speak. 'I'm just thinking aloud, more than anything.' I turned back to my desk and started to gather my things. There were other people I wanted to talk to, but I'd definitely be speaking to Priestley again.

I headed back to my flat and jumped in the shower, turned the temperature to cold in an attempt to reinvigorate myself. I closed my eyes and let the ice cold jets hit me before jumping back out. It'd have to do. I drove to Siobhan's boutique and parked up about a hundred yards from her shop and considered what my strategy should be. All I knew was that she could help me in some way. I could see two men in dark clothing sat in a car parked on the other side of the road. They were staring at me. DI Robinson's team, no doubt. I wasn't bothered by them. They could watch me all they liked, they weren't going to stop me doing my job. The same sales assistant sat near the till. I asked her where Siobhan was. She quickly glanced across to what I assumed was the changing room before reverting back to me. 'She's not in at the moment.'

I walked across to the room. 'I know you're in there, Siobhan.' I looked back at the girl. 'Your assistant isn't a good liar.'

I waited a few moments before calling out again. Siobhan walked out onto the shop floor. I smiled at her. She looked terrible, like she hadn't slept.

'Alright?' I asked.

She nodded, but wasn't convincing.

'We need to talk' I said.

She told her assistant to take a break and closed the door behind her. She found us some chairs and we sat down.

'I'm sorry I wasn't able to find Greg' I said.

'I'm sure you did your best.'

It was my turn to nod unconvincingly. I explained how I worked for Tasker's parents. 'Now's the time to say if you know anything. Anything at all.'

'Why are you working for them?' she asked me.

'I owe them.'

She didn't press me. 'I don't know anything.'

She was clearly upset, but she also had her guard up. She wouldn't look me in the eye. 'We're on the same side here' I said.

'I can't help you.'

I told her how Tasker's parents were suffering. I got nothing back.

She lit a cigarette. I must have been staring. She told me it was her shop, she could do what she liked. 'Have you spoken to that slag, Lorraine?' she asked me.

Her abruptness took me by surprise. Without thinking, I nodded and said I'd spoken to her.

'I can't bear to think about her and Greg. It makes me ill.'

I said nothing. It wasn't my place to get involved.

'What did she say?' Siobhan asked me.

'She wants to know the truth, too.'

'It's none of her business.'

'How did you find out about them?' I asked.

'He told me. He said he didn't want it to be a secret anymore. Can you believe that? He tells me, but expects me to carry on like nothing's changed.' She shook her head, took a drag on her cigarette. 'The arrogance of the man. He was so used to people doing whatever he wanted them to do, he forgot I had feelings. I gave up everything for him to move up here to this shithole and this was how he repaid me. He wouldn't even live with me. I said it was either me or her. He couldn't have both.'

'What did Greg do?'

'Carried on as normal. He didn't think I'd do anything about it.'

'Does Lorraine's husband know about them?'

'No idea. I don't think Greg cared to be honest.'

'Had you left him?' I asked.

She looked up at me and shook her head. 'I couldn't leave him.'

I gave her a minute, found the kitchen and made us drinks. She was busy opening windows when I returned.

'You should have stopped me smoking in here' she said, trying to force a laugh.

I smiled. 'Would you have listened?'

'I suppose not.'

I passed her a mug of tea. 'I spoke to Steve Priestley's wife this morning' I said.

'Never met the woman.'

'She said she didn't want him to be part of the reunion.'

She sat back down. 'I'm not sure Greg really wanted it, either.'

'I thought he wanted to relaunch his solo career?'

'That's what he kept telling himself. To be honest, I think he let himself be talked into it.'

'Major?'

'He could never cut his ties with him.'

'He could have just said no.'

'I think Greg thought he owed him something. He couldn't walk away.'

'But he wasn't so keen?'

'I don't think so, but they both needed the money. Greg's studio wasn't doing too well and he said Kane needed something to happen for him.' She put her empty mug down and walked over to the front door. 'I'm sorry I can't help more, but I haven't got time to be sitting around talking like this. Greg gave me enough money to get started here and his family are going to want it paying back, aren't they?' She turned back to face me. 'Look, there's something I should tell you. The last time I saw Greg, he came in here, didn't say a word to me, just emptied the till and left.'

I missed a call from Julia as I drove away from the boutique. Parking up, I called her back and we agreed to meet for some food. I was pleased there didn't seem to be any awkwardness between us. She'd insisted on eating on Princes Avenue. It was fast becoming her favourite part of the city. I laughed and told her she must be missing London.

The bar was surprisingly empty for early evening, so I had no trouble finding Julia in the corner. Even in the trendiest area of the city, it seemed like some places were trendier than others. I didn't mind. The peace and quiet was welcome. Julia was studying the menu and didn't see me walk in. I spoke as I approached the table. 'How's it going?'

She looked up and put the menu down. 'Alright. You?'

'Had better days. Don thinks we should be walking away from the job and he's not shy in telling me so.'

'What does Sarah think?'

It was a good question. 'I think she's more inquisitive than her father.' My mobile started to ring. It was Major, finally returning my call. I let it go to voicemail. He could wait for an hour. I told Julia that Tasker had emptied Siobhan's till shortly before his death. She had told me she hadn't been to the bank for a couple of days and he'd walked out of the boutique with over £2,000 in cash. Given the price of the dresses, there was every chance the money would mount up like that. It raised more questions, but it helped fill in the timeframe. Greg had told her not to tell anyone that she'd seen him and she'd kept her word. She felt bad over it, but I told her it wouldn't have made any difference to the search to find him. I'd tried to tell her it wasn't important now, but I knew it was going to weigh heavily on her.

'I can solve one mystery as well' she said. 'I know where Greg was hiding out.'

'Where?'

'Bridlington.'

'What was he doing there?' Bridlington is a small seaside resort, thirty miles north of Hull. Not far away, but as good as anywhere if you wanted to lie low, I supposed.

'No idea. He was staying in a cheap B&B. The landlady rang the paper once she recognised who her guest was.'

'What did she say?'

'Nothing of any use. Just that he paid a bit extra to use the room in the day time. Apparently he just stayed in there, playing his guitar. That's how she realised who he was.'

'Right.' There was nothing else to say. He'd obviously wanted to get out of Hull for a bit, like Siobhan and Priestley said he often did, but what had been the trigger? And why had he come back for money? 'Did she say anything else?'

Julia said she hadn't. 'Tell me about your day' she said.

I took her through it. 'I dropped by at Greg's studio' I said. I'd wanted to speak to the people on the site directly. It was a long shot because if they had any information, the police would be all over it by now.

'Anything?' she said.

'No.' I told her that it had cost me £20 to get the security guards to speak to me. And they weren't even the ones who'd been working that night. I explained that they'd called their mate and passed me the phone. The police had already taken statements from them and they had nothing to add. They hadn't seen or heard anything and the CCTV hadn't been working properly. I wasn't surprised. They hadn't seen me walk past them. A dead end.

I moved on and told her how defensive Priestley's wife had been towards me at their house, and how I hadn't been able to speak to him. 'Who do you think really wanted the New Holland reunion?' I asked.

Our food arrived and we ate in silence for a few minutes. Julia put her knife and fork down. 'I assume they all wanted the band to reform. Money. What else?'

I shook my head. 'It doesn't feel right. Priestley's wife said he had to be talked into it and Siobhan said Greg was only doing it because he felt he owed to Major.'

'Greg did have a solo record ready to release, though.'

'Cynical, but true.' It would still be released. Death doesn't stop the music industry. 'Doesn't it strike you as odd? It doesn't seem like he really wanted to be back in the public eye. He was choosing to live in Hull, which I can't imagine is particularly clever if you want to be a musician. I get the feeling he was going against his better judgment on this. I don't think he really wanted to be back in the band.'

Julia considered what I'd said. 'He could have said no to Major.'

She wasn't wrong, but it seemed like a lot of people had a problem saying 'no' to him. Me included. I knew I still had to return his call.

'Don't forget there would have been a lot of money to be made. It would have been difficult to turn down' she said. 'I don't mean to run Greg or Steve down, but they need the band. They wouldn't make anything like the same amount through their solo work. It just wouldn't happen.'

She was right. 'How bad was the falling out between them?'

'They've only just started speaking again. They went their separate ways when the band finished. I don't suppose they had reason to be in touch. It's the way it is when bands fall apart. Too much anger.'

'Long time to bear a grudge.'

'Priestley was always a little bit weird.'

It was difficult to weigh up. I'd read Tasker's drug intake had rendered him all but useless when it came to recording their last album. Maybe he felt like he'd lost face, that the rest of the band hadn't been grateful for his contribution over the years. Equally, Priestley had done what was required. Situations change, the status quo can't always remain. But it was naive to think there wouldn't be any lingering bitterness. Priestley's wife had suggested her husband wanted the reunion to be about the music and not money. I wasn't ready to swallow that unconditionally. If Tasker and Priestley had a volatile relationship, I knew arguments could get out of hand. The smallest thing can be blown up and magnified.

'How do you reckon Greg spent his days?' I asked.

'His studio?' Julia said.

I shook my head. 'Didn't like the place by all accounts.'

Julia shrugged. 'I don't know, then.'

'Neither do I' I said, but I wanted to know. If he wasn't working in his studio, he had to be doing something with his day. It had to bring him into contact with other people. Potential witnesses. Potential suspects.

'I went to the police's press conference this afternoon' Julia said.

'Anything?'

We'd both finished eating and put our empty plates to one side.

'Nothing. DI Robinson said their investigation was following several lines of inquiry, which seems to be their way of saying they're hedging their bets for now, certainly at least until they've got some forensic results. He wouldn't be drawn any further than that.' She checked her notes. 'And he appealed for any witnesses to come forward. Standard stuff, really.'

I nodded. We sat in silence until I broke it. 'Are we ok?' I asked. It needed saying.

'Why wouldn't we be?'

'After last night?'

I stared at her until she spoke. 'We're both adults and we're both single. Why should it be a problem?'

'I was worried I'd taken advantage after breaking the news about Greg' I said.

'You didn't take advantage.'

Our hands were on the table, inches apart. I couldn't decide whether to bridge the gap or not.

My decision was made when she withdrew her hand back under the table.

'I don't want to cause you any trouble, Joe. I wouldn't want to be in your way or anything like that.'

I think I got the point. 'You're not causing me any trouble.' I smiled at her. 'In fact, I quite like it.'

I stepped outside the bar to return Major's call. It had to be done. He wanted to meet me immediately. He gave me the address of where he was eating, a fish restaurant close to his office in the city centre. I knew the place. I terminated the call, went back inside, made my apologies and left. When I arrived, I found Major sat by himself at the back of the room. He was surrounded by paperwork. He looked knackered. He poured himself a shot of whiskey before offering me the bottle. The restaurant wasn't busy. They seemed happy to indulge him.

He asked me what I'd done throughout the day. I gave him a brief rundown of who I'd spoken to and explained how I hadn't seemingly made much headway.

'What are the police saying?' he asked me.

'Not a lot at the moment.'

Major poured another drink. Handed me one. 'It needs sorting. For the sake of his parents.'

I wasn't buying it. 'Cut the shit. How badly did you want this reunion?' I asked.

He smiled, turned away from me.

'It doesn't seem like Tasker or Priestley particularly wanted to go through with it.' I swallowed the whiskey. 'I think they were doing it for you.'

Major shrugged. 'I'm touched.'

'Did you have to force them?'

Major turned to face me. 'How could I force them?'

'You can be very persuasive when you need to be.'

Major stared at me, like he was weighing me up. 'I'm surprised your mouth doesn't get you into more trouble.'

'I say it as I see it.'

Major raised his glass and saluted me. 'I like that, PI. It's why you're so important to me.'

'I'll take that as a compliment.'

'Take it however you want to.'

'You seem to be the one who was pushing for the reunion. There'd have been a lot of money in it for you. Assuming you didn't all argue, because when people argue, things happen. Accidents.'

'Doesn't have to be about the money' he said.

I laughed. 'Come on.'

He stared at me, took the bait. 'Are you saying I killed him, PI?'

I said nothing. I was close enough to smell the alcohol on his breath.

'Why would I kill Greg?' he said, filling the silence. He knocked back his whiskey. Calm now. 'Alright, I'm skint. I've lost out on some bad property investments in London, but who hasn't at the moment? I needed the reunion to get myself back on an even keel.' He poured himself another drink and knocked it back in one. He pointed at me. 'They owe me. I made them what they are. Without me, they were nothing. Reforming to play a few gigs was the least they could do for me. Why would I kill Greg? I needed him alive.'

I swallowed my drink. 'Greg was supposed to be your friend' I eventually said. 'You knew he'd struggled under the pressure of the band, yet you were prepared to put him back in that situation just for your own financial benefit? Some friend you were.'

Major stared at me and wiped his eyes before throwing the last of the whiskey into his glass. 'I was trying to help him.' He stood up. 'I think he was involved with some bad people.'

Fuck's sake. I didn't want to hear it, but asked anyway. 'Who?'

'I don't know. I think he was worried about something, just a feeling I got.' He was pointing at me. 'Maybe you should be looking into that, because that's what I pay you to do.'

He was hardly giving me breaking news. A waiter brought out his food. I stood up and left. The man made me sick.

I left my car in the city centre and walked back to my flat. I needed the fresh air. I was angry with Major. Maybe Don was right. It felt like I was pushing my luck for nothing. What good could come from this situation? Maybe the police should be left to it? I thought about Tasker's parents. They needed me to carry on. I ignored the shouts of the drunks as I walked home, head down through the rain. As I passed a takeaway, a teenager threw a chip at my head, but I didn't respond. I didn't care. Into my flat, I changed out of my wet clothes and put on an old tracksuit and T-shirt. It was getting late, but I wasn't tired now. I flicked through the pile of CDs and put on some early Dylan. I wanted to hear a man with his guitar and nothing else. I wanted it to be sparse and desolate. I wanted to hear the honesty of the music. I found a can of lager in the fridge. Last one. I sat upright when the street-level buzzer went on my door. I checked the time. It had gone midnight. I walked over to the intercom and asked who it was.

'Can I come in?' Julia said back to me.

I swallowed the last mouthful of lager and released the lock. Tomorrow was another day. 'Come on up' I said.

CHAPTER NINE

I woke to the smell of coffee and warm toast. Julia placed my breakfast on the bedside unit. She was wearing one of my old T-shirts.

'Best I could do' she said. 'You should try shopping once in a while.'

'Normally I have fresh juice and croissants with a selection of conserves available.' I sat up. 'Sometimes you run out, you know how it is.'

She laughed and got back into bed after turning the television on. 'Is it always this cold in your flat?'

I said it was, between mouthfuls of toast. 'Storage heaters. They'll kick in soon.'

'They best do.' She pulled the duvet up to her neck.

I put the plate down and thanked her. It'd been a long time since someone had made me breakfast in bed.

The news was covering Tasker's death. The report went to a pre-recorded interview with a tired looking DI Robinson, who urged anybody with any information to come forward. I felt as tired as he looked. We'd spent several hours the previous night listening to the tapes of Julia's recent interview with Tasker. The interview had been wide-ranging, starting from the day he met Priestley, his happiness as the band took off, his difficulty with drugs and the eventual split, through to his thoughts on the imminent reunion. I could have cried as his voice filled the room, his death adding poignancy to his words. Julia had let me burn a copy so I could listen to it again. I reached for my mobile and called Major's number. I listened to the voicemail message.

'He's gone to down London for a couple of days on business' I said to Julia, killing the call without leaving a message. 'He's done a runner.' I threw my mobile onto the bed. Fuck's sake. I should have known from Major's manner that something was amiss. It wasn't a clever move. The police were bound to take a closer look at Tasker's flat. If the police knew about the break-in, they'd be coming for me next.

She put her mug down. 'Don't beat yourself up over it. He's manipulated far more intelligent people than you.'

'Cheers.'

'You're welcome.'

I told her I wasn't doing this for Major. I was doing it for Tasker's parents. But I didn't like being used, or being left to face the music. I checked my emails on my mobile. Sarah hadn't had any luck getting an address for Rusting yet. I looked at the television as the reporter moved onto the sports news. Julia killed the television and checked her mobile. She said she had to go. The story was moving. 'Don't beat yourself up, Joe. You've done nothing wrong, so nothing changes. You told Greg's parents you'd help them, so if I was you, I'd stop feeling sorry for myself, grab a shower, and go see them.'

Once Julia had left my flat, I took her advice and headed for Tasker's parent's house. At first Keith Tasker would only open the door as far as the safety chain allowed. Once he realised it was me, he let me through. He looked awful. I sat down in the front room and asked him how he was doing.

'Muddling along' he said. 'I don't really want to talk to people at the moment. I know they mean well, but it's too soon.'

'It's understandable.'

He disappeared into the kitchen to make us drinks. I took the opportunity to have another look around the room. The first condolence card stood on the mantelpiece. I picked it up and read it before carefully placing it back where I found it.

He walked back in and passed me my drink. I thanked him. 'Where's Kath?' I asked.

'She's in bed. The doctor gave her something to help her sleep.'

'How are you coping?' I asked.

He sat down in the chair opposite me. He looked like he'd aged ten years since I'd last seen him. 'I'm carrying on. I have to. Lots to be arranged.' He passed me a key to his son's flat. 'You might be needing that.'

I took it and drank a mouthful of coffee. Major had lied to me. He'd told me Tasker's parents didn't have a key. I pushed the thought to one side and tried to find the right words. I repeated what I'd told him before; I wanted to help. I owed them that much. I told him that Major had left the city without telling anyone.

'Does that mean Kane was involved in Greg's death?'

I'd thought this over last night as I walked back to my flat from the restaurant. I still didn't have an answer. 'I don't know.' It was the truth. As he'd said, he needed Greg alive. But I couldn't get past the question of why run? 'He told me he didn't kill Greg' I said.

'He can't of' he said to me. 'He was Greg's best friend and he's been a friend of the family for years. It doesn't make any sense to me.'

'Do you think he was capable of killing him?' I asked.

He considered the question. 'I wouldn't have said so a few days ago, but we're dealing with reality. It's not hypothetical, is it? I'm sure most of us could kill if we're pushed hard enough.'

I had nothing to say to that. I knew it was true. I moved us on. 'Did Greg ever mention Kane's financial situation to you?'

'Never. It wasn't something we'd talk about. It wasn't any of my business, I suppose.'

'Have the police spoken to you today?' I asked.

'Not really. To be honest, they haven't really told us an awful lot, but I suppose that's for operational reasons. There must be things they're simply not prepared to tell us. I can't say I've pushed them. I don't think we could bear it if they told us something unpleasant about Greg's death. It would be too much to cope with.'

'I understand.'

'They did tell us we should sever our ties with you. Let them get on with things.'

I wasn't surprised. 'I won't be obstructing the police' I said. I didn't intend to, but I wouldn't be giving DI Robinson and his team an easy ride, either. I'd make sure every lead I generated was followed up as necessary. 'Did you see the news this morning?'

'I did.' He sighed. 'I suppose it's too much to ask them to respect our privacy, isn't it?'

'Have they bothered you?'

'They've been ringing, asking us to give our side of the story. You can imagine the whole tawdry business. I've had their numbers blocked, but I doubt it'll stop them.'

'I know a journalist. Would you like me to see what I can do?'

He shook his head. 'Not at the moment, thanks.'

It was his decision. 'I know we've spoken before about it, but is there anything else you can think of that will help me? What did Greg do with his days? Have you any idea? I'm not getting very far with working it out.'

'I'm ashamed to say I have no idea. It wasn't something we discussed. He led his life how he saw fit and that was the end of it.'

'I'm just trying to build a picture. Had he said or done anything unusual recently? Anything at all?'

'Greg spoke to me last week, which was a little unusual in itself. There was no problem between us, but we just didn't usually speak about what was going on his life. It was his way. He told me he wasn't very happy with things. His relationship with Siobhan wasn't great and he wasn't sure what to do about it. I told him he should do whatever felt right. What else could I say? I've been married for over forty years. What would I know about what goes on these days? Siobhan's a lovely girl, but the fact of the matter is she's a lot younger than Greg. I suspect they wanted different things from life, which is perfectly understandable. It was difficult to know what to say. It might have been nothing, just one of those rough patches that blows over.'

'I've met Siobhan' I said.

'At her boutique?'

I nodded.

'Greg set her up there.'

'So I understand.'

'What was strange about our conversation was that Greg told me he had some big news for us. It was strange because he normally just told us what he wanted to tell us, and that was it, conversation over. I got the feeling that this time our opinion counted for something, that it was something important to him.'

He had my attention. 'What did he say?'

'He said he'd tell us next time he saw us, once he'd made his mind up about whatever it was.'

'He never said?'

He shook his head. 'And I suppose we'll never know now.'

Julia had left me a message whilst I'd been talking to Keith
Tasker. Michael Rusting, the engineer from Tasker's studio,
had called her newspaper. He said he had a story for her.
Julia wanted to see him immediately. I collected Julia and
we drove to the drab looking council flat Rusting lived in.
Tasker's studio can't have paid well. Julia took the lead and
knocked on his front-door. I recognised him when he opened
the door. Julia introduced herself and confirmed we were
from the newspaper. He invited us in. 'Nice to see you
again' I said. A dog sat on the settee, but it ran away as soon
as Rusting raised his voice.

'Might as well make yourselves at home' he said,
indicating we should sit.

'You're not an easy man to find' I said.

'I've not been hiding' he said.

Julia set up her recorder. 'Thanks for agreeing to speak to
us, Mr Rusting.' She passed him a cheque. 'As we agreed'
she said.

He put it in his pocket. 'All helps.'

'Didn't even get as much as a thank you off the police
when I gave my statement' he said. 'So I might as well make
some money from it, know what I mean? I haven't got a job
now, so I need some money from somewhere.'

'Your statement?' I said.

'I found Greg at the studio' he said.

I asked him to repeat what he'd just said.

'I found him.' He offered us drinks, but we both quickly
refused.

'Why didn't you report it to the police?'

'I did.'

'Not straightaway.'

Rusting looked panicked. 'How do you know that?'

'Because I went there after you did and found Greg. I rang
the police.'

Rusting stood. 'I don't want to talk to you.'

I was on my feet. 'You don't have a choice now.' I turned to Julia. She obviously knew what he was going to say. I let it go. Rusting sat back down. I did the same. 'Why didn't you ring the police?'

'I didn't want the hassle.'

'The hassle? He was dead.'

'Exactly. There was nothing I could do for him.'

'Not good enough.'

'I've got a criminal record.' He looked away from me. 'I didn't want the hassle' he repeated.

'So you thought you'd leave it?'

'It wasn't just that' he said. 'I saw these blokes leaving, they didn't look like good news, so I hung back, made sure they didn't see me.'

I rubbed my face. This changed things. 'How did you know they weren't good news?' I asked.

'I just got a vibe off them, like they weren't to be messed with. I didn't even know Greg was in there, he hadn't told me he was coming back. I thought they might have been robbing the place.'

'What happened after you saw them come out?'

'They got into a car and drove away.'

'What kind of car?'

'I don't know. It was too dark to see.'

'Colour?'

'I don't know.' He stared at me. 'I thought I was talking to her about my story. For the newspaper.'

'Once we're done' I said, staring back at him, weighing up whether or not he was holding something back. I decided he probably wasn't. 'Did you hear them speak?' I asked him. 'Were they local?'

'I wasn't close enough. They were arguing amongst themselves, though.'

'What did they look like?'

He hesitated, started to say something, but changed his mind. 'It was too dark.' He at least looked embarrassed by the lack of detail he'd remembered. 'Just average.'

'What did you do once they'd gone?'

'I went into the studio, found Greg on the floor. I could tell he was dead straightaway. It was obvious, so I ran. I called the police once I'd had a drink and settled my nerves.' He shrugged. 'What choice did I have?'

I nodded to Julia. It was her turn.

Rusting gave us no more. I dropped Julia off at her hotel. Having a witness changed things, even if the witness hadn't supposedly seen a great deal. I needed to know what the police were doing. I walked into the reception area of Queens Gardens Police Station. I didn't like the place. It was dull and grey. Institutionalised. The desk sergeant told me DI Robinson wasn't available. I stood my ground and insisted. A couple of youngsters waited in bolted down chairs. They soon got bored of staring at me and went back to whispering and laughing at each other. Eventually, Robinson's assistant, the one I'd given my statement to, made herself available.

'What can we do for you, Mr Geraghty?' she said.

'I understand you've got a witness.'

She looked angry. She walked back to the reception desk, pressed the release button on the door. 'In here.'

I followed her down the corridor and into an empty interview room.

'How do you know about the witness?' she asked.

'He's spoken to the media. You can read all about it tomorrow.'

If she wasn't angry before, she was now.

'He said he saw a couple of men leaving the studio right after Tasker was killed' I said.

We stared at each other. I chanced my arm. 'What did he tell you?' I asked.

She sighed, like she'd heard it all before. 'With respect, Mr Geraghty, I wouldn't tell you the time if you asked me. But please be assured we're looking into it. This isn't a job for you.'

She walked across the room to the door and opened it. We were finished.

I followed her back to the reception area. 'His family want his things back, anything you found on him.'

She stopped walking. 'I suggest you mind your own business.'

'What about the money he took from his girlfriend's till?'

'What money?'

I smiled. She shouldn't have confirmed for me that it wasn't on his person when they found him.

She showed me to the door. 'I'll let DI Robinson know you dropped in.'

I left my car where it was and walked to Tasker's flat. This was my first sighting of it in daylight. It looked like any other nondescript new build block which had sprung up around the city centre in the last few years. Plenty of glass and cheap looking brickwork. Letting myself in, I headed to the front room. It was a mess. CDs had been ripped from shelves and thrown onto the floor. Drawers had been emptied and discarded. Whoever had done this hadn't been subtle. Had Major been responsible? Looking around the room, I could tell the police's Scene of Crime Officers had already been and gone. I stepped over broken glass and walked into the kitchen. Nothing. Tasker's flat was nowhere near as big as mine and probably twice as expensive. I left the kitchen and moved into his bedroom. Tasker's clothes had been thrown across the floor, duvet cast aside. Whoever had been in here had done a thorough job. I was pleased his parents hadn't seen the mess. I heard someone walk in.

'Hello' I shouted. I walked back into the front room. Attack was the best form of defence. A middle-aged woman stood in front of me. 'Sorry, I didn't hear you' I said to her.

'Your colleague said you were all finished here once your scientific people had done their stuff.'

She thought I was a police officer. 'Just a few loose ends to tie up.' I turned to face her. I made a decision. I hadn't lied. I continued. 'Are you a neighbour?'

She nodded. 'Your colleague took all my details.'

'Right.'

'I can't believe it, I really can't. One of my friends told me who Greg was. I had no idea. I'm not a music fan, so it didn't really mean anything to me, but it's terrible to think of what happened to him.'

'It is. Did you hear anything?'

'I hear things nearly every day. He was always playing his guitar loudly and singing. It didn't seem to matter to him what the time was. It was non-stop. If you're talking about the nights your colleagues were asking about, there were some very noisy arguments. I wasn't able to tell them more than that.'

'Did you hear what they were arguing about?'

She shook her head. 'The walls are thin in this place, but not that thin.'

'Was it a man he was arguing with?'

'It was usually a woman, but there have been men around here recently.'

That was interesting. 'Did you ever see the people he was arguing with?'

'I mind my own business. You have to be so careful these days, don't you?'

I decided to come clean. 'I'm not with the police.' I passed her my business card. 'I'm working for Greg's family.'

She looked at my card. 'Why would they need a Private Investigator?'

'Just to keep the police on their toes.' I smiled, hoping it would put her at ease.

'I see.' She put the card in her pocket.

'Is there anything else you can tell me?' I said I hadn't caught her name.

'Mrs Musgrave.'

'Right.'

She shook her head. 'I can't think of anything.'

I thanked her for her time and told her she shouldn't hesitate to ring me if anything came to mind. I didn't want to push my luck. Heading out, I saw the same two men I'd seen at Siobhan's boutique parked up about fifty yards away, staring at me. I picked up my pace and hurried to my car.

CHAPTER TEN

I returned to the office feeling frustrated. There was something on Tasker's mind before his death, but I had no way of knowing what it was. I'd thought Sarah was due to be here, but I was losing track of her movements. She'd left a message to tell me Kane Major had sent someone up from London to deal with his affairs. The man wanted to speak to me. Looking at my watch, he would be visiting in thirty minutes time. Obviously, he was under the impression I was available at his convenience.

I picked up the day's post and walked over to the telephone. No sign of Don and no new messages. I put the post on Sarah's desk and sat down. Going back to basics was the approach I should take. I wrote down what I knew and tried to make connections between people and events. The process didn't clarify my thoughts. Rusting was the best lead, but he hadn't been much help. I left the piece of paper on my desk and logged onto my emails. I couldn't concentrate. I logged off and pushed things to one side. I needed to keep moving, so I looked up Priestley's mobile number and called. I still hadn't caught up with him following Tasker's death. The call went straight to voicemail, but I decided not to leave a message. I'd call again later. My mobile rang almost immediately afterwards.

It was Julia. I told her that I was waiting for Major's man to turn up. 'Do you want to come over and meet him?'

'I can't' she said.

'Why not?'

'Tell you later.'

She terminated the call. I stared at my mobile for a minute before putting it back on the desk. I'd have to wait. The door buzzer went. Looking into the camera, I would have known the man staring back at me was a solicitor. He had the self-confidence of a professional. He was early thirties, in good shape and neat and tidy around the edges. He was a man who looked after himself. I let him up and he walked straight over to my desk and sat down opposite me. He put his briefcase on the floor and took a business card from his pocket. 'Marcus Whittle' he said, handing it over to me. 'I represent Kane Major.'

I put the card on my desk. I didn't pass him one of mine. 'Joe Geraghty.'

He looked around the room. 'It's not what I expected' he said, before getting down to business. 'I assume you know why I'm here?'

'You tell me. I tried to ring Kane earlier and all I got was a message saying he'd left town.' I shrugged. 'No more than that. Odd, wouldn't you say, given what's happened?'

Whittle smiled. 'Kane did say you have a bit of a mouth on you. He's had to attend to some business in London, so he's asked me to come up here to keep an eye on things.'

'Why would he need you to keep an eye on things?'

He passed me an envelope. Money. 'To be frank, you're a Private Investigator, but I'm a solicitor. I can open doors you can't. Kane will need someone here capable of looking out for his interests. Greg was a close friend, so he wants to make sure justice is done. Nothing changes. That's a down payment on what you're owed. Instead of dealing with Kane, you'll deal with me for the foreseeable future. That's all.'

'Says who?' Whittle's attitude was starting to annoy me, money or not.

He feigned surprise. 'You don't want the work? Your choice. Just give me the money back and I'll be on my way.'

I said nothing. He had me. Sarah wouldn't thank me for not taking the money.

Whittle sat back in his chair. 'Right. I think we have an agreement, Mr Geraghty?'

I wanted to argue. I wanted him out of the office. But I had nothing. I said we had an agreement and asked him what he wanted me to do.

'Whatever's necessary' he said. 'Kane needs someone on his side up here, and you're that man. When something needs doing, it'll be you I come to.'

I didn't like what I was hearing. 'How long will you be staying?' I asked.

'As long as it takes.'

'Major told me he was skint. How can he afford your services?'

'No idea. I'm merely a foot-soldier. I do what I'm told.' Whittle picked up the business card he'd put down. He wrote the name of the hotel he was staying at on the back of it. 'You can get hold of me here when you have some news.'

I took the card back and put it in my pocket.

He stood up to leave. 'Don't suppose you can recommend a restaurant to eat in tonight? I assume you have a handful of passable ones in this place?'

I shook my head. I didn't want him using my name anywhere I might want to go to again.

'Not to worry. I'm sure I'll cope.'

'I'm sure you will.'

Whittle leaned over the desk. 'Look, I don't care if you don't like me. Really I don't. It's not the slightest bit important to me, but don't you ever forget which side you're on. You're being paid to do what Kane asks of you.' He straightened himself back up and headed towards the door. 'Let's talk again soon.'

I didn't move from my desk for several minutes after Whittle left. I didn't care much for the man, or for Major, but I was stuck. He was right. He owned me. But I'd come to realise that if I could do what he wanted, I could help the Taskers at the same time. I wasn't happy with the situation, but at least I could turn it to my advantage. It was something. I browsed the Internet for the latest news, but there was little to interest me. The decision on what to do next was made by Priestley finally returning my call. He'd spoken to DI Robinson's team and now he wanted to speak to me. I told him to name a place. He told me he was at Paull. I told him I was thirty minutes away. I locked up and set off.

I had no difficulty in finding an empty space in the car park. The village sits on the banks of the Humber, out to the east of the city and under the shadow of the imposing BP Saltend chemical plant. I knew the area well. When I was a child, my parents would bring me and my brother here and we'd walk on the uneven path along the waterfront. I remembered looking across to the opposite side of the water, thinking at the time that it seemed as remote as the moon. When he was young, my brother had been obsessed with space travel. As well as his records, I'd inherited his poster collection when he'd left home. There had been plenty of space-shuttles and the moon, as well as the usual band posters.

I found Priestley stood at the foot of the path which led along the waterfront. I buttoned my coat up and started walking towards him. You know it's cold at Paull when the ice-cream van isn't there. I nodded to him. He returned my greeting and set off in the direction of the nature reserve. His dog followed obediently.

'You didn't get on too well with Robinson' I said, catching him up. I had to raise my voice to be heard above the wind.

He let the dog off the leash and threw a ball for it to chase. 'You could say that.'

'What did the police want with you?' I asked.

'They're talking to people who knew Greg. Just routine, they told me.'

I didn't say anything for a moment. I hoped he'd continue. When he didn't, I asked him what the problem was.

'He wanted to know where I was the night Greg was killed.'

'What did you tell him?'

'The truth' he said. 'I don't have an alibi. I was out here walking.'

He turned towards me. 'I didn't kill him, Joe.'

'Why did your wife offer me an alibi for you?'

He relaxed. 'Carly's very protective of me. She met me when I was in a bad place and she built me back up again. To tell the truth, I've never quite managed to shake that side of her from me. She thinks she has to look after me all the time. Truth is, I was out walking. I do it most nights. I have trouble sleeping, so rather than keep Carly awake with my tossing and turning, I go out walking. I just drive off somewhere and walk for an hour or so. It clears my head.'

'She should be careful about what she says. It'll cause you more trouble than the truth.'

'Try telling her that.'

I nodded. 'Did Robinson mention anything? Any enemies Greg had?'

'Enemies?'

'Just covering all bases.'

Priestley laughed. 'He was the frontman of a famous band. He probably has more enemies than you can count. He was out of control a lot of the time, upsetting people and causing trouble. It was a long time ago. I wouldn't know. Enough to kill?' He threw the ball again for his dog. 'I wasn't looking forward to the reunion, you know.'

'You told me you were when we last spoke.'

'Just toeing the party line. I thought Greg would be back and we'd knuckle down to it.'

His wife had said as much to me, but I let it go. I could understand why he'd lied to me.

'I can't tell you how much I hated Greg for what he did to me and the band' he said. 'And however much you want to forgive and forget, sometimes you just can't.' He turned to me. 'I was prepared to go through with it. I was being truthful when I told you that. We should close the book on the band properly with some decent gigs. But I'm not stupid, I knew how difficult it was going to be. Part of the reason I'm not sleeping is because of the worry. Greg was always the most popular member of the band and that isn't going to change, but the stick I got towards the end of things was unbelievable. I could have wallpapered my house with hate mail when people thought I was taking over the band. None of it was true. I just wanted to keep the show on the road.'

I thought back to what Lorraine Harrison had told me. 'You weren't trying to take over the band?'

Priestley shook his head. 'I was writing more songs, that's all, and I suppose I was more willing to fight my corner because I thought they were good.' He paused. 'Not that many people agreed with me. But to suggest I'd forced Greg into things, or forced the band to split up over it, is stupid.' Priestley shrugged. 'It was a difficult time for us all.'

'How come?'

'The second album wasn't a huge success in terms of being a band. We were constantly touring and promoting the first record, so things were changing. Greg was becoming a big star, but he took his eye off the ball. We were recording in different studios, bit by bit when we had the time. It was the first real chance I'd had to use a studio properly, and I threw myself into it. It was something to focus on. The others were more interested in the partying, to be honest, and I guess things just became more strained.'

'I suppose it's inevitable. You'd want to enjoy the success, wouldn't you?'

'I suppose.'

I was surprised. Why would you do something if you didn't want to succeed?

'However much I enjoyed it, I was always homesick' he said. 'I like this area. I like walking out here. Just look at it.'

I looked. I liked living near the water, probably because it was in my blood, but all I could see was the industrial sight of the south bank of the Humber. It was remote, not picturesque. 'You didn't want to see the world?'

'Not like Greg and Kane did. By the time of the last album, we were flying all over the world, and it messes you up' he continued. 'We played a lot of gigs in Japan and Greg just lost it with drink and drugs. Cocaine's a terrible idea if you already think the world revolves around you.' He paused for a moment before continuing. 'Japan's weird. When you're in Europe, you can get by, you can read the odd word here and there, even if you can't speak the language. In Japan nothing makes sense and then by the time we'd made it to Tokyo, we were just fried. The place makes London feel like a village. And then we had to come back to England where we'd already climbed the mountain. We were booked into the same venues we'd already played countless times. It felt like we were going backwards. The gigs were shit. I argued with Greg about which songs we were going to play and the whole vibe was wrong. It was the end of the band.'

'Why agree to the reunion? Why not let it lie?'

'Because I couldn't say no. This was a chance to put the record straight. Maybe then I'd be able to move forward.'

I had nothing to add. I looked out towards the marshland. Birds were swooping past, searching for food. I picked one out and followed it on its journey.

'We argued' he said. 'Nearly came to blows in the rehearsal room.'

I knew something was coming. 'You and Greg?'

He nodded. 'The plan was to play a secret warm-up gig at the Adelphi, but we couldn't agree on which songs to play.'

'What happened?' I asked.

'It got a bit heated and we squared up to each other. It was a bit silly, really.'

I knew where this was going. 'Who saw you?'

'Kane Major.'

'Right.'

'It was nothing.'

I continued to stare straight ahead, not liking what I was hearing. 'Do you know how Greg spent his days? Who he dealt with, who he spoke to?'

'Not really.'

I turned back towards him. 'It's important' I said.

'He told me he was working on his album.'

'I didn't think he went into the studio that much.'

'He had some recording equipment in his flat. We were alike in so many ways, not that we'd admit it. He was as plagued with doubt and insecurity about his new songs as I am with mine. I don't go out much. I stay at home with my guitar. It's what I like. I think he was the same.'

Priestley took a dog lead out of his pocket. He flexed it before turning to me. 'We weren't getting on particularly well, but I didn't kill him, Joe. I've got nothing to hide. I'm telling you all this because I think I can trust you to get to the truth.' He started to walk towards his dog. 'You've got to believe me on that.'

Sometimes you get an offer you can't refuse. As I'd driven away from Paull and back towards Hull, my mobile rang. I must have been out of range whilst I was talking to Priestley. I called the number back. DI Robinson. He told me he wanted to meet me straight away. Over the phone wouldn't do. He named a pub, just outside of the city centre. It was far enough away from the prying eyes of the station, but close enough for him to walk to. Twenty minutes later, I'd made it there. Only a handful of customers and a bored looking barmaid in the place.

'You can buy your own drink, Mr Geraghty' he said to me.

'Fair enough.' I ordered a diet coke. With my drink in hand, I walked over to Robinson. 'I'm surprised you've got time for this' I said. I put my glass down, found a stool and sat opposite him.

'I haven't got the time for this' he said. 'But you've been bothering my team, so I wanted to make things crystal clear for you.'

I picked up my drink. 'Another friendly warning?'

'If you won't listen to Don, maybe you'll listen to me.'

'What have I done to deserve this?'

'How about we start with your visit to Tasker's flat?' He smiled at me, knowing he'd scored a hit.

'I had a key' I said.

'You impersonated a police officer.'

I shook my head. 'That's not how it happened.'

'That's not what the neighbour's statement says. It's a very serious offence, Mr Geraghty.'

I said nothing. She hadn't complained at the time, but that was irrelevant. He had me, and he knew it.

'It's a good job I've got bigger fish to fry or I'd be more inclined to make an issue of it. I'm sure you wouldn't work again if people knew what you really got up to. But like I say, this is a friendly warning. You're barking up the wrong tree with this one and you've done enough damage already. For your own sake, leave it to the professionals. You can't help any further. I'm sure Mr and Mrs Tasker will understand. Walk away, stop asking questions, and don't let people take you for a fool.'

I asked him who was taking me for a fool.

He shook his head. 'All you need to be aware of is that this investigation isn't as straightforward as you think. You're getting involved with the wrong team.' He stood up and drained his glass. 'Leave it alone, Mr Geraghty. This is a murder inquiry.'

I stood up and followed him out of the pub, towards the car park. 'I don't need you watching over me' I shouted to his back. 'You can call your team off.'

He stopped and turned around. 'I'm trying to help you here. Walk away or watch your back.'

'Why are your men following me?'

'You think I've got the manpower to waste following you around?' He laughed before turning away and continuing his walk to his car. 'Be lucky, Mr Geraghty.'

I returned to the office and considered what I'd learnt. If DI Robinson's men hadn't been following me around, who was? More importantly, who did they work for? Sarah walked in. I realised I should have updated her on my movements. She went straight over to her desk, sat down and switched her laptop on. Not a word.

'Alright?' I said.

'I saw the reports on the television.'

I told her I hadn't stopped all morning. 'I've had Major's solicitor visit me and then Priestley wanted to talk to me.'

She went back to her laptop. 'Fine.'

I could tell it wasn't fine. 'It's not an excuse. I'm sorry. I should have called. Where's your dad?'

'He got us some extra work today delivering warrants.'

There was nothing more tedious than delivering court papers, but it was a large part of our business. I'm sure it was his way of reminding me of the fact.

'What did Major's solicitor want?' she said.

'Just to tell me nothing's changed. He still wants me on the case to make sure the police are doing their job properly.'

'So why has Major run?' she asked me.

I shrugged. 'Urgent business to attend to.' I didn't believe it any more for saying it aloud.

Sarah grunted, said nothing. We both knew it put a major question mark against him. 'So why did Priestley call?' she asked.

'He's had the police on his back.' I told her I thought Priestley had been honest with me. He hadn't hidden the fact he had issues with Tasker over the reunion. On the other hand, he potentially fitted with my theory of an accidental death following an argument. He could have easily struck out, just the one punch with unexpected consequences. I decided not to tell Sarah about Robinson's warning. I knew how she'd react. I'd speak to Whittle about the men following me. If he was having me followed, I wanted to know why. The doorbell buzzed. I looked into the camera and let Julia up. She walked in, said hello to Sarah and sat down opposite me. I smiled. 'Alright?'

'The paper got a call this morning' Julia said. 'Someone wants to talk to us about Siobhan. He's seen the story on the news.'

I leaned forward. 'Why Siobhan?'

'Don't know. That was the message I got.'

'When?'

'As soon as possible.'

I stood up and grabbed my coat. 'No time like the present.'

Julia followed me towards the door. I stopped and turned to Sarah. 'Coming?'

She looked at me and Julia, and shook her head. 'I've got things to do here.'

You know the recording of the second album isn't going well. You're losing your grip, but you can't admit it, least of all to yourself. Kane is still hammering the drink and drugs. All he has to do is turn up at meetings and sign contracts. Priestley is sober and in control. He's doing more in the studio. Your domain. You hate the fact he has a life in Hull, a million miles away from all of this. He's the one bringing songs in to record. You don't like it, but you go along with it. You're too busy trying to convince yourself that you're having a good time. You know you're jealous of him. You know he's slowly taking over the band. You know you're giving him no choice. You try to hold things together. You switch off from the world and head to a remote cottage, away from all the distractions, and write. You've still got it. You're still a better songwriter than Priestley. The proof is in the songs. You know it. He knows it. The second album is finished. The schedule is relentless. UK tour. European tour. American tour. Time becomes meaningless to you. Travel, interviews, gig, party. That's your life. You think it's what you want.

CHAPTER ELEVEN

The pub we were parked up outside of was run down, many
of the windows boarded up. It looked like it wasn't open for
business. The city of Hull has several large council estates,
but this one had the worst reputation. It was the opposite end
of the scale to the area where I'd met Tasker's parents. I
could see the side entrance door was open. The only sign of
life. The cold drizzle in the air fitted the scene perfectly. It
was an unwelcoming place. I followed Julia to the side door.
The place was dark. The stale smell of last night's beer
turned my stomach. Adjusting to the gloom, I could see a
group of men sat in the corner, smoking and drinking. At the
bar, a woman went about her cleaning duties. Julia led me
across the room. Two of the men stood up and blocked our
path. Julia said we were here to see a man called Trevor
Bilton. They were both huge. Matching leather jackets.
Playing at being gangsters, but I still wouldn't fancy my
chances against them.

'Who the fuck's this, Julia?' the man sat behind them said.

'He's with me' she said.

'Doesn't answer my question.'

'Joe Geraghty' I said, stepping forwards.

'Still doesn't answer my question, pal. Who the fuck are
you?'

'He works with me' Julia said. 'I wasn't coming here by myself.'

The two men at the front laughed. 'What's he going to do?'

'Why would I need to do anything?' I asked, smiling politely.

The third man stood up and dismissed the other two. He waited for them to be out of earshot before turning to Julia. 'You're looking good, babe.'

'I wish I could say the same' she replied.

'Very good. Always had a way with words.' He paused. 'Have you come to repay the money you still owe me?'

'Hardly.'

He turned to me. 'Sense of humour, too.' He pointed to the stools his men had vacated. 'Sit the fuck down.'

I looked across to Julia, puzzled. She wouldn't meet my eye.

'I know you, pal' he said to me.

'I don't think so.'

'We played rugby against each other. Years ago. Junior stuff. Remember?'

I shook my head.

'No reason you would, I suppose. I remember you because you were the star larker for your lot.'

I was no wiser. I didn't remember him.

'And now you're working for Julia. Hardly living the dream, is it?' He laughed and then winked at me.

If we'd played junior rugby against each other, it meant he was the same age as me. If I looked as bad as he did, I'd be worried. His skin was scarred from teenage acne and his teeth clearly hadn't seen a dentist for a number of years. I tried to remember him, but drew a blank. 'The rugby didn't work out' I said.

'Busted leg, wasn't it?'

I nodded.

'Never worked out for me, either' he said. 'No one would take a chance on me, so I played amateur stuff for a while. Soon got bored of it, though. Couldn't be arsed, know what I mean? I found other things to do with my time.'

I said nothing. I wasn't comfortable with the situation. His two men were guarding the door. We were effectively his prisoners.

'How have you been, Julia?' he asked.

'Busy' she said.

'Always knew you'd go far. You were always too good for this place.'

'Nice of you to say so.'

He turned to me. 'I like to keep an eye on my friends. She's doing well for herself. I'm pleased.'

'I am sat here' Julia said. 'Talk to me.'

'I was just explaining it to Joe' he said, before turning to me. 'She always was a bit lively. Know what I mean?'

I didn't like his tone, but I was going to have to listen. 'What do you want?' I said.

Bilton leaned back. 'What do I want?' He grinned at me. 'I'm here to help you. You should show a little more gratitude.'

Julia took over. 'You said you know Greg Tasker's girlfriend?'

'You said you'd bring me some money.'

'I said you'd get paid if you had a story.'

'Always were keen to get the story, weren't you?'

'What have you got for us?' she said.

'I remain anonymous?'

Julia nodded.

'I've seen her in here' he said.

I took the bait and asked the question. 'Why would she need to come here?'

I found us a cafe close to the pub. It was in a supermarket, but it was the nearest place to go. 'What was all that about?' I said. 'You know Bilton?'

'It was a long time ago.'

We sat well away from the other customers so nobody was listening to our conversation. I needed to get some answers. I'd made the connection. 'He was the boyfriend you told me about?'

She shook her head. 'His brother.'

'And he got back in touch through the newspaper?'

'You heard him. He said he'd been following me for years. It's not that hard to do with the Internet.'

We both picked up our drinks and sat in silence for a few moments. I watched people bagging up their shopping, going about their normal business. 'He's a wanker' I eventually said.

'You don't need to tell me that.'

'Sorry.' It wasn't my place to judge.

She shook her head. 'It doesn't look good, does it?'

'What's his brother called?' I said.

'Gary. I was seventeen. He was a bit older and had a car. A job. He was fun.'

'How did you meet him?'

'He'd watch his brother play for my dad's rugby team.'

'We all make mistakes, I suppose.' Once I'd signed for Hull KR, I knew how easy it was to impress girls if you had a bit of money in your pocket. I'd already met Debbie by then, so it wasn't for me.

'I asked around before we came here. Trevor Bilton's your standard lowlife. You can fill the rest of the picture in. He uses kids and a few trusted individuals to stay below the radar. He doesn't get his hands dirty.'

'Cleverer than he looks.' Contacting the media demonstrated that he felt untouchable. It was going to be all on his terms.

Julia turned away from me and looked out of the window. 'I don't want to talk about it, Joe.'

I reached across the table for her hand. She pulled hers away and took a deep breath. 'I want to go back to the hotel, please.'

We drank up and left. I dropped Julia off and said I'd call her later. She shut the car door and walked away from me. My mind turned back to what Trevor Bilton had told us. It helped explain why Siobhan was nervous when I'd spoken to her. Bilton was bad news. I knew she had been holding something back from me.

Sarah was still at the office. 'Alright?' I said. Still no sign of Don, but I said nothing more.

'All done.' She told me she was finished and was about to head off for the day. 'Where's Julia?'

'I dropped her at the hotel' I said. 'She had things to do there.'

I checked my mobile. There were no new text messages. I told Sarah about the meeting with Trevor Bilton. 'Can you get some background on him for me, please?' I asked. 'He's got a brother, Gary, who I want to know about, too.'

'I'll see what I can do' she said, writing it down on a notepad.

I told her about his connection to Siobhan.

Sarah sat back down. 'Tasker was back into drugs?'

'Maybe.' It was certainly a thought that had crossed my mind. It potentially opened up a whole new dimension to the investigation, but there was no proof yet. My mobile rang. Marcus Whittle.

'I need an update from you, Mr Geraghty' he said.

'I'm working on it' I said.

'Have you spoken to Priestley yet?'

'Earlier today.'

'That's a step in right direction. What did he have to say for himself?'

'Not a lot. He hasn't got an alibi. The man's an insomniac. He was out walking.'

'Do you believe his story?'

'I'm not sure.' Priestley's farm was about fifteen miles away from the centre of Hull. He'd have needed transport, which I knew he had. He could have driven into Hull, killed Tasker, and returned home. Maybe even without his wife knowing. Maybe CCTV would have picked him up as he drove into the city, but the technology wasn't infallible. It wasn't guaranteed.

Whittle laughed. 'There are plenty of reasons to doubt him. I've spent best part of the last few hours outlining them to the police.'

'Want to share them with me?'

'I have a conference call to take in a moment, but after that we'll talk.'

I gave him the address for Queens and told him I was looking forward to it.

'Pleased to hear it. The sooner we get to the bottom of this, the better.'

'Indeed.'

I was relieved to finish the call with Whittle. I busied myself at my desk, waiting for Sarah to speak. She walked over to my desk and told me that Lorraine Harrison's mother had visited the office earlier in the day. 'She said her daughter doesn't know anything about Greg's death and doesn't like you harassing her.'

'I'm not harassing her' I said. 'She came to me.'

'That's pretty much what I told her. She said we should be talking to her daughter's husband.'

'How do you mean?'

'Apparently it was a whirlwind romance. She didn't approve. She told me he's very controlling. Lorraine fell pregnant almost as soon as she met him, certainly within weeks, and since then he's had a hold over her. She regularly goes back to her mum for a shoulder to cry on.'

I was interested. 'Did she say whether or not he'd been violent?'

She shook her head. 'I asked, but not so far as she's aware. But she's worried for her daughter's safety when he loses his temper.'

'Did she say how things had been recently?'

'Seemingly it had been alright until all this business with New Holland started up again. Her husband never liked her involvement with the band.'

It wasn't news. 'Maybe he's jealous? She knew the band.' I shrugged. 'They were famous.'

'Hardly worth getting upset about, is it?'

I didn't have an answer. 'Did she say what she thought Jason Harrison was capable of doing?'

'That's why she came. She thinks he's capable of anything.'

We called it a day so I headed back to my flat. I checked for messages before heading to Queens. I left my car where it was. The fresh air would do me good. Whittle walked up to where I was sitting. 'This is your local?'

'This is it' I said. 'It's just been redecorated.'

'It's not too bad' said Whittle, looking around the room. 'I've seen worse.'

'I'm sure.'

He went to the bar for our drinks. Diet Coke for me. I was still on the clock. I thought about Jason Harrison. His mother-in-law had confirmed he had a temper. I couldn't ignore that. The pub was quiet, the late afternoon lull before people dropped in for a drink on the way home from work. I found us a quiet corner away from the sports screen.

'You spoke to Priestley' he said, putting the drinks down in front of us.

I nodded. I'd already told him that over the phone. 'I'm doing my job. You don't have to worry' I said.

'I have to check.'

I could understand his reasoning. He didn't know me. It was a test of my loyalties, but I was a step ahead of him. 'Have you spoken to Major?'

'Why would I?'

'Because he's wanted back up here.'

'I'm not his keeper.' He sipped his drink. 'Tell me what Priestley had to say, then'

'He wanted to tell me he hadn't killed Tasker.'

'That's all?'

I nodded.

'Not much of a defence, is it?' he said.

'Depends if he needs one or not.'

'Did he mention Lorraine Harrison?' Whittle asked.

The question threw me. 'Why would he?'

'You know who she is?'

I said I did. I didn't offer anything further.

Whittle made sure he had my attention. 'I'm led to believe Priestley has a thing for her.'

I thought about it. 'Major told you this?'

He nodded his confirmation. 'I'm sure I don't need to tell you Tasker and this Harrison woman had a relationship in the past. Seemingly, it caused a lot of tension in the band. I don't suppose we'll ever know the full story, but I would suggest if there was some jealousy between them, it gives Priestley motive as a potential suspect. Maybe you should speak to this Harrison woman and see what you can find out?'

I said I would. Lorraine definitely hadn't said anything like this to me about Priestley. And nor had he.

He drank up and got ready to leave. 'Keep me informed, please.'

'One other thing' I said, stopping him leaving. 'Now you know I'm doing my job for you, you can call off whoever you've got following me.'

Whittle looked puzzled. 'Why would I need to have people following you?'

Once Whittle left, I sat in the corner of the pub and stared at my drink, thinking things over. If it wasn't Whittle or DI Robinson having me followed, I had no idea who it was. It was beginning to weigh on my mind. I was sure they'd introduce themselves before too long, but it was the manner in which it would be done that worried me. I didn't expect it to be a civil chat. My mobile vibrated in my pocket. I answered it.

'Fancy a chat, Mr Geraghty?'

It was Robinson. 'When?'

'I'm in the car park.'

'Where?'

I heard a car horn sound.

'Your assistant told me where I'd find you.'

'She's my partner.'

'Of course. Don's daughter?'

'That's right.' I put the phone back into my pocket and left the pub. I spotted Robinson, walked over and opened the passenger door. 'What can I do for you?' I said.

'We've got a few things to talk about.'

'I thought we might have.' I got into his car.

He drove out of the car park, turned left towards Beverley Road. 'I've spoken to Mr Whittle, who I believe you know' he said. 'He tells me that Kane Major has had to return to London on urgent business.'

'That's right.'

'Are you happy about that?'

'About as happy as you, I should think.'

He smiled. 'I'm pleased we're on the same page. Now, to be frank, I don't know who this Mr Whittle thinks he is. If he thinks he can come into my station and demand I answer his questions, he's very much mistaken. Kane Major remains a person of significant interest to me and I haven't finished with him yet. I want him back here in Hull immediately.'

'I'm not his keeper.' I used the line Whittle had used on me. I looked out of the window. He turned onto Cottingham Road. A hundred yards further, he indicated left again. Newland Avenue. We were heading back to where we'd just left.

'I assume you can speak to him. Tell him I'll be much happier if he comes back and makes himself available to me.'

'I've been trying his mobile. It's switched off.'

'Try harder.'

'I've tried.' I didn't like the situation any more than he did, but I didn't like his attitude either. 'You must have contacts down there who could give him a knock.'

'No luck so far.' Robinson pulled up. We were halfway down Newland Avenue when he pulled over. I was about twenty minutes away from my flat. He turned towards me. 'I warned you, didn't I? I told you to leave this alone, Mr Geraghty, but you didn't listen to me. You had your chance.' He turned away again. 'I'm not going past your flat, so you best get out here. You and Mr Whittle had best get your heads together on this and make Major reappear or there's going to be trouble.'

CHAPTER TWELVE

Julia rang my mobile. She apologised for earlier. I told her there was no need. I understood. She was calmer now and ready to talk about it some more. I said I'd go to her hotel. It was cold, but the walk to the city centre would help me think.

Her hotel room was a mess. Her laptop was on the bed, in the middle of notes, newspapers and various printouts. I put them into a neat pile and sat down. She looked better. She'd had a shower and changed.

'I wasn't expecting it to hit me so hard' she said, sitting down opposite me. 'It's only his brother, after all. It wasn't even Gary.'

'It's only natural' I said.

'It's been so many years since I've seen either of them. I didn't think it'd bother me anymore.'

'A bit of a shock to the system' I said. 'It's understandable.'

She smiled. 'You could say that. I don't know what I was expecting, really. He just looked so old and nasty.'

I'd read somewhere you get the face you deserve when you hit forty and Trevor Bilton didn't look like a five-a-day man to me.

'I used to think Gary had an edge to him. Nothing serious' she said. 'I suppose being a stupid teenager, I did it to annoy my parents. Eventually, they gave me an ultimatum. I either had to stop seeing him or leave home.'

'Really?' It seemed a bit extreme.

'I ignored it at first. I didn't think they meant it, but it blew up into a massive row. I packed my bags and moved into Gary's flat with him.'

I nodded. 'How long did you stay there for?'

'A few months. At first it was great, but it didn't last long. His brother started to get involved. Trevor was always digging away, encouraging Gary to stop me from seeing my friends and having my own life.' She shrugged. 'That was the way he treated his girlfriend. I used to hate Trevor. Really hate him. If he told Gary to do something, he'd do it without question. If Trevor hadn't been around, it might have worked out better, but in the end, I had to get away from both of them.'

I reached across for her hand. This time she let me. 'We don't have to talk about this' I said.

She took a deep breath. 'I want to. If we're going to deal with them, you need to know what they're like.'

'How did you get out?'

'I ran away. I stole some money and got on a bus to London. I had a friend who was studying down there and she was kind enough to let me stay with her whilst I got myself sorted out. I told her I'd fallen out with my family, but nothing more than that. You're the first person I've really told about this. I couldn't go back home after the arguments. I wasn't there when Mum died and Dad never forgave me. It was a horrible time, but it made me grow up fast. I knew I didn't want to become reliant on anyone ever again. I wanted to go back to my studies and be me again. I found a part-time job and got myself sorted. Made a life for myself. Maybe in a perverse way, it helped me to focus. I knew what

I wanted and I was so desperate to start again, I threw myself completely into it and here we are. I've got everything and I've got nothing. I've got a career, but I haven't got a family.'

I paced the room. I wasn't sure what to say to her. Or what she wanted me to say. I turned the conversation back to Trevor Bilton. 'Can we trust him?' I asked.

'Of course we can't trust him.'

'He's the best lead we have.' I said, thinking aloud more than anything. Once he'd told us he knew Tasker's girlfriend, we'd left the pub. Julia had to go back to her editor to get permission to pay him for his story. As we'd left, he'd given us twenty-four hours to sort it out, otherwise he'd go elsewhere. Holding off for old times' sake, he'd said.

'I'm going to contact him tomorrow and set something up' Julia said.

'Right.' We needed him. If Julia could cope with the situation, I would have to.

'How are things with Sarah and Don?' she said to me.

'Sarah's doing her best, but she's caught in the middle. She wants to help, but she doesn't want to upset her dad. I haven't seen Don. He's staying away from the office.' I knew a gulf had opened up between us all, but I didn't know how to go about fixing it.

Julia changed the subject. 'I've been speaking to some contacts in London about Kane. Let's say he has some problems. Things haven't been going so well for him of late.'

'You do surprise me. They build you up and they knock you down.'

'It's not for those without a thick skin.' Julia looked at her notes. 'On the back of his initial success, he'd pumped a load of money into a new nightclub in London. At first, it was a big success, glitzy opening, the place to be seen, but these things change like the wind. One week you're the big thing, the next you're staring at an empty club wondering where everyone's gone.'

'It's a tough life.'

'It's collapsed like a pack of cards and it's taking its toll on him. He's paranoid and thinks people hate him. The word is that he's hitting the drink and drugs pretty hard.'

'How hard?'

'Hard enough for it to have been noticed. He's stressed out. New Holland's reunion was his get out of jail free card. He'd seen other bands do it, so why not New Holland? It would have gone a long way to digging him out of his financial problems.'

And he'd got Greg's new demos, I thought. He'd said he was going to make Tasker a star again. It sounded more like it was a plan to dig himself out of a hole.

'What if he hadn't been able to persuade them to reform?' I couldn't imagine the demos would be much good to him if Tasker didn't have the profile to launch them.

Julia shrugged. 'Sounds like he'd be in serious trouble.'

There was a text message from Sarah to say she'd finished running the searches on the Bilton brothers. I needed to know what she'd found out. The hotel was next to the remodelled travel interchange. I jumped on a bus. I wasn't sure how pleased to see me she would be, but it wouldn't wait. I sent a message back so I wouldn't wake Lauren.

We sat in her front room, the television down low.

'Don't tell Dad I've been doing this for you' she said.

I said I wouldn't. She was still prepared to help me and I didn't want to throw that away.

'I'm still working on some of the stuff you asked for, but this is what I have so far.'

She passed me a copy of her notes. 'I had to speak to some of Dad's old contacts about Trevor Bilton. He's well known to them. He's not a massive player, but he seems to keep a lid on things on the estate in his own way, so I think they just prefer to keep an eye on him to make sure he doesn't get too far out of line.'

I nodded. That was the harsh reality of the situation. If it wasn't him, it'd be someone else. Better the devil you know.

'I can't believe she wants to deal with him' Sarah said. 'He's hardly a reliable source.'

'It's her job, I suppose.'

Major had told me that he thought Tasker was involved with some bad people. And I knew his girlfriend was involved with Trevor Bilton. It wasn't a good situation.

'What are you going to do?' Sarah asked me.

It took me a moment to register what she was asking me. I pushed aside the thought of Siobhan. Sarah repeated the question. I answered this time. 'Julia's going to set up a meeting tomorrow' I said. 'It's her call. What did you find out about his brother?'

She passed me another sheet of paper. 'Gary Bilton is an interesting case.'

I read. He worked on the estate as a community worker. I smiled at the irony of the situation. 'Do they still get on?' I asked.

'Like peas in a pod apparently. Work's work and blood is thicker than water.' She cleared the empty mugs away and sat back down. 'What did Whittle have to say?'

I told her about our conversation. 'He was testing me. He wanted to make sure I was asking the right people the right questions.'

'I suppose you can understand that.'

Sarah brought me up to date with the news coverage. The investigation was going quiet, which meant they were either very close to a breakthrough or nowhere near to solving the case. Judging by how harassed DI Robinson looked when

I'd spoken to him, I thought it was probably the latter. I suspected we'd be talking again soon.

'I've got something else for you' said Sarah. She passed me another printout. 'Jason Harrison. I wanted to check him out.'

'Good idea.' I read the notes on Lorraine's husband. He'd had been arrested in the city centre ten years previously for fighting and received a fine and conditional discharge. It was clear that Harrison had been the aggressor. Exactly the kind of man who might lose his temper if he was involved in a confrontation with someone he didn't like. And it tallied with what his mother-in-law had told Sarah. I rubbed my face and tried to think through what it meant. I thanked her for her work.

'You should go home and get some sleep' Sarah said.

I said I would. I had one more visit to make before I called it a night.

I couldn't leave it. There was still an hour left before closing time. I walked back to my flat and collected my car. Heading across the city, I parked up on the road opposite the pub I'd met Trevor Bilton in earlier. The main entrance was open this time, but I headed for the same side entrance. That way, I knew the layout. A gang of teenagers rode quad bikes around the car park and shared a bottle of cider. If they were shouting at me, I wasn't interested. The place was busy, a duo on stage singing a Beatles track. Nobody was listening, rather they were huddled in small groups, talking and laughing. I nudged my way through the drinkers and made it to the bar. No sign of Trevor Bilton, but this was the place to start. I could feel people staring at me. I was willing to bet everyone knew everyone else in this place. I was an outsider. The barmaid made sure she'd served everyone else before making her way over to where I stood.

'What can I get you, love?' she asked.

'I want to speak to Trevor Bilton' I said.

She was in her fifties, but she looked like she knew how to handle herself. She carried on chewing her gum. She looked me up and down, shook her head and walked away to pour a pint of lager for someone else.

I waited for her to finish before repeating myself.

I felt someone barge into the back of me. 'Are you deaf, cunt?' he said to me.

I turned to look at him. It was one of the sidekicks I'd met earlier. 'Talking to me?' I said.

'Who else?' He smiled and leaned in. 'Cunt.'

I smiled back. 'Where is he?'

'I suggest you fuck off while you still can.'

'I'm going nowhere' I said.

The other guy from earlier appeared and told me to follow him.

I ignored the stares as we headed to the corner of the room. We went around the back of the stage, one of them in front of me, one behind. I was told to go up. I tensed as we climbed the stairs, ready for their attack. It didn't come. I was directed into a room which was a make-shift office. Trevor Bilton closed his laptop and stared at me. I smiled. 'Does the landlord know you're up here?' I said, attempting to lighten the mood.

He walked out from behind the desk and headed across to the window. 'You're beginning to get on my fucking nerves.'

It was dark outside. I had no idea what he thought he could see. He wasn't in the mood for banter, but I still thought I might get more out of him if Julia wasn't with me. 'Am I supposed to be scared of you?' I said.

He turned to face me and smiled. 'That's up to you. I didn't want to be rude in front of Julia, but you were always a right cunt as a kid. Do you remember me now?'

I shook my head. 'No.'

'You always thought you were God's fucking gift. To be honest, I wish I'd broken your legs back then.' He grinned. 'But there's always time for that.'

We eyeballed each other. He eventually let it go.

'You're here because of Julia?' he said.

'I don't want you taking her for a ride' I said.

He smiled. 'That was always Gary's job' he said. He winked at me. 'I'm sure you know what I mean.'

I'd heard enough. I stepped forward and threw a punch. It connected perfectly with his jaw. He fell backwards against the wall. I told him to watch his mouth.

He slowly pulled himself back up. Blood trickled out of his mouth. He sat down at his desk. 'That wasn't a very wise thing to do, but I'll let it go, seeing as we're business partners.' He grinned through the damage I'd done to his teeth. 'You tell Julia to give me a call' he said, before spitting blood onto the floor.

I walked back down the stairs and into the pub. Punching him had been a mistake. I'd let my emotions get the better of me. It was momentarily satisfying, but I'd probably pay for it when he sent his men after me. I pushed my way through the groups of drinkers and out into the car park. I saw the same men I'd seen earlier sat in their car, watching me. I was still angry, my first thought was to walk over to them and ask who they worked for. If DI Robinson and Whittle were telling me the truth, were these men connected to Trevor Bilton? But why would they stay outside as I'd attacked their boss? It didn't make sense. It wasn't the right time to be confronting them, though. If I was going to approach them, it was going to be on my terms.

I drove home through the busiest roads I could think of, before weaving my way around the side streets of the Avenues to make sure they weren't following me. Once I was sure I couldn't see another car in my rear-view mirror, I quickly pulled over and switched my lights off. I sat and waited for a few minutes until I was sure I wasn't being followed. Satisfied I was alone, I headed to my flat.

Splashing cold water on my face in the bathroom, I walked into the front room. I pulled the curtains together, leaving a small gap to peer out of. I couldn't see the car that had been following me. It had been too dark to get its registration number. I couldn't even guess the make or model of it with any accuracy. I moved into the kitchen and seeing no beer in the fridge, poured myself a glass of water. I wanted something stronger. The adrenalin was starting to fade away, replaced with feelings of stupidity and fear. I'd have to watch my back. I'd also have to tell Julia what I'd done and I doubted she'd be very impressed. I stretched out on the sofa and put my headphones on. I flicked through the CD interchanger until Dylan's 'Blood on the Tracks' came on. I was asleep by the time the third track started.

CHAPTER THIRTEEN

I woke early after not sleeping well. Pulling on a tracksuit for warmth, I brewed a pot of coffee and rummaged around in my cupboards for something to eat. Settling for a cereal bar, I switched the television on. They weren't talking about Tasker, so I booted my laptop up and checked my emails. I quickly forwarded on a couple of general enquiries to Sarah, checked the latest sports news and shut it back down.

The coffee was ready, so I took a mug back into the front room. I'd made an enemy of Trevor Bilton last night, possibly for little reason. I unwrapped the cereal bar and started to eat. I thought about cleaning my flat and getting some food in before I knuckled down to some work. Maybe Julia would want to visit again, if she would still be talking to me once I'd brought her up to date.

DI Robinson appeared on the television, prompting me to search for the remote control. Finding it, I switched the volume up. He was repeating himself, as he explained police inquiries were ongoing. He finished by appealing directly to Tasker's killer to contact the police. I smiled and nodded. Nicely done, but it was going to need more substance and less style. I could tell he was struggling in front of the cameras. The report cut to a pre-recorded article, detailing the now familiar story of Tasker's rise to fame and subsequent fall. There was nothing new. I started to channel hop and finished my drink. Shopping and cleaning would have to wait. I had plenty of work to do.

I headed to the Old Town. My walk took me down Spring Bank, towards the city centre. I walked past the job centre, noting the ever increasing crowd of people stood outside. I crossed Ferensway and headed down Jameson Street and the side of the City Hall. The wind whipped my face as I passed Princes Quay. Five minutes later and I was at the office. I walked up the stairs and opened the door. The place had been turned upside down. All the desks and cupboards were empty, their contents on the floor. My eyes finally settled on Sarah, sat on the floor in the middle of the mess.

'What's happened?' I said.

'What do you think's happened?'

She was calm, but I could read her. She was controlling her anger. I closed the door behind me and went over to her. I tried to put my arms around her, but she resisted.

'Just look at the place' she said.

'It's a mess.' I stood up, embarrassed she didn't want me touching her. I made a token effort to start tidying up the paperwork.

'What's going on, Joe?'

'Places get burgled all the time' I said. 'It could be anything.' I didn't say it with much conviction. I thought about my attack on Trevor Bilton last night. And the people following me.

'If places get burgled, things like laptops tend to go, too' she said, pointing at her desk.

I hadn't looked properly. Sarah was right. Poking out from under the mess was a laptop. It wasn't a normal burglary. But I already knew that.

She stood up and walked across to her desk. 'Why have they done it?'

'I don't know' I said.

'It's gone too far, Joe. I've tried to help you, I really have, even when Dad was telling me not to.'

'We don't know it's connected.'

'Don't treat me like an idiot, Joe. Just don't.'

I looked around. I had to tell her. 'There's more' I said. 'I'm being followed.'

'Followed?'

'That's right.'

'Why would anyone do that?'

'I don't know.' It was the truth. I didn't want to tell her how much it was freaking me out. 'And I got myself into a bit of a situation last night with Trevor Bilton.'

'Joe.'

'I'll sort it out' I said.

She shook her head and walked over to the coat-stand. 'I've got to think of Lauren, too.'

I watched her leave. I shouted that I'd tidy the mess. She'd gone. I sat back in my chair not knowing where to start.

I spent an hour tidying, trying to put things back as they were. Paperwork had never been my thing, so the process was slow and painful. Thinking I had things back to how Sarah liked them, I needed to get away from the place for a while. I decided to speak to Lorraine Harrison. I was sure the answer to Tasker's death was close to home and it was time to rattle her cage a bit. I also wanted to speak to her away from her husband. I headed to the office she worked at. It was down Scale Lane, a two minute walk away. She wasn't on reception. I told the woman that I needed to speak to Lorraine. She looked at me suspiciously before eventually deciding to call her colleague. She was photocopying in another room, but didn't look too pleased to see me. I told her it was important. We went into one of the firm's small interview rooms.

Lorraine closed the door behind us. 'Have you got any news?'

I got to the point. 'How well did you get on with Priestley?' I asked her.

She looked surprised by the question. 'Alright, I suppose. Why?'

I ignored her question and pressed on. 'Nothing more than that?'

'What do you mean?'

'Anything beyond friendship?'

She looked appalled. 'Of course not. Why would there be?'

'I've been told he had a thing for you.'

'Who on earth would say that?'

'It doesn't matter.'

She was doing the calculation. 'Are you saying he killed Greg because of it?'

I said nothing, hoping she'd offer me something.

'He was always a bit weird' she eventually said. 'But I don't mean that in a particularly bad way. He was just always really quiet and intense. I never really thought he was interested in women, to be honest.' She shrugged. 'Or men, either. He just wasn't that type of person.'

'He must have shown some interest, surely?'

'He certainly never gave any signs that he was interested in me. I haven't seen him for years, so it doesn't make sense. Even if he had been carrying some sort of a torch for me, he'd have gotten over it by now.'

'Why do you say that?'

'He's a got a wife, hasn't he?'

She looked at me. I nodded.

'It can't mean anything in relation to Greg's death?'

I'd known people to act with seemingly little motive. It sounded fanciful, but I wasn't ruling anything out. 'I'm in touch with his parents' I said. 'They think Greg had something to tell them. Some important news.' I was sure she knew what I was talking about. I could see it written all over her face, but I wasn't ready to push her on the matter just yet. It'd keep.

'He wouldn't tell them about us. We'd agreed.'

'What else might he have wanted to tell them?'

'Maybe something about Siobhan?'

'Did you ever speak about her?'

'No.'

'Never?'

'Not very often.'

'You didn't like her?'

'Of course I didn't like her, but I respected Greg's position.'

I nodded. She'd said previously he wouldn't leave Siobhan, given that she'd moved up to Hull for him. 'But things weren't right between them?'

'Of course they weren't.'

I found it difficult to understand. Even if he felt obligated, Greg had to be in charge of his own life. He couldn't stay with Siobhan out of pity. 'She was a bit young for him' I said, thinking of what his mother had said to me. 'They probably wanted different things.'

'We never spoke about it.'

'You must have an opinion?'

'Of course I have an opinion. She was a leech who was only interested in Greg because he was famous and had some money. There was no other way she was going to launch her fashion career. Look at her. All she has is a shop in Hull. She's hardly setting the world on fire, is she?'

I ignored her bile. 'Did they argue?'

'All the time. Greg would sometimes tell me things. I think he needed to get it off his chest and have someone listen to him.'

'I don't think Greg was happy, do you?'

She calmed down. 'He wasn't. He was always talking about needing something, but I don't think he could ever figure it out for himself. I suppose music was his rock. He'd spend hours recording things in his studio. I've been putting some of the tracks onto a CD this morning. I didn't want to do it at home in case Jason saw me. Greg was going to use them for his new solo album.'

I asked for a copy. I wasn't sure what it'd tell me about Tasker, but it seemed worth a shot. She reluctantly agreed and disappeared to burn me a disc. She returned and passed me a CD-R.

'I'll do another copy for myself, but please don't spread it around' she said.

I said I wouldn't. 'Was Siobhan supportive of his music?'

'I don't think so. I don't think he ever let her listen to anything like this.'

I asked the big question. 'Would you have left your husband for Greg if he'd asked you to?'

She shook her head. 'I couldn't do it to Jason.' She paused again before continuing. 'What we were doing was wrong. I know that. I think we both needed a friend more than anything.' She paused. 'I think we both knew it wouldn't work out for us this time, either.'

I turned the conversation towards her husband. 'Jason's never been a fan of the band?'

'He's not into music, but he's a good man. We can rely on him. He's right for me and Jay.'

'He's got a temper' I said.

Her eyes narrowed before she turned away from me. 'Why do you say that?'

'I had him checked out.'

She turned back to me. 'It was a long time ago when he used to drink. He made some mistakes and he's paid for them. He's doesn't need people like you dragging it all back up again. It's not fair.'

I said nothing, let her continue.

'I know what you're thinking' she said. 'He didn't like Greg and he had a temper, so he must have killed him. I thought you were better than that. I thought you wanted to help. I've already had the police asking about him and I told them what I told you. My husband didn't kill Greg. He's not like that.' She stood up and opened the door. 'I've got work to do.'

The front door to the office was unlocked. I tried to think whether or not I'd locked it. It didn't matter. I went inside. Don sat at his desk.

'Don't look so surprised to see me' he said.

'I'm not.' I sat down opposite him. 'How's Sarah?'

'Not so good.'

We stared at each other.

'Who's done this to us, Joe?' he asked me.

'I don't know.'

'You don't know?'

'No.' It was the truth.

'What about these men who are following you?'

'I'm trying to find out.'

He sat back and shook his head. 'You've made a right mess of things' he eventually said.

There was nothing I could say. He was right. I was going to have to listen whilst he tore a strip off me. Truth was, I probably deserved it.

'I gave you an opportunity when no one else would' he said. 'I've always tried to show you that there's a right way and a wrong way to this job. There are things we do and there are things we don't do. This was never a job for us and now you've put all I've got left of my family in danger. I said last time that I couldn't let that happen again, so it's time to say enough's enough. I can't have people breaking into our office like this. Not when it's my name above the door. You've gone too far this time' he said. 'Way too far. You don't even know what you're dealing with.'

'And you think we should leave this to DI Robinson and his team?' I said, arguing back. 'Because this is real now. I'm sorry for the position it's put us in, but it's not going away. I have to sort it out.'

Don pushed aside my objection. 'Robinson's an old colleague and a friend. I'd trust him with my life.'

'He's hardly covering himself in glory.'

'Hardly the point, is it? He's doing his job to the best of his ability.'

'So am I.'

'There's a difference.'

'Not from where I'm sitting.'

'Why are you doing this to us?' Don asked me.

'Because I'm involved. I have to.' It was for Tasker's parents. There was no point explaining this to Don. He was a head over heart type of person.

'Kane Major hired you to help the band. Obviously, it's sad what's happened, but it's not your problem, Joe. Can't you see that? The only way to succeed in this business is to distance yourself. Don't get too involved. Leave it to the police when you have to.'

I shook my head. 'Have you checked the bank statements recently?' I wanted to scream at him that he was the one being naive. We couldn't back out now. I told him about Tasker's parents and how upset they were. How I owed them.

Don looked at me like I was stupid. 'Of course they're going to be hurting, it's only natural, but you can't help everyone you meet. You can't change the world like you want to, you just can't.'

'I've got to try.' I had a lot of time for Don, but I couldn't let him talk to me like this. 'It's not about the money. They need answers and I owe them. I let them down.'

'How on earth did you let them down?' he said. 'That's stupid talk, and you know it.'

'I let Major convince me Tasker's disappearance was nothing to worry about and that he'd be back. I should have done more.'

'You wouldn't have found him. It was needle in a haystack stuff. Nature of the job, Joe. You can't win them all.'

I shook my head. 'I didn't do enough.'

Don looked at me. 'How are you going to sort it out?' he asked me.

I didn't have a proper answer. 'I'm getting closer' I said.

'Who killed him?'

'I'm getting closer' I repeated.

'Not good enough.'

'I've got to finish it' I said. 'It's the only way.'

'You're kidding yourself. Listen to Robinson. If he's telling you to let it go, let it go.'

'I can't.'

Don stood up and walked over to the window. He stopped and turned back to face me. 'Have you totally lost the plot? I thought you were more switched on than this, Joe.' He headed towards the door, but turned around to point at me. 'You don't even think about contacting Sarah. Are we clear about that? I'm not having her and Lauren put in danger because of your stupidity. We're flying out later today to my sister's place in Spain for a couple of days. I want this mess cleared up before we come back.'

He was gone before I had chance to say anything further.

It was times like this I wished I kept a bottle of whiskey in the desk drawer, like all good Private Investigators are supposed to. I sat at my desk, the office silent. I glanced at Sarah's desk. Don's words were harsh, but I knew I'd let him down. He had been the one person who'd seen something in me when I was in danger of falling to pieces. He'd taken a chance on me and invited me into his business. His way of working might have been different from mine, but I should have shown him more courtesy. The last thing I wanted to do was cause him or Sarah any trouble. Aside from my brother, they were the nearest thing I had to a family. Or used to have. The bottom line was that I thought I'd taken the job on for the right reasons, but I needed to make amends to Don now, show him that he could still rely on me. I needed to straighten things out for everyone's sake.

I knew where to start.

I walked into the pub, looking for Trevor Bilton. I couldn't see him, so I headed to the stairs. One of his men appeared and tried to stop me, but I wasn't in the mood. I pushed him aside and increased my pace. Bilton was on the telephone. He smiled at me, finished his call. His mouth was a mess. He'd lost a front tooth when I'd punched him.

'I thought you'd be keeping a low profile' he said to me. 'Given the circumstances.'

He stood up and walked around his desk to face me. The man I'd pushed aside as I'd made my way up walked in. Bilton shoved me into him. My arms were behind my back before I had chance to defend myself. He smiled, punched me in the stomach. 'What a pleasant surprise this is.'

I struggled for breath, tried to shake myself free of the man's grip. I was going nowhere. I looked up at Bilton. He smiled, punched me in the stomach again. I fell to the floor.

'We'll call that quits, shall we?' he said.

I slowly stood back up, trying not to show that he'd hurt me too much.

'Consider yourself lucky' he said. 'I've let you off lightly. Now, what the fuck do you want?'

'I want you to stay away from my office.'

He looked puzzled. 'Why would I want to visit your office?'

I told him what had happened.

He was jabbing at me with his finger. 'If I want to speak to you, cunt, I'll speak to you face to face. Why would I pull that kind of stunt? You need to get a grip of yourself.' He gave the nod to his man to get rid of me. 'See you around, Geraghty.'

I struggled back to my car and drove away from the pub. My mobile rang. I thought twice about not answering. I knew that Julia would call back. I relented, deciding to get it over and done with. The day couldn't get much worse. 'Now then' I said.

'What the fuck are you playing at, Joe?' she said.

I said nothing and let her continue.

'You never mentioned your plans for last night.'

'I was going to ring you' I said.

'What stopped you, Joe? What stopped you calling me after you made this decision of yours?'

'I don't know.'

'You can do better than that.'

I pulled over so I could take the call properly. I didn't need telling what a stupid decision I'd made. I apologised.

'You think I can't fight my own battles?' she said. 'I've managed this long without a knight in shining armour.'

'I know.'

'You just don't go pulling stunts like that. Not for me. Is that clear?'

There was a moment's silence. She'd said her piece. I'd acted without thinking and crossed a line. Nothing more needed saying. I told her what had just happened at the pub.

'He's doubled his price' she said.

'Bilton?'

'Compensation for you punching him. Dental work costs.'

I was sure I detected a hint of pleasure in her voice as she told me, but I didn't push my luck. 'I guess your paper's not happy?'

'Not particularly, but they'll pay it.'

'Good.'

'I've come to an arrangement with him.'

'What kind of arrangement?'

'I told him if he wanted his money doubling, we wanted something in return.'

'What do we want in return?' I asked.

'Siobhan's been in touch with him. They've set up a meeting and we're going to be there.'

I had intended to approach her at the boutique where she wouldn't want to cause a scene. This sounded like a much better plan. 'When?' I asked.

'Tonight.'

'That's quick.'

'At the pub.'

'Right.' It wouldn't be my choice to go back there, but it made sense.

'Tell me I'm not the only one working here, Joe. What do you know?'

'I've found out Priestley had a thing for Lorraine Harrison. Did you know that?'

'Where did you hear it?'

'Major's solicitor, so I assume it must have come from Greg.'

'Have you spoken to Priestley?'

'Not yet. I've just had a word with Lorraine.'

'What did she say?'

'It was news to her.' I told Julia about Jason Harrison's criminal record. 'She wasn't impressed I brought it up.'

'I don't suppose she would be.'

'What do you think about Priestley?'

'If you're asking whether he could have had an argument with Greg and accidently killed him, why not? It happens, doesn't it?' She paused. 'He was always a bit weird.'

'How do you mean?' It wasn't the first time she'd said this.

'Just a feeling I got off him. The rest of the band were great, but he was always a bit reserved. It might have been shyness. It might just be that he was weird.'

Her opinion of him was the same as Lorraine's and I didn't like coincidences. I told her about the break-in at the office and that Don and Sarah had left for Spain.

'They've just walked away?'

'That's about the size of it.' Not that I blamed them. 'She's got to think about her daughter.'

'Even so.'

'I've put her through a lot in the past. She doesn't need this.'

'What are you going to do?' she asked me.

'Keep asking questions, I suppose' I said, before terminating the call and pulling back out into the traffic.

CHAPTER FOURTEEN

I didn't want to go back to the office, so I sat in the cafe I'd met Lorraine Harrison in previously. I'd barely touched my coffee when Marcus Whittle called. Major had listened to reason and returned to Hull on the day's first train from London. It was something. He wanted to talk to me. Immediately. I was just as keen to talk to him. I walked through the city centre, towards his office. The receptionist sent me straight up to his suite. I walked in, no knocking.

Whittle looked up. 'Thanks for coming so promptly' he said. He indicated I should sit down.

I ignored him. The conference desk was covered in newspapers. They were still poring over the details. Major looked up. Winked. 'Alright, PI? Solved the case yet?'

'I'm not in the mood' I said. 'Where have you been?'

He sat back in his chair. 'Who the fuck do you think you're talking to?'

'I've had DI Robinson on my case, wanting to speak to you.'

Whittle stepped in, defused the situation. 'Let's not worry about him just yet' he said. 'We're here to talk about the progress being made.' He glanced at Major. The message was clear. He was saving me the bother of telling Major to watch his mouth.

'Fucking hate this city' Major said, throwing the newspapers to one side. 'It's no wonder anyone with any talent leaves. Shithole of a place.'

I turned to Whittle and raised my eyebrows.

Whittle ignored me and got proceedings underway. 'If we're quite ready, gentlemen. Obviously we need to keep things moving in the right direction' he said. He turned to me. 'What about Steve Priestley? What does he have to say for himself?'

'I need to speak to him' I said. I saw Major shaking his head. 'Problem?' I said to him.

'Fuck's sake, PI. Are you just pissing my money up the wall, or what?'

Whittle told him to be quiet. 'Shall we start again and assume we're all acting in good faith?'

Major eventually nodded. I followed suit.

'Priestley's next on my list' I said. 'I spoke to Lorraine Harrison earlier this morning and she said she had no idea he was carrying a torch for her. I get the impression people think of him as being either a bit weird or a bit intense.'

'I never really liked him' said Major. 'New Holland was never about Priestley. It was me and Greg who got things moving because he never had the same vision as us. He couldn't see the band's potential like we could. It was like it was something for him to do before he got himself a proper job. Became a fucking accountant or something. I never got that kind of attitude. He never seemed to want to enjoy the ride. He was always a bit weird like that.'

'He held the band together when Greg lost it' I said.

Major shook his head. 'Not really. He wrote some songs, but it didn't mean it was his band. The gigs were always about Greg's songs. Nothing really changed.'

'Priestley's wife said the reunion was a chance for him to get the credit he deserved for his songs.'

'It was going to be Greg's songs.' Major laughed. 'What else? Priestley wasn't willing to accept the fact people weren't going to pay to listen to the later stuff. It's obvious, isn't it? They want to hear the good stuff, the hits. Greg's songs.'

He was right, but I could see how the situation might escalate in the rehearsal room. Neither Tasker nor Priestley would want to back down.

'I think we need to pin Priestley down on his alibi' Whittle said.

'He's already said he doesn't have one.'

'All the more reason, then.'

I held my hands up. 'I'll try again.'

'What about me telling you I thought Greg was involved in something?' Major said. 'Have you sorted that?'

I told them about Trevor Bilton and his connection to Siobhan. 'I might know more on that later' I said.

'Fuck's sake, in your own time. What about Lorraine Harrison? Her husband didn't like Greg very much. I'd be looking at him, too, if I were you, PI.'

'How did you know about her and Greg?' I asked him.

'They go way back. It wasn't a huge surprise to me that they'd got back together. It's not a big deal.'

'That wasn't what you said before. You said you didn't know what they were up to.'

'I didn't want to tell you.' He shrugged. 'It was Greg's private life.'

The man was incapable of telling the truth. 'What about Siobhan?' I asked.

'It's not my place to judge.'

'She'd followed him up to Hull.'

'In exchange for her own boutique. She didn't do bad out of Greg.'

I turned the conversation back to Lorraine Harrison. 'Did you know Jason Harrison's got a conviction for assault?'

Whittle nodded. 'There you go.'

'He's on my list of people to talk to.'

'Good' Major said. 'He was probably jealous of what Greg had achieved. He's ordinary, got nothing going for him. I'm not surprised their marriage is dead.'

'It's not dead' I said.

Whittle stepped back in. 'Kane's right. Priestley's got every reason to resent Greg. Plenty to be getting your teeth into, Joe.' His mobile rang. He said he had to take the call. He stood up and left the room.

Major waited for him to leave. Leaned forward. 'Just the two of us, then.' He stared at me before smiling. 'Cards on the table time, PI. Do you reckon I killed Greg?' Do you reckon I ran away because I was scared? Go on, tell me what you think.'

The time away from Hull hadn't dulled his arrogance. I pointed at him. 'I'm going to find out who killed Greg and I don't care if you're paying me' I said. 'I'll play the cards I'm dealt. If they lead to you, they lead to you.'

Major shook his head, like he was pained by what I was saying. 'I thought we'd been through all of this and got it straight. I didn't kill Greg.' He spoke slowly. 'It doesn't make any sense, does it? I was going to use this to relaunch his career, make us both some money. I needed him alive.'

'Where have you been?'

'I told you. I had to go back to London for some meetings.'

'Just after Greg was found?'

Major leaned back in his chair and smiled at me, like I was simple. 'That's exactly right, PI.'

It took me a moment to realise what he was saying. I was appalled. 'You set some deals up on the back of his death?'

Major shrugged. 'The band's never been hotter. There's a lot to sort out. The label wants something in the shops as soon as possible.'

'You heartless bastard.'

'I'm not going to apologise to you. I'm looking out for the family's long-term interests. There was nothing I could do here. I was in the way. I like to delegate, leave things to the professionals.' He laughed. 'Or at least the so-called professionals.'

I ignored the jibe. 'What did you tell the police?'

'I gave them a statement through my legal team.'

The big question. 'Where were you the night Greg was killed?'

Major sat back upright. 'I'm getting fucking bored of this chat, now. I was in the hotel, in my room, working. Satisfied?'

'Did anyone see you? Receptionist, room service?'

'No.'

We sat in silence for a moment, listening to Whittle on the telephone in the other room. Major spoke. 'Why don't you believe me, PI?'

'I'm following the leads.'

'Maybe you're following your dick?'

'Say that again?'

'Still fucking Julia, are you?'

I leaned forward. 'Mind your own business.'

Major sneered at me. 'Don't be so touchy. I'm only asking. I like to know to what my people are up to.'

I looked away. Controlled my temper. 'Robinson tried to warn me off' I said. 'He told me I shouldn't be working for you. He said I was getting involved in something way over my head, that I should back off. What did he mean?'

Major shrugged. 'He's not going to like you trampling all over his territory, is he? You should know that. You're still here, aren't you?'

His was right, but his attitude was infuriating. 'Doesn't explain why he took the time out to speak to me.' I pressed on. 'I'm being followed.'

'Who by?'

'I wouldn't be mentioning it if I knew.'

Major laughed. 'Don't be so paranoid, PI. We're in Hull. Who the fuck would be following you here?'

'That's what I want to know.'

Major shook his head and turned away. He'd had enough of our talk. 'I've really got no idea' he finally said.

I needed to calm down and talk to someone else after leaving Major's office. I didn't want to stand still. I drove out to Priestley's farm. His wife told me he was in his recording studio. She pointed me towards a barn at the end of their yard. I walked across and let myself in. Priestley sat in front of his mixing desk, strumming an acoustic guitar. I coughed to get his attention.

He spun around and nodded to me. 'I can't say this is a surprise.' He put the guitar down. 'I've just finished some recording with my brother, Richard. He's a got a band together.' He smiled. 'He doesn't know what he's getting himself into.'

I found a chair and sat down. 'I've been hearing some unpleasant things about you.'

'Is that right?'

'It is.'

'Shall I say it? You want to know if I killed Greg?' He paused. 'Do you really think I could do such a thing?'

I didn't answer straightaway. Probably because I didn't know. 'When we spoke at Paull, you told me you had nothing to hide, so let's say I'm open-minded.'

He picked up his bottle of water. 'You're taking a chance coming here, aren't you?'

'I'll take my chances.'

'The searchers will be out if you don't report back within the hour?'

'Something like that.'

He nodded. 'What have you heard, then?'

'I've heard you weren't very popular within the band.'

Priestley shrugged. 'I told you we'd had a falling out. It wasn't a big deal. It wasn't the first time it'd happened over the years.'

'Even though you'd have been playing his songs on the reunion tour?'

Priestley took another mouthful of water. 'Nothing like that had been decided.'

'I'm sorry to be brutal, but it would have been Greg's songs.'

'There would have been a balance.'

I tried another tack. 'Major wasn't very complimentary about the way you took over the band when Greg lost the plot.'

'It makes him a hypocrite, then, doesn't it? We never really got on, that's true, but don't let him fool you. He's a businessman. He was never a musician or someone who cared about the music. His thing is doing deals, seeing who he can screw a little bit more out of. It's all a game to him. When I stepped up to the plate with the songs, he carried on like we were best buddies. The bottom line was money, and to get money, he needed the band to function when Greg had his troubles. I made it happen for him, whatever he says about it now.'

I wasn't going to argue with his assessment. Not after Major had gone back to London, touting for business on the back of what'd happened. But I had to keep an open mind. 'If we're talking about Greg's murder, you see it gives you motive? There was a professional rivalry between you and Greg. The arguments could have become heated, neither of you wanting to back down. Sometimes things happen which we don't intend when we're angry.'

Priestley shook his head. 'I loved Greg like a brother. It was always about the music for me, and that was what was most important to us. We'd argue and he was difficult to deal with, I can't deny that, but any bad feeling never lingered.'

I'd listened to the tapes of Julia's interview with Greg again. 'Didn't you resent him taking over your band?'

He shook his head. 'There wasn't much to take over. Sometimes you've got to know when to make sacrifices. Did I want to be a big fish in a small pond, or a smaller fish in a much bigger pond? Greg could do things I couldn't do. I was happy when he came along.'

I wasn't sure if I believed him. 'Tell me about Lorraine Harrison' I said.

He smiled. 'I wondered how long it'd take you to find out about that.'

Priestley picked up his water again. I didn't like it. It was a stalling tactic. I could see him working out what he wanted to tell me.

'It was a private matter' he eventually said.

'There's no such thing at the moment.'

He put his bottle down and explained how they'd argued over her. 'I assume you know she was seeing Greg?'

I nodded. 'She's told me.'

'They go way back. I had a stupid crush on her. That's all. I wouldn't have embarrassed her by making a move.'

'I think it was more than that.'

Priestley took a deep breath and toyed with his water. Drummed his fingers on the mixing desk. He looked away from me after nodding his agreement. 'I'm not happy, Joe. It's like I'm living a lie out here.'

'Your marriage?'

He nodded. 'I owe Carly everything. She saved me when I was a mess. She's a great woman who sorted me out when I needed it the most. I owe her everything.'

'But you don't love her?'

'No.'

We sat in silence. I already knew his wife was protective and it was obvious she was in charge of their relationship.

Priestley sipped at his water before continuing. 'I always had a thing for Lorraine, but Greg got there first. Story of my life. I suppose I was always too shy to do anything about it. It was never the right time. You know how it is with these things? And then the band moved down to London, so that was that. I didn't see her again for years until I heard about her website.'

'Did you approach her?'

'No.'

'Did you argue with Greg about her?'

'She deserved better than him.'

'Did you argue over her?'

'Yes.'

'Recently?'

He nodded. 'He always knew I had a thing for her. He used to enjoy rubbing my nose in it, letting me know he had what I wanted. He told me he was seeing her again.'

'What did you about it?'

'Nothing. I did nothing. What could I do? I'm not stupid. I knew she was only interested in Greg. It was always that way.'

'But he wouldn't let up about it?'

'He was very keen to let me know he'd won.'

'How did it make you feel?'

He shook his head. 'I've already told you I didn't kill him. Don't try to twist my words.'

I stood up, unsure whether I felt sorrow or pity for him. 'If you didn't kill Greg, you've got to give me something' I said. I looked him in the eye. 'You've lied to me once before.'

'I explained that, but it doesn't change anything. I've still got nothing to give you. The cards will have to fall where they fall.'

'It doesn't give you an alibi, does it?' I decided to leave him to his recording. He'd argued with Tasker about Lorraine Harrison. Priestley said it himself: she deserved better. I wondered if their argument had spilled over into violence and how it had finished. And he'd lied to me. Even if he was toeing Major's line about the reunion, he'd still lied. 'You must have seen somebody on your way to Paull' I said. 'Passed a petrol station or something?'

Priestley picked his guitar back up and turned away from me. 'What's the point?'

I called Julia to bring her up to date with my movements. As I'd headed back towards Hull, I'd dropped in at the garage where Jason Harrison worked. I wanted to check out his alibi. The garage was on an old industrial block, out towards the eastern edge of the city, not far from Paull. The area was deserted and decaying. It wasn't the sort of place which attracted passing custom. You went there for a purpose. The businesses which could afford it had relocated, leaving behind several empty units and those which obviously didn't have any real need to move. It was maybe ten miles away from Siobhan's boutique, but it felt a world away. I'd had to wait in my car until I saw Harrison leave for a break.

I told Julia what Harrison's boss had told me. 'They did go out for a drink' I said. 'They went into town, had a couple of pints, planned to get a curry to round the night off. Same old story.'

'So his alibi stands up?' she said.

I smiled. 'Not quiet. His boss said when they got onto the subject of family, Harrison started to get a bit agitated. He went off on one about Tasker and how sick he was of the man. He got himself really wound up about it and then disappeared, leaving his boss stood by himself in the pub.'

Julia got it. 'Early in the evening, was it?'

'Correct.'

'So, theoretically speaking, he would have had time to get to the studio?'

'Correct.' I ended the call, threw my mobile onto the passenger seat and drove off.

I wanted to know more about the Bilton brothers. The ring road was as busy as ever, heading to the estate's shopping centre. Several of the shops had closed permanently, shutters down, covered in graffiti. I walked into the newsagent's. The man behind the counter physically backed away from me when I mentioned Bilton by name. He told me he wasn't prepared to say anything. The shop was dirty, tired and anything of value was kept behind the till. The sign on the door said he was open until ten p.m., so I could only guess at the level of trouble he had to contend with.

I left and walked down the arcade of shops. Spotting the library, I went in and headed straight to the notice board. I found what I was looking for; a flyer for a forthcoming Neighbourhood Watch meeting. I leaned forward to read it. The group was meeting next week to discuss a course of action. The flyer gave the name and address of the group leader. I made a note of it.

Betty Page's house was to the north of the estate, a disorientating five minute drive through symmetrical housing along identikit roads. It had been a while since I was here, playing rugby on the large playing field as a boy. There hadn't been many reasons to come back to the area over the years.

I explained I was a Private Investigator and she let me straight in. Betty Page was well into her sixties and clearly very house-proud. Nothing was out of place. Immaculately tidy. The air in the house was stale. It looked like she never opened any windows. The number of locks and bars she had on them was staggering. What depressed me most was how flimsy they were. They wouldn't stop anybody. She settled me down and disappeared to make drinks. I passed the time by looking at the photographs on her mantelpiece. They portrayed three generations of her family. The way she quietly crept back into the room took me by surprise.

'My husband, Ernest' she said, pointing to the photograph I was looking at. 'He died seven years ago.'

I put the photograph back in its place. 'I'm sorry to hear that.'

She passed me my coffee. 'You never get over it properly.'

'I know.'

She didn't press me. She sat back down in her chair and asked what she could do for me.

'Do you know a man called Trevor Bilton?' I asked, getting straight down to it.

'Of course I do.'

'What can you tell me about him?'

'What do you want to know?' She leaned forward in her chair. 'This used to be such a lovely place to live, especially when me and Ernest first moved here. We all moved together from Hessle Road when they pulled a load of the old houses down.' She laughed, shook her head. 'It was supposed be an improvement. Move people out of what they called the slums. Biggest mistake they ever made. These were decent people who worked and instilled some manners and discipline into their children. Now it's the complete opposite and it's people like Trevor Bilton who are to blame. He's made life for everyone around here a misery. You know what the do-gooders are like. Nobody nipped his behaviour in the bud when they had a chance. Did you know his brother is a worker on the estate? I don't know whether to laugh or cry, I really don't.'

I agreed with her. 'It's a bit unusual' I said. 'What's Gary like?'

'I often deal with him at the Community Centre where he works. He's not a bad lad, really, which is more than can be said for his brother. At least he's trying his best to make things better around here. Problem is, these kids don't think there's anything better for them. They idolise Trevor, but they don't see that they're the ones taking all the risks. They can't see the truth.'

I looked around the room, letting her continue.

'Their parents don't care' she said. 'Bilton and his like rule this place at the expense of us decent folk. The kids are out of control, setting fire to stolen cars, posting dog muck through doors, you name it. Even the fire brigade are too frightened to come out here unless the police will escort them.'

'What do the police have to say?'

She laughed. 'They tell me they can't do anything. They've got no proof, but we all know that he directs things from the pub, and if he's not there, he's gambling on the horses. He's a man of habit and he thinks this is his kingdom.'

'I bet your viewpoint hasn't made you popular around here' I said.

'I don't care. Somebody has to say, it's time to put a stop to it. We can't have people too scared to leave their own homes. Enough's enough. It's not how it should be. It's not a community anymore and I'll keep shouting until the police do something.' She struggled to her feet and picked up a folder from her bookshelf. She took out a photograph of Trevor Bilton. 'They keep telling me they need evidence, so I take photographs.' She passed me one. 'You can keep this. It's a copy.' She moved across to her mantelpiece and looked at the neat framed photographs she had on display. 'If my Ernest was still alive, he wouldn't stand for this kind of thing either, I can tell you.'

You're a mess. A total mess. You measure time in terms of the wait to your next drink. Coming up with the third album is like torture. The lure of the road has gone. You're sick of seeing the same towns, the same countries, the same venues. The relentless monotony. Kane tells you it has to be done. It's what pays your wages. You're beyond caring. Priestley is effectively running the band. He's still sober, still splitting his time between Hull and London. He can deal with the things you can't. You know the songs you're writing are shit. You know the songs Priestley's writing are the best he's done. You're angry and jealous. You can't express your despair in any other way. You lash out. Kane keeps the band together. You get up on stage night after night and sing the words Priestley has written. You hate it. You spit the words out. You can see the crowds are thinning out. Times have changed. Newer bands are now the darlings of the music press. You hate it. You know you're yesterday's news. You know the band is finished. You know you're finished.

CHAPTER FIFTEEN

I decided to go home for some rest. It had been a long day and it wasn't over yet. The cupboards were still bare, so I made my signature dish of pasta surprise. The surprise this time was that the only thing I had to go with the pasta was some carrot. I tried to concentrate on the rolling news as I ate, but I was too distracted. I was nervous ahead of the meeting with Trevor Bilton and Siobhan. I left my flat, collected Julia from her hotel as agreed and drove across Hull towards the pub. My earlier visit to see him went unmentioned between us. I suspected neither of us wanted to dwell on it. Not at the moment. This time the car park was quiet. No teenagers. I locked up and we headed into the bar. Despite it being early evening, it was still busy. Some had clearly been in the place most of the day, some had just arrived and were settling in for the night. Bilton's men were in their usual positions. No live music tonight. One stood at the foot of the stairs, one stood at the bar. I nodded to the closest one and told him we were expected. Eventually we were allowed up the stairs. Bilton sat in the corner of the room. He looked up as we walked across to him.

'Got my money?' he asked Julia. He didn't take his eyes off me.

Julia passed it over.

'Do I need to count it?'
'I shouldn't think so' I said.
'Think I'd trust you?'
'It's Julia's money.'

He counted it anyway and put it in his back pocket. We followed him over to the corner of the room, towards a large curtain.

'Behind there' he said.

Five minutes later we heard Siobhan enter the room. It felt childish being hidden behind the curtain and it made me want to laugh. I glanced at Julia and smiled. She was thinking the same thing. We heard Bilton and Siobhan discuss why she was there. Julia nudged me. It was our cue. I nodded to her and stepped out into view. Siobhan looked confused. Bilton headed towards the door, leaving us to it.

'Bastard' she shouted at Bilton's back. I introduced Julia, making sure I mentioned she was a journalist.

I waited until he'd left. 'We just want to find out who killed Greg' I said. 'Nothing else. Whatever else you get up to is your business. We're not interested in that.'

'I knew something was wrong.'

'Them are the breaks' Julia said.

'This is blackmail.'

I smiled. 'Not really.'

'She'll write a story if I don't talk to you.'

I took three chairs off the stack and put them down next to each. 'Shall we?'

Siobhan hadn't wanted to stay in the pub, and having nowhere else to go, we headed to my flat. I washed out the cafetiere and started to brew a fresh pot. Siobhan and Julia sat in the front room. I joined them and looked out of the window.

'You've got the same depressing CDs as Greg' Siobhan said, flicking through the pile of cases on the coffee table.

I turned around and smiled.

She put the CDs down. 'I was doing it because I felt numb' she said. 'I've lost Greg and no one cares about me.'

I moved away from the window and sat down. 'Have you spoken to Greg's parents?'

She shook her head. 'His mother never liked me.' She looked like she was going to start crying. 'Only on the phone a couple of times, but nothing more than that. '

'Right.'

'He was cheating on me, yet it still hurts. I keep telling myself what a bastard he was, but it doesn't make any difference.'

I went back into the kitchen to finish making the drinks. I hoped Julia would say something comforting in the meantime.

I rejoined them and passed her a mug. 'What does Lorraine have that I don't?' Siobhan said.

I assumed an answer wasn't required. 'Was Greg back into drugs?' I asked.

She put the mug back down and shook her head. 'No.'

'They were yours?'

She nodded. 'I'm trying to stop, I really am. I just need it for now, for a couple of days to get me through all this.'

I didn't want to push her, so I let it go.

We sat in silence for a few moments. Siobhan spoke again. 'I felt like I was losing Greg. I had to do something to try and get his interest back. Stupid, I know.'

'The age difference?' Julia said.

'And other things. We'd been arguing a lot recently. Whenever I went to his flat, it seemed like we argued. Stupid thing was it was over nothing in particular. Lots of small things which we kept going over and over. The same things. Lorraine, the reunion, all that kind of stuff.'

It confirmed what Greg's neighbour had told me. 'You should get help' I said.

She sat upright and looked at me. 'I just need to get past the next couple of days.'

I understood what she meant. I'd gone to pieces when Debbie had died, but this wasn't the way to deal with things. I knew that much. 'What are you going to do?'

'What do you mean?'

'When this is over.'

She looked puzzled. 'I've got no idea.'

Half an hour later and I'd put Siobhan into a taxi and sent her home. We told her we might want to speak to her again. Julia produced a bottle of wine she'd been carrying in her bag. I smiled. 'Excellent idea.'

'I think we've earned it' she said.

I took it from her and went for it. It needed saying. 'About earlier today' I said.

'It doesn't need to be said, Joe. Let's just leave it, shall we?'

I nodded my agreement. Remembering the CD Lorraine had given me, I passed it over to Julia, explaining what it was. She told me to put it on. We listened to what would have been Tasker's comeback album. The songs were simply Tasker and his acoustic guitar. Whether he planned to overdub a band onto them later, we'd never know. The songs were good. Some were very good. It'd been a long day and the wine was making me drowsy. Before the CD was finished, I'd fallen asleep.

Breakfast was an apple and a coffee. And I was alone. Julia had left. I showered and headed out to speak to Jason Harrison. His boss had told me on my previous visit that he was going on holiday, taking his caravan up the coast, leaving Harrison to look after things. There was a red MG on the ramp and two more cars parked outside of the garage. I walked around the car and peered into the office. It was a mess. Two chairs were placed next to the desk. Boxes of spare parts piled in the corner. There was no one there. I turned around and saw Jason Harrison. I hadn't heard him climb out from under the car he was working on. He was holding a large wrench in his hand.

'I've got nothing to say to you' he said.

I smiled. 'Do you want put that down?'

'No.'

I moved closer and stood next to the car. He might want to do me some damage, but he wasn't going to risk damaging the car. 'I need to talk to you.'

'I've got nothing to say to you.'

The car was nice. If I ever had the money, I could see myself driving it. I paused. I did have the money, though. I could afford it. I'd bought into the partnership with some of the insurance money from my wife's death and put the rest in the bank and forgotten about it. I pushed the thought to one side. I wasn't going to waste it on a car. I turned back to Harrison. 'Anything you want to tell me?' I asked.

He laughed. 'Why would I want to talk to you?'

I took another step forward. 'I know you've got a temper on you. '

Harrison grinned. 'And you think it means I killed Tasker?'

'Give them enough time and the police will eventually get around to you' I said.

'You're not very quick, are you?' He looked at the wrench then looked at me. 'They've already spoken to me.'

I nodded. Sometimes I'm stupid; sometimes it pays to let people tell you what they know. If it helps them underestimate me, so much the better. 'Did you tell them about your wife and Greg?'

He looked like he wanted to punch me. 'It was a long time ago. She had a relationship with him before we met. So what?'

'Did you give the police an alibi?'

'What's it got to do with you?'

I shrugged. 'I might be the best friend you've got.'

He looked at me like I was mad. I told him what my involvement was. If he had nothing to hide, it was in his interests to tell me.

'I was out with the boss, having a drink.'

'All night?'

'Until the pubs kicked out.'

'And then what?'

'I had a kebab and went home.'

'Don't lie to me.'

'I'm not.'

'I know you left your boss standing around in the pub like a spare part.'

He waved the discrepancy away. 'I'd had enough for the night. I just needed to get some fresh air.'

'You didn't like Tasker being back on the scene, did you?' I said.

'I thought I'd made that clear last time.'

'Jealous?'

'Why would I be jealous of him?'

'He was a famous musician who'd had a relationship with your wife.'

'Long time ago.'

'But they were still in touch.'

He moved towards me. 'What the fuck are you saying?'

He was challenging me. It was time to say it like it was. 'It must have made you feel second best. I know that's how I would have felt if I was you.'

He shook his head. 'I don't think about him.'

'No?'

'He's in the past.'

'The band was reforming. He wasn't in the past.'

'Why would I give a shit about the fucking band? It's her who needs to sort her priorities out. She should be doing something more useful, like taking some of that overtime she's been offered. If I get laid off here, we'll need the extra.'

'She isn't going to stop with the website, though, is she?'

He shook his head. 'She never shuts up talking about him and the band. Never gives it a rest.'

'Where did you go when you left the pub?' I repeated.

'You really think I killed him?'

I shrugged. I knew he had plenty of time to leave the pub and get across Hull. Certainly at that time of night. His alibi was worthless.

The fight seemed to leave him. 'I went to Tasker's flat, alright?'

'His flat?'

'I'd had enough. I wanted to sort it out, man to man. Tell him to leave us alone.'

'It must be tough for you' I said. I knew that had to be true. I could feel some sympathy for him.

'You don't know the half of it' he said.

I walked around the car, looking at the upholstery and finish. It was beautiful. I gave him the time to get his thoughts together and continue. 'What happened?' I asked. 'At his flat?'

'He wasn't there.'

'Did anyone see you?'

'No idea. Look, I really don't give a shit that he's dead' he said. 'I don't care what you think. I just never wanted my son anywhere near the man. That's all. Have you ever felt like you can't do right for wrong, like you're some sort of idiot?'

I nodded and moved closer to him. 'Of course.' Probably more than he knew.

'I hated the man and the way he was always there in the background.' he said 'Like he was part of our lives.'

I snapped back into our conversation, pushing my own thoughts to one side. His alibi wouldn't stand up. I looked again at the car, admired the finish. I turned, looked him in the eye, wondering how far I could push him. 'You said it was in the past. Maybe you're the one with the problem?'

He threw the wrench at the wall, shouting at me to get out. 'If you want the truth, go speak to my wife.'

I nodded and told him I'd be doing that.

Lorraine sat at the reception desk. The office was quiet. I waited for her to finish her call before speaking. 'I've just spoken to your husband.' She looked up. She wasn't pleased to see me. I wasn't bothered. It was time to start sorting things out.

'Why are you bothering him at work?' she said to me.

'We had things to discuss' I said.

'I told you. My husband didn't kill Greg. You're wasting your time talking to him.' She walked out from behind the desk and opened the front door to the office. 'I can't believe you've got the nerve to come back here, saying these things. This is where I work. I want you to leave. And don't bother coming back.'

'I know, Lorraine.'

She looked at me. 'What do you know?'

'I've put it together. I know.'

She nodded. The decision made. She relented. 'How did you find out?' she said.

'Maths.' Priestley had told me she'd always stayed in touch with Tasker, even when they'd moved down to London. It hadn't seemed important until now, but thinking on it, it was strange. Friendships come and go. Some are only made for a specific moment, and hers with Greg Tasker seemed like a classic example. Their lives had taken very different paths, yet they'd stayed in touch. And her husband's dislike of Tasker went far beyond normal jealousy. He hated the man, and for that, he had to have good reason. I knew from his reaction in the garage that there was more to the story. 'Your husband more or less confirmed it for me.'

'Wait there a minute.' She said it was almost time for her break. She made a call and we waited in silence until another woman appeared to take her place on the reception desk. Lorraine led me out of the building. We walked to Queens Gardens. Less than a hundred years ago, it had been a working dock. Now it was one of the few places you could find some peace in the city centre. We found a bench next to one of the ponds. I angled myself away from the Mick Ronson band stage. It was hardly a fitting tribute to one of the city's most famous musicians and nor did it seem appropriate when we were talking about another one. My city was terrible when it came to commemorating its past and coming to terms with its history. I looked at Lorraine. It was like she'd had a weight lifted from her shoulders.

'Jay is Greg's' she said, turning to face me. 'But Jason is his real dad.'

I nodded my understanding. 'Of course.'

'It doesn't make any difference to me.'

'But Jason knows?'

'We don't talk about it.'

He knew. I was sure.

'I met Jason as Greg left and went down to London with the band' she said. 'He's the complete opposite to Greg. Jason is a family man who puts us first. He was the kind of person I needed after Greg. Jason was very good about the pregnancy. I think he wanted a child as much as I did, so we never had the conversation. We took it as being a nice surprise. It was quick, but it was what we wanted. End of story. We never discussed it again.'

'Did you tell him about Greg?'

'He knew I'd had a relationship with him, but he wasn't bothered by it. Not then. He never asked the question about Jay, so I never said anything.'

'He never questioned it?'

'Neither of us wanted to upset things.'

'But things changed?'

She nodded. I sat quietly and let her work out what she wanted to tell me.

'It's not fair' she eventually said. 'It's not fair on me or Jason, but it's especially not fair on Jay. It didn't seem like a problem when he was younger, but now he's a bit older it feels like I shouldn't be lying to him like this.'

'Did you speak to Greg?'

'He'd worked it out.'

'How?'

She laughed. 'Jay looks like Greg.'

I hadn't particularly noticed the resemblance. He'd probably done the maths, like I had.

'What did Greg want?' I asked.

She looked at me, as if I was stupid. 'His son.'

I looked around the Gardens. Office workers on their lunch breaks and pupils from the nearby nautical school running around. I turned back to Lorraine. 'What about Jason?'

'I haven't told him.'

'Why not?'

'It'd destroy him. I couldn't do it to him. I'd hate myself.'

'He must have had his suspicions?'

'His name's is on the birth certificate. I thought it was enough.'

'But Greg wanted to be part of Jay's life' I said.

'He wanted to leave Siobhan and start again with me and Jay.'

'He was going to tell his parents about Jay?' I said. That made sense to me now.

'I think so, but I told him he couldn't do that.'

'When did you speak to Greg about Jay?'

'Not that long ago.'

'What did you want to do?' I asked.

She held my stare. 'I wanted to believe Greg. I really wanted to believe what he said, but I'd made my decision years ago. I couldn't do it to Jason. He stood by me when I needed it the most, so now it's my turn to stand by him. It cuts both ways.' She paused. 'Do you have family?'

I thought about my brother, but pushed it to one side. I hadn't made the time to ring him since our night out, but I'd promised I would. 'You don't owe Jason your life' I said.

'Just leave it, please.'

I felt sorry for her. She was trapped in a marriage she didn't want with a man she didn't really love. It was sad she felt she couldn't make a change, that she owed him so much. I wondered if Tasker had told Kane Major about his son, that he was willing to move away with Lorraine. I wondered if that would have meant there'd be no reunion. I couldn't see Major receiving that news happily. Equally, Jason Harrison stood to lose everything. He'd treated Jay like his own, probably believed it, too, but he had to know the truth. It gave him a powerful motive in relation to Tasker's murder. Tasker would have brought Harrison's life crashing down around him.

We were finished here. Lorraine stood up, ready to leave. I told her she could call me whenever she liked.

'Please don't speak to my husband again' she said, before walking away from me.

CHAPTER SIXTEEN

The office was cold and empty. I'd spent the time as I walked down Whitefriargate thinking over what I'd learnt. It struck me Tasker's parents didn't realise they had a grandson. Sarah would know whether I should tell them about Jay or not, but she wasn't around to ask. It might be some small compensation after losing their son that he would live on through his child. Sat at my desk, I busied myself by updating my notes. It was a habit I'd picked up from Don. He called them 'Case Management Reviews', like he was still in the police force. He was right. It made sense and it helped me stay on top of things. Easily distracted, I checked the BBC website for any updates on Tasker. There was nothing new from DI Robinson and his team. I called Julia to see if she'd made any progress. She was just about to leave the press conference she was attending.

'I was going to call you' she said.

I asked why.

'Gary Bilton wants to talk to us. Now.'

I drove to the police station and waited for Julia. I wondered if I should tell her about Jay Harrison, but decided to sit on the information for now. I wanted to tell her, but it was an explosive story. Other people had a right to know first. I leaned on the bonnet of my car and watched DI Robinson push his way through the remaining reporters, heading towards the exit. I noted the media crowd had started to thin.

'Now then' I shouted to him. I waved to make sure he didn't miss me.

He changed direction, walked across to me. 'Mr Geraghty. I understand you've had a spot of bother at your office?'

I wondered how he knew. 'Nothing serious' I said.

He stepped closer to me. 'You should be careful.'

'I'm fine.'

He turned away from me. 'Well, best of luck. If you'll excuse me, some of us have proper work to be getting on with.'

I saw Julia walk out of the station, stuffing papers into her bag. 'Best of luck to you, as well' I shouted after Robinson.

'What have you been up to?' Julia asked me, as we pulled away.

I told her as we drove across the city, before changing the subject and asking her about the press conference.

'There was nothing new, really' she said, then she pointed. 'Down there.' I turned the car around and parked outside the house she was indicating.

'Are you alright?' I asked.

She looked at me and nodded. 'I'm fine.'

'Right.'

We got out of the car, knocked on Gary Bilton's front door.

'At least he's moved since I was last in Hull' Julia said, as we stood and waited.

He eventually opened the door. He looked terrible. His left eye was closed, his mouth swollen. Someone had given him a proper going over. But you could see he was in better shape than his brother. Maybe five years younger.

'Nice to see you, Julia' he said. 'It's been a long time.'

She ignored him. He let us into his house. We followed him into his front room. I unplugged his Xbox and turned the television off. The curtains were still closed, the room smelt stale.

'What do you think you're doing?'

I pointed to the big cardboard box in the corner. 'New television?' I told him to sit down. 'You wanted us to come here. You can talk to us properly.'

'Who did this to you?' Julia asked him.

'If I knew, I wouldn't be talking to you about it, would I?'

'What happened?' I said.

'Jumped as I walked home from the pub. Some bloke appeared out of nowhere and asked me what time it was. I went to have a look and he cracked me one. The next thing I knew, him and his mate had picked me up and thrown me into the boot of their car.'

'What did they look like?' I asked.

'How would I know? I didn't get a proper look. The bloke who spoke to me had a cap pulled right down over his face. They weren't local.'

'Where did they take you?' Julia asked, ignoring me.

He turned his head to look properly at her. 'I was in the boot of their car. I've no idea.'

'What about when they got you out?'

'No idea.'

'You didn't recognise the area?'

'No. It was the middle of nowhere.'

I turned to Julia. 'We're wasting our time.'

'What did they do to you?' Julia asked, turning back to Bilton.

'What do you think happened?' He held his left hand out for us to look at. 'They didn't take me out for a nice meal.'

I looked away. I didn't want to see.

'They used me as an ashtray' he said. 'Is that enough detail for you?'

'Have you been to the hospital?' Julia asked.

He shook his head. 'Don't be stupid.'

'You could have some internal damage.' She looked at me for confirmation. 'We'll take you.'

I shook my head. I couldn't believe what I was hearing. I wasn't sure if Julia saw me out of the corner of her eye.

'I'm not going anywhere' he said.

'What did they want?' I asked.

'They wanted their money' he said to me.

'Right.' I walked over to the window. The estate was quiet, like it was asleep. I didn't like it. It made me feel uneasy. I turned back and shrugged, no idea what he was talking about. 'Give it to them. It's nothing to do with us.'

He pointed at me. 'It's everything to do with you.'

I walked towards him. 'Say that again?'

Julia told me to be quiet and turned to Bilton. 'What are you talking about?'

'They said they were owed money and they were going to collect.'

Julia looked at me. I got a sinking feeling in my stomach. I got it. Mistaken identity.

He smiled at me through his broken face. 'That's right. You were supposed to lead them to my brother. But they got me instead.'

I told Julia to call Major as I drove. She did as I asked and told him we'd made a breakthrough. Nothing more than that. He told her where he was eating. It was the same fish restaurant as last time. I told Julia I'd got the address and headed straight there. We found him eating by himself in the corner. I sat down opposite him. 'You're lucky I don't knock you out in here' I said to him. 'So everyone sees.'

'I don't follow you, PI' he said. I was willing to credit him for being a good actor. He was unmoved.

'Trevor Bilton's brother has been given a good kicking.'

I could see him doing the calculations. He eventually shrugged. 'I'll get you both a drink.'

'I don't want a drink off you' I said. 'I assume you don't want to do this in public?' I stood up. 'Outside.'

Major told the waiter he'd be back shortly. We walked out and got into my car. Major was in the back, me and Julia in the front. I eyeballed him using the rear-view mirror and told him about Gary Bilton's injuries, describing them in detail, right down to the cigarette burns. 'Somebody wanted to hurt him badly' I said. 'But they got the wrong brother.'

'I'm not with you' he said.

I smiled at him. 'You're with friends now. You don't have to lie.'

'I've no need to lie to you, PI.'

'Try again' I said. I held his stare. 'I told you about Trevor Bilton, remember?'

He nodded. 'So what?'

I took my eyes off him and turned to Julia. 'His brother said the beating was my fault, didn't he?'

She agreed with me.

I searched for Major's eyes again in the mirror. 'He also told us I led them to his door.' I turned around. 'Remember I told you I was being followed? I mentioned it to the police and I asked Whittle. Neither of them knew anything about it and I believed them. Why would they need to follow me?' I pointed at him. 'You know exactly what I'm talking about. You said Greg was involved with some bad people and you wanted them off your back. You told them Trevor Bilton was the man they needed to speak to.' I looked at Major again. 'You know who they are.'

We sat in silence for a few moments. I never took my eyes off Major I'd locked the car doors to make sure he wouldn't leave until I was satisfied I'd heard the truth. 'Why did you do it?'

'I didn't have a choice.

'You can do better than that.'

He flashed with anger. 'Who the fuck do you think you are?' He jabbed his finger at Julia. 'You bring a journalist along with you and expect me to answer your questions? Have a word with yourself, PI.'

I shrugged it off. 'I'm the man who has the police on speed-dial. This is off the record for now, but it can soon become on the record. Do I make myself clear?'

Julia nodded. 'I can have it ready for tomorrow's paper.' She knew how to play along.

'Look, you don't know what you're messing with, alright? These are bad people, seriously bad fucking people.'

'So why are they chasing you?' I already knew the answer, but held out some small hope he'd surprise me.

'I owe them money.'

Of course he did. Drugs. Hence the disappearing act. It wasn't just business taking him away from Hull. 'Couldn't you borrow some?'

'Who from?'

'You tell me.'

'There's no one' he said. 'Don't you think that option has crossed my mind?'

I let it go. 'Who are these people?'

'The less you know, the better.

'Too late' I said.

'These aren't the kind of idiots you have running around in this shithole. I was using their stuff and they said it wasn't a problem sticking it on the tab. You know how it is, the money started to mount up and I couldn't pay them. I thought they were my mates, but as you find out in this business, no cunt's your mate.'

'What are they doing up here?' I asked.

'My secretary told them where I was.'

I got it. Hide in the most visible and obvious of places. Hull would be the last place people would think to look for him at the moment.

He smiled at me. 'What can you do? I didn't have a better plan. I just need to set things up with the band and then I'll get them their money.'

'So you decided to put Trevor Bilton in the frame, tell them he stole your money?' I did the calculation. He'd told them I was tracking the guy who'd ripped him off. 'They bought that?'

'They were prepared to give me the benefit of the doubt. I can still open doors for people. I'm still a face in London. I know a lot of people who want to buy what they're selling.'

'You're a face?'

'Fuck off, PI. You wouldn't understand. I had to tell them I'd been ripped off.' Major leaned forward, putting his head between mine and Julia's. 'Come on. You're not really saying you give a shit about Bilton and his brother? Fair enough, it's a bit unfortunate, but Trevor Bilton is a fucking scumbag. Greg told me all about him.'

'It's not the point' I said.

Major slumped backwards. 'They're going to come back for me.'

I couldn't resist smiling. 'Good.'

Julia took a call on her mobile. She turned to me. 'We've got to go.'

I unlocked the doors and told him not to choke on his meal.

I fed the parking meter and looked up at the imposing concrete monstrosity which stood in front of me. Hull Royal

Infirmary was a place that had brought me only misery in my life. I stuck the ticket on my windscreen and caught Julia up. She was looking at the list of wards on the wall next to the lifts. The area was congested, so we took the stairs. Heading straight onto the ward, I saw who I was looking for. Carly Priestley looked up at me.

'How are you doing?' I said.

'What are you doing here?' She looked at Julia. 'Who's this?'

'She's with me.' I explained who she was. 'Her colleague rang us after he took the call. You can't keep a secret in this city.'

Carly said nothing. I dug out some change from my pocket and asked Julia to get the coffees. I waited for her to leave. 'I just want the truth, like you do.'

'Try telling it to him' she said, pointing to her husband, lying in the bed asleep, hands bandaged up.

Carly passed me the note Priestley had left in his recording studio. I read it and passed it back to her. I looked at him and wondered if it was a serious attempt to kill himself or a cry for help.

'When did you find him?' I asked. It can't have been long after I'd seen him. Another thing on my conscience.

'When I came home from work. The ambulance people told me it wasn't as bad as it looked. Apparently, if you slash your wrists in a certain direction, it's not so dangerous.'

I nodded. It still sounded like a gamble. 'He said he couldn't take it anymore?'

'The press and the police have been all over him and it's getting worse and worse. He couldn't take their continuous questioning, repeating themselves over and over. It wasn't fair on him.'

'It's a high profile case.' I walked over to the corner of the room and picked up a chair. I put it down next to her at Priestley's bedside. 'You can't control it, I'm afraid.' Priestley was a suspect for Tasker's murder. I assumed she didn't know her husband's true feelings, or anything about Lorraine Harrison. I certainly wasn't going to enlighten her. This was hardly the time or the place for it.

'I can't believe they're saying such things. He didn't kill anyone' she said to me.

We sat in silence for a few moments, both looking at her husband, listening to the rhythm of the hospital machinery. I knew I was at least partly responsible. I hadn't stopped asking him questions, either.

'I should have put my foot down about the band' she said. 'I knew it was going to be more trouble than it was worth.' She shook her head. 'I shouldn't have let Kane Major anywhere near him.'

I couldn't disagree. He was the catalyst for all this. Julia returned with the coffees. I changed my mind, stood up and told her we were leaving before passing Carly my mobile number. 'Stay in touch' I said.

I told Julia we shouldn't be there. We were intruding. Her hotel was less than ten minutes from the hospital, an easy drive late at night with little traffic on the roads. I pulled up at the entrance.

'Thanks, Joe' she said.

'Not a problem.'

She started to get out of the car. 'Do you think it was a cry for help?'

'I hope so' I said. I was weighing up how much slack to cut Priestley. He was still a legitimate suspect for Tasker's murder. It could easily be an act of guilt. 'Tell me you're not going to write the story?' I said to her. 'At least let him get home first. Let him have a bit of dignity.'

She turned away from me. 'I don't have a choice, Joe.'

I needed a drink. I decided to leave my car at Queens for the night. It'd been a long day and things were weighing heavily on me. I tried to rationalise it by remembering Major had manipulated me for his own purposes. He'd been the one who baited the trap. No wonder the people following me hadn't made a move. They thought I'd eventually lead them to their money. They'd professionally worked Gary Bilton over, so I knew I was messing with serious people. It was obvious they wouldn't stop until they got what they wanted. I thought about the way Major had used his influence to keep them at bay. It made me sick.

I finished my second pint and decided to call it a night. I couldn't shake the image of Priestley's bandaged wrists, either. I'd played my part in pushing him to it. Things were getting out of control. I needed to keep a grip on things and drinking wouldn't help. I walked back to my flat, head down, hands in my pockets. As I was about to turn down the path that led to the front-door, I saw a figure hunched down, close to the ground floor window. I altered my path and went straight past. Pure instinct. The extra seconds I'd bought myself might save me from a good beating.

I heard my name being called. A female voice. I stopped and walked back. 'Julia?' I said, looking down the path.

She stood up. 'Can I come in, Joe?'

I let her in and told her to sit on the sofa. I put the fire on and made drinks. When I returned, she was quiet and calm.

'Why didn't you ring me?' I said. She told me she'd sat on my doorstep for over an hour.

'I thought you were mad at me.'

'Why would I be?'

'The story I was writing.'

I'd considered that, too, whilst sat in Queens. 'If it wasn't you, it'd be someone else' I said.

'I still feel bad about it' she said.

I passed her a hot drink. 'Warm yourself up on that.'

'Thanks.'

We sat in silence for a few minutes. I put the stereo on. Greg Tasker's demo CD was still in the machine. The songs really were excellent. I was disappointed he wouldn't be making the comeback he deserved with it. It might all have been so different. It was the chance of a fresh start for everyone which had turned into a nightmare. Julia was still quiet. I turned around to face her. 'What's up?'

'I was just thinking' she said.

I turned back and put my mug down. We both knew what needed talking about.

'I hate the man. I really do' she said to me. 'But he didn't deserve to be beaten like that. We've got to help him, Joe.'

'Gary?'

She nodded. 'I never thought I'd say it, but we've got to.'

I knew she was right. I didn't like it. Things were likely to get worse before they got any better.

'Hold me, Joe' she said.

CHAPTER SEVENTEEN

Julia hadn't stayed overnight in my flat. She'd called a taxi and left once we'd finished listening to Tasker's CD. I woke early and headed to the office, hoping the walk and fresh air would help me think more clearly. I sat at my desk and tried Sarah's mobile. Still no answer. I clicked on the Internet and went to the local news pages. Nothing new, just the usual sound bites from DI Robinson and his team. I was interrupted by someone walking up the stairs to the office. 'Help you?' I said to the man who'd walked in. He said nothing. He was a man mountain. Muscle, shaved head and dark clothes. This wasn't a social visit. I looked around my desk for a suitable weapon.

He smiled, like he'd read my mind. Pointed at me. 'You come' he said.

Eastern European accent. He walked over to my desk. I stood up, ready to face him. I was giving away both height and weight. I recognised him as one of the men who had been following me. I'd seen him in the passenger seat of the car. The people who'd beaten Gary Bilton in error.

'You come' he repeated.

I shook my head.

'You come with me.'

'No.'

He stepped forward and punched me. Hard. I fell backwards into my chair. I quickly tried to sit up to cut down on my embarrassment. I could taste blood in my mouth. He was quickly around my desk, taking hold of me.

'I said, you come.'

He bundled me out of the office. Outside a car was waiting. The back door was being held open by another man mountain. He nodded to his colleague and I was pushed into the back and we sped off. Nobody said anything to me and I stayed quiet. I wasn't giving them anything. The car headed to Hessle Foreshore and pulled up in the car park underneath the Humber Bridge. At least it was a public place.

'Take a walk with me, Mr Geraghty' the man in the front passenger seat said. I hadn't been able to get a proper look at him. He'd not turned to face me during the journey. The door was opened. I was told to get out. It was three against one. I did as I was told.

The man was already on his way towards the path which took you directly under the bridge and ultimately back towards the city centre. I hurried my pace, caught him up. I put him around the same age as me, early to mid-forties. His eyes told me he wasn't a stranger to violence.

'Who are you?' I asked.

'Doesn't matter' he said, pointing at the bridge. 'Look at that' he said to me. 'Very impressive. I bet you don't even notice it, do you? How long is it?'

'Not sure' I said. 'Couple of miles, maybe.' I wasn't sure where the civic pride had come from, given the circumstances. He was older than the Eastern Europeans. Better dressed, too. London accent.

He continued to stare at the bridge. 'Certainly impressive.' He stopped walking, turned to stare me. 'I assume we've got your attention now?'

The break-in at the office. 'You could have just called me' I said. 'I'm in the book.'

'I find actions speak louder than words. You talk to people, they make all the right noises, like they're listening, but they're not really. It's much better to do these things face to face.'

'This is between you and Kane Major. It's nothing to do with me.'

The man laughed. 'You're a Private Investigator who stuck his nose into our business. That was your choice, so you're involved now.'

'What do you want?' I said.

He turned to face me, relaxing back onto the railings. 'I want my money.'

'Can't help you.'

'That's not the attitude I was hoping for.'

'It's what you're getting.'

'Major owes a lot of money' he said. 'I'm here to politely request payment of his debt, but so far, no luck, and that's not acceptable. We'll be staying around until we get it, though I must say he's testing my patience.'

'I wish I could help you.'

He took a step forward and smiled. 'You've got no choice in the matter.'

I didn't like the way this was going. 'I don't think I'm able to.'

'We're owed.'

'You should speak to Major.'

'He pointed us towards Trevor Bilton, and as a sign of goodwill, we thought we'd have a chat with him, see if we could it all out amicably. But he denies all knowledge of having our money, despite our efforts to prompt his memory for him.'

I didn't tell he he'd got the wrong brother. Gary Bilton had kept his mouth shut throughout the beating.

'I don't like the situation very much' he continued. 'Major owes the money, but we don't really want to have to touch him. He's a man with contacts.' He shrugged. 'It's the way of the world. We've tried to cut him some slack, so we'll accept payment from either Bilton or Major. It doesn't matter which. It's not my argument to resolve.'

'Nor is it mine' I said.

'Wise up. You don't have a choice. I can understand you must feel disappointed to have been used in such a manner, but at least we're grateful for your hard work, even if no one else is.'

I looked out at the muddy water, watched a boat slowly head down the estuary towards the North Sea. I said nothing.

'You're going to help us get our money back. We're friends here, Mr Geraghty, but that can change.' He turned to face me. 'How's that assistant of yours? And her pretty daughter, Lauren?'

It took me a moment to register the information. I felt sick. I stepped towards him, my fist bunched and ready. He met me halfway. 'Think very carefully about this' he said. 'You don't want to make an enemy of me. You best be a fast worker because I'm beginning to run out of patience with people in this fucking dump. You try to be reasonable, but people take advantage.' He jabbed a finger at me. 'Time is running out.' He turned away from me and started to walk back to his car. 'I suggest you make an immediate start in finding my money.'

I was looking at a five mile walk back to the city centre, so I was fortunate to quickly flag down a passing taxi, especially given the state of my face. The door to the office was unlocked. I hadn't been given the chance to close up before my enforced departure. I walked in and took a quick look around. I was satisfied nothing was missing. I washed my face in the toilet sink before grabbing my coat and my mobile. I locked the office up and headed towards Queens Gardens Police Station. I wanted some answers.

The desk sergeant told me DI Robinson was unavailable. I made him call Robinson and tell him that I'd spoken to the man from London. The desk sergeant nodded to the seating area, told me to wait. I was looking at the same, tired posters when Robinson eventually appeared. He had his coat on. 'Let's take a walk, Mr Geraghty' he said.

I followed him out of the station and down George Street.

'I remember when there used to be honest pubs down here, don't you?' he said to me. 'Now it's all late-opening bars and pole dancing clubs. I often wonder why.'

'Progress' I said.

He cut down a side street and led us to a small cafe. He greeted the owner like an old friend before turning back to me. 'I'll just have a cup of tea, Mr Geraghty. It's too early to eat.' He told the man I was paying.

I ordered myself a coffee and joined him at a corner table. We were the only customers in the place. Robinson studied my face. It was sore to the touch and starting to swell.

'Have you heard from Don?' he said.

'No.'

'You were given fair warning about these people' he said. 'I've tried my best to help you. And so did Don.'

It was going to be like that. I just wanted to know the score. I didn't want the lecture. 'Who am I dealing with?' I asked.

The drinks were brought over. Robinson sipped his tea.

'He's not the top man. He's just been sent here to collect the money they're owed. The Eastern Europeans are extra muscle.' He stirred his tea. 'But you'd already guessed that.'

'Who's the top man?' I asked.

'An Albanian. I doubt he'll be bothering you in person. They're drug dealers, which given the nature of your client, won't be a surprise to you.'

'Why are you giving them the freedom of the city? Why haven't they been arrested?'

He put his mug down and stared at me. 'It's not my decision to make, Mr Geraghty. I'm under orders not to touch them at the moment.'

'Why?'

He shrugged. 'A wider investigation. I'm not privy to the details.'

'So you're going to let them do as they please?'

Robinson smiled. 'We're keeping an eye on things' he said. 'They haven't broken any laws since they've been here, so far as I'm aware.'

Easy for him to say. I'd have to buy some Ibuprofen before the pain really kicked in.

'Unless you want to press charges?' He was smiling at me, but he knew the answer.

Robinson leaned in towards me. 'Look, I want these people out of my city just as much as I suspect you do.' He finished his drink quickly. 'Don't let me hold you up. You've probably got things you need to be getting on with.'

DI Robinson left me sat in the cafe. I had a refill before leaving. I needed to think through what my next move should be. I was under no illusions as to how dangerous the people Major owed money to were. I hadn't really taken them seriously, thinking I was worth more to them if I was in one piece, but feeling the pain in my mouth, I was revising my opinion quickly. Robinson had left me in no doubt I was involved with heavy people. To be fair, he'd gone out of his way to warn me, but I hadn't listened. He was right; I'd made my bed and now I was going to have to lie in it. I finished my coffee and settled the bill. I walked back towards the office to collect my car, stopping at the newsagent to buy some painkillers. I dry swallowed two down and headed off to see Gary Bilton. New Holland's 'Welcome to Hell' was playing on the radio as I drove. It couldn't have been more fitting.

Bilton wasn't home. I headed to the estate's Community Centre. The place was quiet. I looked around. On a table leaflets advertised the facilities. There was a well-equipped gym and a recording studio for local residents. A small library offered free Internet access. I'd thought it would be all nasty tasting beverages and cold meeting halls.

I found Gary Bilton in the office. I knocked and walked straight in. I pointed to my face. 'Snap. They've had a word with me, too.'

He wasn't impressed. 'What do you want?'

'We need to talk.' His desk was covered in paperwork. It looked like his job kept him busy.

'Julia sent you, has she?' he said.

I looked for somewhere to sit. 'She doesn't know I'm here.'

He looked at my face. 'Looks like you've just got a few scratches compared to me.'

I couldn't claim I'd taken a similar beating. I changed the subject. 'What's it like working on the estate?'

'You mean because of my brother?'

'If you like.' The phone rang, but he ignored it.

'I'm not his keeper' he said.

'Must be embarrassing.'

'He does his thing, I do mine.' He swivelled in his chair to face me properly. 'Do you think people like us have got options? My brother got himself into some bother when he was a kid and he's had to live with the consequences. Who's going to give him a job? I've long since given up worrying about it. After I lost Julia I did nothing for years until I started studying.' He laughed. 'Me studying? I got the bug for learning, fuck knows where from, but I realised I could make a difference around here, do something good.'

'Even though your brother causes most of the misery?'

'If it wasn't him, it'd be someone else.'

'But you're happy to turn a blind eye if it suits?'

'You don't know fuck all about this place. There are too many good kids on the estate to just give up. Have you seen the facilities we've got here? There was nothing like this when I was a kid, that's for sure.' He stood up. 'I'll show you around.'

He locked the office door behind us. I followed him into the main hall area. A man and a woman were putting chairs out. 'There's a meeting on tonight' he said.

I stopped walking, forcing him to do the same. 'You don't want to let your brother win, is that it?'

'Something like that.'

I wasn't sure how to feel about the Bilton brothers. I put the thought to one side. 'Tell me about the blokes who jumped you.'

We left the hall and went into the kitchen area. 'Why do you want to know?'

'It's important. You said they weren't local. Where do you think they're from?'

'They were Poles or something. And there was a southern sounding guy who was in charge.'

It sounded about right. I doubted his geography was that good, but he was probably close enough.

'So why did they attack you?' he asked me. 'You gave them what they wanted. You led them here.'

'They want their money.'

'I've spoken to Trevor again. He hasn't got it.' He shrugged. 'He's my brother. He wouldn't lie to me. And I certainly haven't got their money. I'm always skint. Like I said, I'll be out of work once the funding for this place runs out.'

I caught his eye, made sure I had his attention. 'I need to know what you know' I said. 'If I have to work with you and your brother to sort this mess out, I'll do that.' I paused. 'And if I can sort this mess out, you might live to tell the tale.'

'We haven't done anything. They'll have to get the message.'

'They won't' I said. 'They're going to come back for you and your brother. I can guarantee it.' I thought about what Julia had said. I owed the brothers, however distasteful I found it. 'The police have tried to warn me off, but it's gone too far for that. These people aren't playing at being gangsters, these are the real deal.' I let him digest what I'd said. It was sinking in. He knew he and his brother were in serious trouble.

'What do you want from me?' he said.

I made sure he was looking at me. 'I need your help.' I told him to ring his brother.

We went back to his office and waited. I watched him check his emails and file some paperwork. It didn't take long for Trevor Bilton to arrive.

He nodded to his brother. Turned to speak to me. 'I thought we'd said our piece to each other.'

I smiled at him. 'It's not that simple, is it?' I glanced at Gary Bilton. 'Things have changed.'

'Nothing we can't handle ourselves.'

'You'll be next' I said to him.

Trevor quietened down, taking on board what I was saying. Both me and his brother were walking advertisements for what was in store for him. I asked him if he'd ever met Kane Major.

He found a chair and sat down with is. 'The cunt wouldn't be walking if I had done' he said.

'What about Greg Tasker?' I said.

'What's he got to do with this?'

'I need to know.'

'Through his girlfriend' he said eventually. He looked to his brother and then back to me. 'I thought you wanted to know about Major? Why are you asking me about fucking Tasker?'

'I don't care if you were dealing, or it was someone else doing it for you. I'm not interested in any of that stuff' I said. 'If Gary can live with it, so can I. It's none of my business, alright? Just tell me about Tasker.'

I watched him weigh things up. He eventually spoke. 'He sometimes came along with his bird, but more recently he'd started coming by himself.'

Siobhan hadn't told me the truth. 'Who was he buying for?' I asked.

'Didn't ask.'

'Was he using his own money?'

'How would I know?'

'Was it a regular thing?'

He smiled. 'I don't think he could take the pressure of the band starting up again. Needed a bit of medicinal help.'

I wanted to wipe the smirk off his face, but carried on. 'Did he ever mention Major?'

'No.'

'Right.' I turned the possibilities over in my mind for a moment.

'You're thinking these people killed Tasker?' Gary Bilton said to me.

'It's a thought' I said. I wasn't convinced, but it was possible. An argument. A punch. It could happen. I'd definitely struck a nerve. Trevor Bilton was experiencing being on the wrong end of things for a change. All the misery he'd brought people like Betty Page was being paid back with interest. I wasn't upset by that. It doesn't matter how big you think you are, there's always someone bigger.

'What can you do to help to us?' Gary Bilton said.

I stood up, wanting to get back to the office and think. 'I'll do what I can' I said.

I'd agreed to meet Julia for a quick lunch. I was pleased we were getting back to being on something approaching an even keel. The Priestley story had broken, so time was limited for both of us. She'd offered to buy the sandwiches and I left the office to meet her a short walk away in the grounds of the Museum Quarter on High Street. The jewel in the crown was the restored house of William Wilberforce, which stood as a monument to the man's role in abolishing slavery. I made my way through the parties of school children and headed towards where Julia was sitting on a bench, waiting for me.

'What happened to your face?' she said before I'd even managed to sit down next to her. I tried to angle myself away from her so she wouldn't see the worst of it.

'Someone wanted a word.'

'Who?'

I told her about being followed. I told her how it was linked to the break-in at the office.

She passed me my sandwich. 'Why didn't you tell me, Joe?'

I bit into my sandwich and shrugged. 'I didn't want to worry you' I said. What I didn't say was that I didn't trust her with the information. We sat and ate in silence. I watched the school party being shepherded into the Transport Museum by their teacher. We stood up and walked out of the grounds. 'I spoke to the Bilton brothers earlier' I said.

'What did they say?'

'Let's say we've come to an understanding.'

She seemed to accept it, asked me if I'd spoken to Major.

'He's keeping a low profile' I said. His mobile was switched off, but he'd keep for now. 'I had a word with DI Robinson as well' I said.

'What did he say?'

I repeated what he'd told me, explaining that he was probably embarrassed by the fact he wasn't calling the shots here. It sounded like the London mob were being tracked by more powerful people. Robinson would have to swallow it down and do as he was told. 'What have you got planned for the afternoon?' I asked her.

'Work.'

I didn't ask anything more. I didn't want to know. Rightly or wrongly, Priestley would be in the headlines. Julia would have to work out for herself how far she was willing to go with things. As I watched her walk away, I suspected I knew the answer.

You're depressed. Kane wants you back in the band, but it's over for you. You know it, he knows it and Priestley knows it. Your girlfriend leaves you. You're a mess. Your friends aren't really your friends. You can see that now. You have nothing and no one. You stay in your flat in London because it's the easiest option. This way you don't have to see people. This way you don't have to answer their questions. Priestley makes no attempt to contact you. Kane tells you Priestley has bought an old farm property outside of Hull. You hate the fact he's happy. You know what it is – self pity. You try to convince yourself that you're a free man again, that your life is still in front of you, not behind you. You can't cope. You overdose. It's the stupidest thing you've ever done. You call your ex-girlfriend, tell her what you've done. She calls Kane. You're taken to hospital. You're taken to rehab. You start to sort your life out.

CHAPTER EIGHTEEN

I still had unfinished business with Siobhan. Walking up to the boutique, I wasn't surprised to see a closing down sign in the window. She didn't look pleased to see me. The place was quiet. I closed the door behind me, flicked the sign over and told her we needed to talk. I didn't want us disturbed.

'Moving on?' I asked her.

'It's the right time' she said. She looked at my face. 'What happened to you?'

I told her I'd had a disagreement with someone. Nothing more than that. I looked around. Already a lot of the stock had been sold. 'I need to speak to you about Trevor Bilton again.'

'I told you everything I know.'

I found a chair next to the till and passed it to her. She sat down. 'Have you been back to see him?'

She said she hadn't. 'I told you. I just needed something to get through this. I've stopped now.'

'Pleased to hear it.' I moved us on. 'What about Greg's involvement with Bilton?'

'He didn't have any.'

'Don't lie to me, Siobhan' I said. 'I know he was in far deeper than you told me.'

She nodded, like she'd made her mind up. 'I dragged him into it. It's my fault. No one else's.'

I found another chair and sat down next to her. 'Tell me about it.'

'I knew how hard it had been for Greg to get clean, but it was me. I was buying the stuff. I hate myself for it, I really do. We'd even moved away from London so he was out of temptation's way and I let him down. Moving back here was supposed to be a fresh start. It was a chance for us both to get things back on a positive footing. It was probably harder for him than me, truth be told, because he could blend into the background a bit more in London. It wasn't so easy for him here. Too many people knew him' she continued. 'He deserved much better than me. I let him down.'

'He was big enough to make his own decisions' I said. 'You can't take all the blame.'

'But he didn't need me to make it worse for him.'

'He started to visit Bilton with you?'

'After a while. I got Bilton's name through a friend who comes in here. At first, Greg just let me get on with it. It was stupid.'

'He wasn't impressed?'

She laughed. 'He was always more interested in Lorraine.'

'Did he want to start using again?'

'He told me I didn't need to worry about him. He could handle it.'

'Why did he want the money from your till?' I asked.

'I didn't ask. He wouldn't tell me. He never told me what he was up to.'

She turned away from me. We both knew. 'Kane was involved?' I said.

'I don't know.'

'Didn't you ask?'

'He wouldn't talk to me.'

'Why didn't you say something?' I asked. 'People would have wanted to help you.'

She snorted. 'Who would? His parents?'

I realised I didn't have the answer.

'I didn't say anything because I was trying to protect him' she said. 'I know how much he hated the way the band had finished. How it'd all fallen apart. He carried the guilt over it. He knew he'd behaved badly, especially towards Priestley. The least I could do for him was help keep his reputation intact. He didn't deserve any of this hanging over him.'

I needed to speak to Tasker's parents. I hadn't spoken to them for a while and I didn't want them to think I wasn't keeping them up to date. I called Kath Tasker. She told me she was in Pearson Park, trying to get some peace and quiet. It was picturesque, Victorian, and despite it being on the doorstep of my flat, I rarely made the effort to visit. I found Kath sat on a bench next to the pond. I sat down next to her. There was a family feeding the ducks. A small group of men kicked a football about between them. Otherwise she was right, at this time of day, the park was quiet.

'Keith's at work' she said to me.

I must have looked surprised. She told me she wasn't complaining. 'It'll do him good to get back to some sort of normal routine.'

I didn't know if she was right or not. Everybody has different ways of dealing with grief.

'I'm sorry I wasn't available when you last called' she said.

I waved her apologies away. 'I spoke to Keith. It's not a problem.'

'What can I do for you?' she asked.

'I wanted to let you know I'm still working on things.'

She nodded. 'That's good to hear.'

I smiled. 'I'm getting there, I hope.'

She threw some bread crusts at the ducks. 'I'm well aware Greg was no angel. I know we're old and out of touch, but we know what people in his position get up to. I know he was no different. It was difficult for us, but we loved him.' She stopped and looked at me. 'You've heard all of this before.'

I told her to continue. It was interesting to get her perspective on things.

'To be honest, Greg was a selfish man' she said. 'I don't know whether it was the band or not, but he'd never call and he very rarely made the effort to see us. Everything was on his terms. To me, it doesn't matter whether you're in a famous rock band or you work in an office. There's always a telephone, and it's not a huge effort, is it?

'Is that why you don't have photographs up of him and the band?'

'I suppose it is. It's not how I want to remember him. Keith was always more forgiving, but I wish Greg had just led a normal life. There's no shame in that, is there?'

I was surprised by her attitude. I'd always assumed if I had children, I wouldn't mind what they did with their lives, so long as they were happy. But then again, I wasn't sure how happy Greg had been. I also had to think about Jay. Should I tell her she had a grandson? It wasn't something to be thinking about at this moment in time.

'Are the media still bothering you?' I asked her.

'I've unplugged the telephone and I ignore them at the door. They'll get the message eventually.'

'I can imagine it's difficult.'

'I'd like to speak to the journalist you know, please. I've spoken to Keith about it. It's what I want to do.'

I watched a child throw some bread into the pond. I told her I'd sort it.

'So how are thing progressing?' she asked me.

'I've got a few leads to follow up.' I didn't want to tell her the police had warned me off. I also didn't want to be pointing the finger at anyone yet. 'The police are working hard' I said. 'They're doing a thorough job.'

She looked like she wanted to say something. But she didn't. I promised her I was doing my best.

'We both appreciate it' she said. She offered me money again, but I told her it was covered.

'I don't think Greg knew what he wanted from life. It pains me to say it to you, it really does. He was my son, but in so many ways, he was a stranger to me.'

'He had Siobhan' I said, hoping to offer her some comfort.

'To be frank with you, I'm not convinced she wasn't part of the problem. We never thought it'd last, but they were obviously fond enough of each other to stay together. I suppose we should be grateful she brought our son some happiness.'

'Do you like her?' I asked.

She shook her head. 'She was wrong for Greg. I never understood it, really. You'd think they'd want different things from life, wouldn't you? It's only natural, given the age gap, but Keith is much more laid back than me and always said we should let people get on with living their lives. I never liked the woman. I never trusted her.'

Julia called my mobile and asked me to collect her from the hotel. I left Kath Tasker alone to enjoy the peace and quiet in the park.

'Where's the fire?' I said to Julia, starting to walk back to my car.

She paused before telling me the fire was at Trevor Bilton's flat. I hadn't expected that. By the time we'd driven east across the city and parked at the top of his street, the Fire Service looked to be on top of things. We walked as close to the flat as we could. A make-shift cordon had been set up, stopping us getting any closer. I saw DS Coleman directing the police's activity. No sign of DI Robinson. I tried to get Coleman's attention. No luck. Damage limitation was underway. It'd drawn a crowd. A mix of rubber-neckers and people no doubt delighted to see Bilton on the receiving end for a change. I spotted Betty Page, the Neighbourhood Watch leader, and pushed through the crowd towards her. 'What happened?' I asked her.

She looked at me like I was stupid. 'Fire.'

I could see Julia out of the corner of my eye, laughing.

'Anybody in there?' I asked her.

'No.' She turned to face me. 'More's the pity.'

'Right.' Trevor Bilton's flat was the downstairs of a shared house. 'What about the people above him?'

'Empty.'

It made sense. Who'd want to live above him? I looked at the damage. If there had been people upstairs, I doubt they would have made it out safely.

'Any idea how the fire started?' I asked.

She looked at me. 'How would I know? But I'd shake the hand of the man who did it.'

I thanked her and turned to Julia. I was done. It wasn't difficult to work out. I already knew who'd started the fire. The watching crowd had grown during the ten minutes we'd been there. We pushed our way back out and headed to the car.

'London calling' I said, once we were in and the door was closed.

'Could be anyone' Julia said.

She was right. But we both knew who was responsible. I started the car up and pulled away.

'Where next?' she asked me.

'We best find him' I said. 'See what he has to say about it.'

I drove us to the pub. It wasn't busy. Most of the regulars were probably watching the fire. The hardcore drinkers standing at the bar ignored me. I could sense an edge in the place. I wasn't going to be giving Bilton breaking news.

'What can I get you, love?'

I ignored the barmaid and led Julia towards the stairs. Bilton's men stepped out of the shadows and blocked our way. I went for jovial and told them how pleasant it was to see them again. The biggest of the three men stepped forward. 'Geraghty, is it?'

I nodded. 'I need to speak to your man.'

He laughed and took another step forward. 'No chance.' He looked over my shoulder at Julia. 'He said if she came along I definitely wasn't to allow you to go up there.'

'Tell him I can help' I said.

All three of them had now moved forward and stood around us in a tight semi-circle. The leader spoke again. 'You can help him? All you've done, cunt, is make things worse. I don't know about you, but we look after our own in this part of the city. We don't grass and we don't bring trouble to our own door, so if I was you, I'd fuck off right now.' He dismissed me. 'And don't think about coming back.'

It was a stand-off. There was only one winner. I took the hint and led Julia out of the pub. No one made eye contact with us as we left. The barmaid didn't repeat her offer of a drink. I drove us back to the city centre. It hadn't been a good day so far. The London gang had stepped things up and they were holding me responsible for finding their money. I knew I was in their firing line.

I pushed the thought to one side and told Julia I'd spoken to Siobhan again. 'She's leaving Hull' I said.

Julia shrugged. 'Nothing here for her now, I suppose.'

I repeated what Siobhan had told me, how her relationship with Tasker was falling to pieces, how they'd argued following the New Holland reunion, how she didn't know how to make him happy.

'Because of Lorraine?'

'I'm sure she was a significant factor.' I explained about Tasker's link to Trevor Bilton. 'It wasn't just her buying from him.'

'So why did he only tell us about Siobhan? Why didn't he mention Tasker?'

It was a reasonable question. 'I assume because he was trying to sell a story. Maybe he was holding it back as his ace, to drive his price up. Maybe he didn't want the attention it'd bring.'

'I suppose.'

She didn't seem convinced. I let her catch up with my train of thought.

'When did Greg start buying again?' she asked.

'Around the time the reunion started.'

She was getting there. 'So you think he was also buying for Kane Major?'

I nodded. If he was clean, it made sense. Major had said he knew about Bilton through Tasker. We lapsed into silence again, both thinking events through for ourselves.

'Have you heard from Sarah?' she asked me.

Events had overtaken me. She would be enjoying the sun in Spain. A million miles away from my problems in cold, grey Hull. I shook my head. 'Not a word' I said.

Julia asked me to drop her at the hotel so she could work. I was left to my own devices. I wasn't happy at not being able to talk to Trevor Bilton. The fire wasn't an accident, that much was obvious. If he wouldn't talk to me, Major would have to. He had plenty of questions to answer. I walked into his office block as the workers were leaving, done for the day. His office door was closed. I walked straight in. Marcus Whittle was heading for the door, pulling a suitcase along behind him. I blocked his exit. 'Going somewhere?' I said.

He looked embarrassed.

I pushed him backwards, closed the door. 'Sit down' I said. I wasn't expecting this, but I quickly weighed the situation up.

He reluctantly let go of his luggage and walked backwards to the sofa in the far corner. 'I've got a train to catch' he said.

'I don't give a fuck. Where's Major?'

'I've no idea.'

'No?'

He shook his head. 'None at all.'

I took my mobile out of my pocket, held it out towards him. 'Want to give him a call?'

Whittle said nothing.

I put it back in my pocket. 'Surely it's not that bad here?' I said.

'You can't get a decent meal, that's for sure.'

I smiled at his joke and made a show of looking at my watch. 'Not long until the last train leaves.'

'Look, I'm not paid to do this kind of thing, alright?'

'What kind of thing?'

'Deal with animals. What Kane does is his own business, but I can't afford to be involved. I've got a family to think of.'

The thought of missing the train was opening him up. He knew he wasn't going anywhere until I let him. Of course he didn't want to be involved. I didn't want to be involved like this, but I had no choice, either. 'Have you been threatened?' I said.

He nodded. 'They wanted to know everything.'

'What did you tell them?'

'The truth. I don't know anything about their money.'

'What did you tell them?' I repeated. At least he hadn't been physically attacked.

'I don't know anything about Kane's personal life. I don't know who these people are, alright?'

I told him to calm down. 'What's the situation with Priestley?' I asked.

'What about him?'

Fuck's sake. 'I thought you might give something approaching a shit, seeing as he's in the band.'

Whittle shrugged. 'There isn't going to be a reunion now, is there?'

'You haven't tried to speak to him?'

'I haven't been told to.'

'Has Major spoken to him?'

'I've no idea.'

I couldn't believe it. Priestley was lying in a hospital bed and he genuinely didn't care. I stood up and walked across to the door. 'Who killed Greg?' I said.

Whittle looked surprised. 'How would I know?'

'Take a guess.'

'I really have no idea.'

I took a last look at Whittle before leaving. 'Have a safe trip' I said. It was Major I wanted to talk to.

Whittle had every reason to be worried. Drugs and money made people act unpredictably. I headed to the Black Boy on High Street. The pub had been there nearly three hundred years, all dark wood and quiet corners. It was one of my favourites in the Old Town. I bet it had some stories to tell. I ordered a pint of lager and sat in the corner, well away from the other drinkers. I wasn't sure how seriously I should be taking the gang's threats. Sarah was out of harm's way, so they couldn't get at her, or at Lauren. My mobile rang. It was the office phone on divert. DI Robinson wanted to speak to me immediately. I told him where I was. Take it or leave it. I wasn't in the mood. Twenty minutes later he walked into the pub. He nodded to me, offered to buy me a drink. Surprised, I took a pint off him.

'I assume it's not been a pleasant day, Mr Geraghty' he said.

'Not really.'

'I don't suppose it would have been, under the circumstances.'

'No.'

He stared at my face. 'It'll be a black eye this time tomorrow. It'll hurt less.' He sat down. He took his coat off, folded it neatly before speaking again. 'What do you know?' he asked me.

I wasn't sure how much I knew. Or what I wanted to tell him. 'Not a lot' I said.

He smiled and picked up his glass. 'I thought as much.'

I wasn't sure if he was being serious or taking the piss. His face was unreadable. He was good. I had to give him that.

'What's the score with the fire?' I asked.

He took a drink before speaking. 'The fire. Could be something, could be nothing.'

'But we both know it's not nothing.'

Robinson put his glass down. 'Correct.'

'I saw Coleman there.'

'Did you speak to him?'

'I didn't want to disturb him.'

'Pleased to hear it.'

'Major's solicitor is leaving town' I said. 'He'll be on the last train back to London now.'

'Like rats deserting a sinking ship' Robinson said. He looked at me. 'Those who can still get out, should do so.'

'Easier said than done, I'd imagine.'

'Like I said before, you should choose your clients more carefully.'

I laughed. 'Too late for that.'

'Consider it a tip for the future.'

'I will do.'

I watched Robinson straighten himself up, fiddling with his wedding ring. I knew something was coming.

He started. 'I don't like this any more than you do, Mr Geraghty.' He paused. 'I assume we can talk openly?'

I nodded. 'Of course we can.' I trusted him as far I could throw him.

'We both know who set Mr Bolton's flat on fire, and why they did it. To be frank, I'm getting pretty fucking sick of it now.'

He had my attention. 'What are you saying?'

'I'm saying you need to start seeing things more clearly, Mr Geraghty.'

'My vision is twenty-twenty.'

'Not from where I'm sitting it isn't.'

'How about you give me a clue?'

'There's only so much I can do, but let me tell you, you're barking up the wrong tree.'

I was starting to get bored of hearing him talk in riddles. 'Spit it out.'

He placed a photograph on the table. 'Max Fitzjohn.' It was the man who'd threatened me, who wanted his money back. 'Nasty piece of work' Robinson continued. 'Not the kind to take no for an answer. The people with him are dispensable muscle, but don't let it fool you. These are bad people, the kind who'd enjoy extracting information from you, if you follow me.'

I followed him. I could feel my heart pump a little faster.

'I'm not going to bullshit you, Mr Geraghty. There's only so much information and protection I can give you, and I know you've not listened to me or Don so far, but I want you to take on board what I'm telling you and act accordingly.'

'Act accordingly? What does that mean?'

'It means start looking closer to home.'

I offered to buy him another pint. I had more questions. He said no. He stood up, said he was expected home. 'Don't be a stranger.'

CHAPTER NINETEEN

I took DI Robinson at his word. I left the pub and walked across the city centre to Major's hotel. With Whittle on his way out of Hull, I wanted to make sure Major had no plans to go anywhere. I wasn't facing this alone. The lobby was empty; quiet music in the background and bright lighting. I waited for the receptionist to finish checking in her customer before walking over. I asked if Major was in his room, and when she confirmed he was, I told her he was expecting me. I knew which room he was in and made my way to the lift. There was no one in sight when I stepped back out of the lift. I made my way to his room and knocked on the door. 'Room service' I shouted.

I heard him moving around inside. 'I didn't order anything.'

I knocked again.

He undid the chain on the door and opened it. I didn't give him a chance to react, pushing the door open, sending him to the floor. I stepped into the room, closed the door behind me. 'Thought it was about time we caught up' I said.

He picked himself up, looked surprised to see me. He sat down on the bed and waved a bottle of whiskey at me. 'I'll forgive you for that, PI. Have a drink with me. You look like you need one.'

I found a chair and sat down, waved his offer away. 'Not for me.' He looked like he'd had plenty already.

'What do you want?' he said to me.

'Your friend from London had a word with me this morning. Max Fitzjohn. He wants the money.'

'I haven't got it.'

'Not good enough.'

'I told you to sort it, PI.'

'How can I sort it? You owe them money. They want it back. They're not going to think twice about hurting someone like me. They'll take me to pieces and where will that you leave you? You need to sort it out.'

'Do they know I'm here?'

I shrugged. 'They didn't say.'

He stood up and paced the room. 'I haven't got their fucking money.'

He was scared, but I didn't really care. I had my own back to look after. 'Trevor Bilton's flat was set on fire today.'

He swallowed his drink and stared at me. 'Fires happen all the time, don't they? People drop cigs, leave the fucking chip pan on, whatever?'

'Not this time.'

He sat back down on the bed. 'Shit.'

'Indeed.'

'Was he hurt?'

'No.'

'Have you spoken to him?'

'Couldn't get close to him when I tried earlier. Last time I spoke to him, he wasn't best pleased with you.'

He smirked. I couldn't believe he actually smirked.

'Has he spoken to them?' he asked me.

'He told them he's never had their money.'

'Do they believe him?'

'No idea.'

He picked the bottle back up. 'Have a drink.'

I shook my head, wanting to press on. 'What are you going to do?'

He drank straight from the bottle. I watched him put it down and shake his head as the alcohol burned down his throat. 'I'll get their money.'

'How?'

'I'm talking to people all the time. I'm trying to put deals together, but it takes time. There's a lot of interest in Greg's music and life. I'll get something sorted. I just need the time to firm things up and get the paperwork done. You've got to stall them, tell them I'm close. I'll get them their money. I'll pay interest, but I just need a bit of space to get it right.'

I wanted to shout in his face that he was wrong. These people were running out of patience and wouldn't wait much longer. But then I thought about Sarah, and the danger I might be putting her in. Fitzjohn knew all about me and my life. I needed him to do the deals for my own reasons. I nodded, hating myself. 'I'll see what I can do.' I took a drink off him. Slugged it back, but I didn't really want it. 'Whittle's gone' I said.

'Gone?'

'Left the city. Doesn't want to know you.'

I watched Major digest the news. He shrugged. 'He can't help me now.' He poured himself another. 'Fuck him.'

'Nice.'

He stood up. 'What do you expect me to say? He's fucked off and left me in the shit.'

'What about Priestley?' I said. 'How's he?'

He looked at me like I was mad. 'How would I know?'

'You haven't even rang the hospital?'

'Why would I?'

He was one heartless bastard. No wonder he had no one left. I told him I wanted the truth. He offered me another drink. I wasn't interested. 'The truth' I repeated. He laughed. I told him I was entitled. 'Was Greg back into drugs?'

Major sat down, seemingly calmer. He said nothing. I told him I was the last friend he had. If he didn't talk to me, I'd walk away. It'd be his problem to sort. It wasn't strictly the truth, but it did the trick. He relented.

'He was getting them for me. I needed something and he sorted it. I don't know anyone here anymore. He was helping me out.'

And Tasker was getting the drugs through Siobhan and Trevor Bilton. The chain of events made sense.

'He kept telling me he was skint' Major continued. 'Reckoned he couldn't keep doing it.'

It might have been the truth. I thought back to Tasker emptying the till in Siobhan's boutique. He obviously didn't have easy access to money.

'Was he using again?' I asked.

The man was a mess; a shadow of the one who was the centre of attention only a few days ago in the Princes Avenue cafe bar. He looked stressed and tired. But if I was in his position, I wouldn't be sleeping comfortably, either.

'Of course he was fucking using' Major said to me.

'He wanted you out of his life.'

He laughed. 'I made Greg. He was only a star because I spotted his potential. Look, all you need to know is that when all's said and done, we were best mates. We did everything together.'

I told him Siobhan was leaving the city.

Major put his glass down. 'So what? There's nothing for her here, is there?' He stared at me. 'Are you still fucking Julia?'

I let it go. Didn't answer him. 'What did Greg say about Siobhan?'

'I asked you a question, PI. I warned you about Julia. She's poisoning your mind. I can tell. You're not thinking straight.'

'We're talking about Greg.'

He laughed. 'Don't be a killjoy.'

'Tell me about Greg and Siobhan.'

'Why?'

'I want to know.'

'I knew he was seeing her, but I don't really know much about her. Why would I?'

Because he was supposed to be your friend, I thought. 'Don't you have regrets?' I asked him.

He stared at me and eventually nodded. 'Of course I do. I've lost everything. I've got nothing left apart from people chasing me for money.'

'Sarah's left me' I said. 'I'm on my own.' I wasn't sure why I was talking like this to him, but it felt like a release. I needed answers for Tasker's parents and to get some self respect back. It wasn't working.

He looked confused. 'How do you mean?'

'Her and Don were never keen on me taking the job. They've gone away until it's sorted.'

Major shrugged. 'You can't rely on people and that's the truth. You can have that bit of advice for free, PI.'

I was trying to please everyone and failing miserably to please anyone, including myself. What should have been a straightforward job had spiralled out of my control. And I still hadn't had seen the final tab for my actions. I stared at him. DI Robinson's warning was still at the forefront of my mind. I should be looking closer to home. Major was drifting away from me, drinking himself into oblivion. It was probably going to be the only way he would sleep tonight. I wasn't going to get anything more out of him. I left him to his own misery.

I walked home, the cold night air not bothering me much. Julia sent me a text message to ask if she could come around to my flat. I sent her a message back, telling her it was fine. I crossed Ferensway and stopped at the Tesco in St. Stephen's shopping centre to buy food. The centre was the flagship building in the area's regeneration, but as usual, it was practically empty. A handful of people were leaving the cinema. A handful of people were out late night shopping. I thought back to a man I'd met during a previous case. Christopher Murdoch had a genuine vision for the city's regeneration. This wasn't it.

I wasn't in the mood for cooking, so I paid for a couple of ready meals and a bottle of wine and continued on my way down Spring Bank. Julia was waiting for me outside my flat. We went inside and I put the food in the oven, opened the wine. I watched her flick through my CDs.

'Anything you like?' I said, passing her a glass.

She laughed. 'Joking, aren't you?'

I knew she'd interviewed Tasker's mother earlier in the day. I asked her how it'd gone.

'Poor woman. She comes over as quite calm and detached, but she's not. How could she be? She's lost her son.'

I wasn't surprised. We sat down on the settee. 'I had a drink with DI Robinson earlier' I said.

'Didn't have you down as mates.'

'Neither did I.' I repeated what he'd told me about Max Fitzjohn.

She said she'd see what she could find out about him. 'Sounds like Robinson's had enough, too.'

I figured him as a proud man, not the kind who'd take kindly to being told what to do in his own city by outsiders. But his co-operation was only going to go so far. I was still very much out on a limb. I should be looking closer to home, he'd said. 'Seems like the fire at Trevor Bilton's flat was the last straw.' I asked her if she had any news for me.

'The police are saying nothing about the fire, won't say if it was arson or just an accident.'

I nodded. A stalling tactic, but while I appreciated their hands were tied, it didn't mean I had to like it. And clearly, neither did Trevor Bilton. I didn't like the thought of him placing himself beyond my reach, either. It had been made clear I should leave him to look after his own business, but I wasn't going to be doing that.

'Has Bilton got their money?' she asked.

I'd thought about this some more as I'd walked home. 'I really don't know' I said. Trevor Bilton was a typical small-time operator. I'd be surprised if he'd go head-to-head with someone like Fitzjohn. He ruled his area by fear, and if you want to maintain that level of fear, it's easier to prey on the weak and the vulnerable. Maybe he'd bitten off more than he could chew and was now regretting it. Maybe he'd tried to make an example of Tasker and it had gone wrong. Helping him didn't sit well with me, even if Julia was genuinely concerned for his brother. I could see through him. What was more important was that Fitzjohn thought he had the money. I switched the television on and flicked through the channels. Nothing worth watching. I went back into the kitchen and plated up the food, wishing I'd made more of an effort now. It was supposed to be Spaghetti Carbonara, but all the plastic tray contained was a depressing looking mess. I wasn't hungry. I passed Julia her food. She took it from me without a word. We ate in silence. Neither of us cleared our plates.

'Robinson told me to look closer to home' I said, breaking the silence. 'Implied that I should be looking at Major.'

That got her attention. She thought about it and shrugged. 'Anything's possible.'

I told her about Jay Harrison and Greg Tasker. It didn't come much closer to home than that. It took her a moment to digest the news.

'You didn't think to tell me this?' she said.

I put my food down and walked across to the window. I looked out onto the street. I rubbed my face. I hadn't told her because I knew I couldn't trust her. Recent events had confirmed that for me. I'd been wrong from the start. I watched a young couple hurry past on the other side of the road, wondered where they were going. I turned around and faced Julia. 'I wasn't sure what to do' I said. It was the truth.

'Because I'm a journalist?'

'Partly.'

'Thanks a lot.'

'Don't take the moral high-ground, Julia. You wrote the story about Priestley's suicide attempt and you'd been in contact with Rusting without telling me. This goes beyond the story. It could ruin people's lives if they knew the truth.' I paused. 'Can I trust you? You tell me.'

She said nothing.

I continued pacing the room. I told Julia I'd gone looking for Major earlier in the evening, but bumped into Whittle at his office. 'He was on his way out of Hull' I said.

'I don't blame him.'

'I found him in the end.' I brought her up to date and told her it was off the record for now.

'Off the record? What do you think I am, Joe?'

I wasn't sure what to say. There was no right answer.

'Do you think I'd do that?' she said. 'Really?'

I had nothing to say. She stood up and got her coat.

I sat there with the bottle of wine to myself. Seeing the fire at Trevor Bilton's flat had stirred bad memories for me. I'd taken my guilt out on Julia, which was wrong of me, but my thinking was valid. First and foremost, she was a journalist and she wanted the story. If that was incompatible with our friendship, then that was the way it had to be.

I put the first New Holland CD I could find on the stereo. I'd picked up the second album. Steve Priestley had told me it had been recorded in between tours. I knew the cracks were already starting to appear in the band by then. It was clear from the lyrics that Greg Tasker wasn't happy, even when the band was at its peak. Lorraine Harrison had told me he wanted Kane Major out of his life. I wondered if he'd argued with his friend. If they had, how far had it gone? How violent had it been?

I put my glass down and thought about calling Julia to apologise. Whatever my feelings were, she'd gone out on a limb for me by keeping the full story away from her editor. I felt like shit. I needed all the friends I could get and I'd blown it with her.

I thought about my talk with DI Robinson. I had no reason to doubt him, but I didn't like the way I'd been continuously played. How far could I trust him? I poured another drink. My suspicions were turning towards Major and Fitzjohn, but Priestley and Harrison had motive, which I couldn't ignore. It was late and I was getting tired. I drained the last of the wine and sprawled out on the settee. The CD had finished, but I didn't move to replace it. I sent Julia a text message. I waited in silence for a reply. I didn't get one. I tried to figure out how I'd got myself into this whole mess, but I was too tired to think clearly. I couldn't be bothered to move. I fell asleep where I was.

CHAPTER TWENTY

I woke feeling rough. It took me a moment to realise I was still on the settee. My back ached. I slowly sat up and headed into the kitchen for a glass of water. I drank it down in one, poured another and stretched, feeling better for it. I searched for my mobile. I hadn't missed any calls. I had a new text message from Julia. It was short and to the point. I should call her. I jumped in the shower, scrubbed myself clean. I towelled myself dry and sat back down in the front room. The New Holland CD cases were spread about where I'd put them down the previous night. I looked at the band photo on the first album and wondered where it had all gone wrong. I decided Julia would wait for now. I tidied them up, called the hospital.

'I'm ringing about a patient' I said to the receptionist 'Steve Priestley.'

'Are you family?'

I hesitated. Her tone suggested I wasn't the first to be calling. No doubt the media had been bothering them. I remembered my conversation with him in his studio. I said I was his brother, Richard. I waited. I could hear her tapping away on her computer. 'It would appear your brother has discharged himself.'

'Right.' I thanked her and put the phone down. I was going to have to speak to him. I headed out, locked the door behind me and switched on my mp3 player, ready for the walk into the city centre and the office. As I walked down the path, someone shouted my name. I turned to look. Max Fitzjohn.

'Good morning to you, Mr Geraghty' he said.

'Same to you, Mr Fitzjohn' I said. He looked surprised I knew his name. He was leaning on the bonnet of his car, his men sat in the back, watching me.

'I'm impressed' he said. 'You've done your homework on me.'

I didn't like the fact we were doing this outside of my flat. 'What do you want?' I said.

He walked to the back of his car, opened the boot. 'Get in'.

I laughed. Didn't move.

He stepped towards me. 'Get in.'

'Are you mad? It's a public street.'

It was his turn to laugh. 'And who the fuck do you think gives a shit?' He told his men to get out the car. I thought back to what Gary Bilton had told me of his beating. The same thing was going to happen to me. I wasn't walking away from this. But I had no choice. I got in the boot. The journey was uncomfortable. I curled up in a ball to reduce the impact of the blows as the car cornered. I had no idea where I was being taken, nor did I have any sort of plan. The car stopped, the sun dazzling me when the boot was opened. I was hauled out and thrown onto the ground. Any thoughts of escaping were soon driven away by the first kick to my stomach. I rolled over and vomited. Fitzjohn laughed and told his men to take me inside. We were in a disused factory of some sort. Maybe agricultural. I had no idea where I was, most probably out in Holderness somewhere. There were no landmarks I recognised. Just fields. I was thrown into a chair, my hands quickly tied behind my back.

'The money' Fitzjohn said.

'I haven't got it' I said.

'I don't think you're trying very hard.'

'I'm doing my best.'

He smiled and took a step towards me. Took some leather gloves out of his pocket. 'I don't think you are.' He nodded to one of the men, who stepped forward and punched me in the stomach.

I shut my eyes, waiting for the worst of the pain to pass.

He continued. 'You know my name, so you know exactly who I am.'

We both knew the situation wasn't my fault, but that was no help to me at the moment. 'I've spoken to Major' I said. I had to take deep breaths to get my words out. 'He's putting some deals together. He'll have something sorted soon.' I repeated his words. 'There's a lot of interest in the band.'

'I dare say, Geraghty, but cash is king.' Fitzjohn walked behind me, out of my eyeline. He grabbed my hair and pulled me backwards. I screamed in agony.

'Can't do it, I'm afraid' he said, before releasing my head 'Do you think I'm stupid? Are you trying to take me for an idiot?'

'He just needs to sort the deals out and you'll get your money' I said.

He walked back around the chair to face me. He stepped forward and punched me in the mouth. I swallowed back the blood. A tooth was loose.

'I think you're taking the piss out of me' he said. 'I know your assistant isn't in the country. Do you think I'm stupid? I asked her neighbour. He told me she'd gone away.' He smiled at me. 'Take that as a warning. I'm smarter than you, so you better shape up. Do I make myself clear? I want the money and I'm running out of patience. I thought you had more about you than that idiot who works for Major. Nearly shat his pants when I spoke to him.'

I said nothing.

'Give me your finger' he said to me.

I shook my head violently, desperately trying to move my wrists away from him.

He stepped closer, smiling. 'Your finger.'

He held my wrist tight, undoing the rope.

'Open your eyes. I've got all day.'

I opened my eyes. He leaned in, inches from my face. I waited for the pain to hit. I'd dislocated fingers playing rugby. I knew what it felt like. He smiled as he pulled my little finger back. This time I couldn't stop the screams. Once he was done, he stood up and left his men to pick me up. Moments later I was back in the boot of the car. I curled up in a ball, willing the journey to be over. Eventually I was thrown out on the grass verge next to my flat.

'Remember our problem takes priority' he said before getting back into his car and driving off.

I kept a first aid kit in both the office and my flat. I wasn't sure if it was commonsense or a damning indictment of how things were turning out for me. I found the antiseptic and went into the bathroom to clean myself up. The cuts on my face stung and my finger was bent out of shape, but ten minutes later I was feeling almost human again. I knew what I needed to do. Both my flat and office were now compromised. I found an old jiffy bag and went to work. I taped it up and addressed the contents to Sarah before heading out.

At the office, I sat at my desk and put my hands to my face before quickly removing them. The stinging was still intense. I started my laptop up and surfed the Internet for news. There was nothing new. Closing it back down again, I sat back in my chair and tried to make connections in my head. I looked up as Lorraine Harrison walked straight in and sat down opposite me.

'I want to talk to you' she said.

She didn't mention my face, or stare at it for longer than necessary. 'I've left my husband in HMV, looking at computer games.'

'With Jay?'

'He's at his grandparents. It's just me and Jason in town.'

'Right.'

'How's Steve?' she asked me. 'I saw it on the news.'

'On the mend. I'll pass on your regards.'

She ignored my comment. 'My husband didn't kill Greg.'

'You said.' I didn't mean to sound rude, but I wasn't hearing anything new from her. 'But somebody did.'

'It wasn't him.'

'I'm not really in the mood' I said. 'Why have you really come, Lorraine? We've been through this before.'

'Greg was doing really well, happy within himself for the first time in ages. He'd made his mind up. He said he was going to tell Siobhan he was leaving her, whether or not I wanted him. He wanted to release his new music and start again.'

'Were you tempted to start again with him?'

She hesitated. 'Of course I was. I might have done it, but it was Greg. He doesn't live in the real world. He only knew how to please himself. I was worried he'd get bored of us. What would he do if Jay was ill? Would he take him to the doctors? Would he go to the supermarket for me? He wouldn't be able to change, and deep down, I knew it.'

'Did you speak to your husband about it?'

'No, but he knew something was wrong. I couldn't think straight. I couldn't bear him touching me. I needed some time to think it through properly.'

'He hated Greg. Surely you can understand that?'

'Of course he hated him. I'm not stupid.'

I said nothing and waited for her to continue.

'DI Robinson spoke to me earlier' she said.

She had my attention. 'When?'

'This morning.'

'What did he say?'

'He said you'd been asking questions about Jason. That you thought he might have killed Greg.'

Robinson had certainly been busy. 'It's not a secret.' I didn't think his alibi really stood up. He was still a decent suspect to my mind.

'He was fishing. Seeing what you were up to.'

I could buy that. 'What did you tell him?'

'Nothing.'

'What did he tell you?'

'That he wasn't interested in Jason. He told me a witness had come forward. She heard Jason shouting outside of Greg's flat, just like he'd said. This woman had been away on holiday and didn't realise that what she'd seen was important.' She smiled at me. 'He was where he said he was. He wasn't at the studio. It wasn't my Jason who killed Greg.'

'Right.' I sat back, surprised. Harrison had been a legitimate suspect. He had to answer the questions.

'There's nothing to say, is there?' she said. 'We've sorted everything out. There'll be no more police coming to the house, nothing. I want you to stay away from me and my family. You don't bother me. You don't bother my husband. You certainly don't bother Jay. Do I make myself clear?'

I understood. Jason Harrison walked in. He told her he wanted to speak to me. Alone. We sat in silence until she left. He said nothing, just staring at me.

'Join the queue if you want to hit me' I said.

'I don't want to hit you.'

That was something at least.

'My record is a long time in the past. I hit the kid when I was pissed in town. I can't justify it, but stupid arguments sometimes happen, especially when you've had a drink. I was young and stupid. I was lucky, I suppose. No real harm done. I think. I paid the price and took my punishment. It's people like Lorraine's mother who can't let it go.'

He'd been luckier than whoever had killed Tasker with a single punch. Luck of the draw.

'Do you think I don't know?' he said.

'Know what?'

'About Jay. I've always known.' Harrison shrugged. 'What can you do? He's my son. I've tried to put all that stuff with Tasker to the back of mind and move on. Why do you think I was out drinking so much, acting like an idiot? It took me a long while to work out that it doesn't make any difference to me. It really doesn't. It wasn't important until you came along, raking it all up again. I knew I couldn't compete with Tasker. How could I? I'm a car-mechanic, he's a rock star, but he wasn't around when it counted. It was me who picked up the pieces and put Lorraine back together again and took care of Jay. But I didn't kill him. Why would I? We don't want him back in our lives. We just want to put this behind us, before Jay realises something's wrong.' He stood up. Looked at me. 'I didn't kill him.'

I looked up and met his eye, difficult though it felt. 'Had to ask the question.'

'Whatever the consequences?'

I turned away from him, nodded. Was I doing the right thing or not? How could I weigh up trying to find answers for Tasker's parents against the damage I'd caused Jason Harrison and his family? I'd walked into the man's life, turned it upside down, and now I was just going to leave him to clear up the mess. I watched as he headed towards the door.

'I'm not a bad person, Mr Geraghty, but I'd do anything for my family. To people like you, you think it means I'd kill someone. But it's not like that at all. To me it means I say nothing. It means I push it all to the back of mind and try to forget about it, say nothing, even if it cuts me up inside every single day.' He looked at me. 'That's what it means.'

CHAPTER TWENTY-ONE

I called Julia. She was working from the new Hull Truck Theatre cafe on Ferensway. I decided I could use the fresh air and walked across the city centre to meet her, stopping at the small florist's booth outside of Princes Quay. I hoped the flowers would say sorry, without making me look like I was trying too hard or was too desperate. I understood how things stood, but I had to put that to one side. I was going to need her help.

She was hard at work on her laptop when I arrived. The cafe area of the theatre was busy, filled with people eating and drinking, talking and laughing. It was my first visit to the place, not that socialising was top of my list of things to do at the moment. Julia had already ordered drinks and found us a quiet corner. She closed her laptop down as I approached.

She pointed at my face. 'What happened this time?'

I smiled and pulled away. I couldn't bear the thought of it being touched. 'I'm not flavour of the month.' I told her what had happened to me before trying to offer some kind of apology for the previous night.

'I overreacted, too' she said, taking the flowers off me. 'It's a difficult situation. We need to be able to respect each other's position.'

'We're ok?' I asked. I was expecting it to be more difficult.

'Mates' she said.

I nodded, understanding. I told her about my visit from the Harrisons. 'He didn't kill Greg' I said. 'If this witness had come forward quicker, it would have saved us all a lot of bother.'

'Did you really see him as a suspect?' she asked.

'He had motive.' He knew Greg Tasker was Jay's father, but he'd kept it to himself, saying nothing. I wasn't sure it was something to be admired or be saddened by. It wouldn't have surprised me, but I was still thinking things over. Something else was nagging away at me. I needed to think it through properly, but I was sure I was beginning to get closer to the truth.

'Any word on Priestley?' she asked.

'He's improving. I'm going to speak to him again a bit later on.' He was another unhappy man, but he still had questions to answer. I walked to the bar and ordered a sandwich before sitting back down.

'This is very cosy.' We both turned around. Max Fitzjohn walked up to our table. He pulled up a chair. 'Can't say I rate your choice of venue.'

'What do you want?' I said, my appetite gone. It was only a couple of hours ago that he was taking me out for a drive. He was following me.

'Aren't you going to introduce me to your friend?'

'No.'

Julia smiled at him and introduced herself. 'I wondered when we'd meet.'

He looked her up and down. 'I should have made it sooner.'

'What do you want?' I repeated to him.

'Take a guess.'

I nodded. I'd had enough. It was time to finish things. Whatever it took. 'Give me twenty-four hours. I'll call you.'

The offer took him by surprise. He eventually relaxed and smiled, gave me his mobile number. 'It'll be good for the rest of the day, so I'm going to trust you on this. I like to think a man's word should count for something. Don't let me down or I'll be disappointed.'

Julia waited for him to leave before asking me what I was playing at.

'It can't go on forever' I said. 'I've got to sort this out.'

'How?'

It was a good question, but I was getting closer. I could feel it.

I left Julia at Hull Truck, collected my car and drove to Trevor Bilton's flat. It was a mess. The damage looked extensive, the windows boarded over. There was no way he was staying there. I pulled over and flicked through the sports pages of the newspaper, looking to see if the horse racing had already started for the day. It had, so I hedged my bets and headed towards the bookies in the shopping precinct. I pulled up right in front of the shop. No windows. It looked like an old school kind of place, nothing like the light and airy ones you see in the city centre. I was prepared to wait it out, but I hadn't had the chance to read past the headlines before he walked out of the shop. I smiled. Betty Page was right. He was a man of habit.

I locked the car up and followed him on foot. He turned left and disappeared behind the shops. I caught him up and shouted his name.

He turned around. 'What the fuck do you want, Geraghty?'

'A word.'

'How about two – fuck off.'

I smiled. 'You can drop the hard-man act, no one's watching' I said.

'You're fucked in the head. Look at the state of your face. You need to have a word with yourself.'

I pushed him down the nearest alley. I'd had enough. 'Just shut your mouth and behave' I said. I wasn't taking a lecture from him. Shrinking back against the wall, he looked like a cornered animal. 'What happened in the pub?' I asked him.

'What do you mean?'

'I tried to speak to you.'

He shrugged. 'So what?'

'We said we'd help each other.'

'Things change.'

'The fire?'

'What do you fucking think? You set these people on us and then expect us to play along with your stupid game?'

I stepped away, leaned on the opposite wall, trying to show him I wasn't a threat. I didn't want to get involved in a fight with him.

'I don't need your help' he said. 'I'll take care of myself. I always said you were a cunt, thinking you were the big shot when we played rugby. Fucking hated you, I did.'

I ignored his comments. Pressed on. 'What do you know about the fire?'

'It was your friends, dickhead. The ones from London. They came to the pub, straight up the stairs and told me they wanted their money. I told them I didn't have it, like I keep having to fucking say to people. The one in charge said he didn't believe me and told me if I didn't get him his cash within the hour, I'd be hearing from him.'

'So they set your flat on fire?'

'Bit of a coincidence otherwise, wouldn't you say?'

'They were outside my place earlier.'

'You expect me to care?'

Probably not. 'Have you heard from them since?'

'Nothing.'

'They're going to come back for you.'

He nodded. 'I know.'

'You can't beat them by yourself.'

'Want to bet?'

He smiled. I needed him more than he needed me. This was his territory. Everything was set up to his advantage. Max Fitzjohn wouldn't pull the same trick again. But I had nowhere to hide. I had no backup. He walked away. I shouted after him. 'They'll come back for you.' He didn't stop or turn around.

I sat in my car, staring out the window, the radio turned off. I couldn't even remember the rugby properly. I was a teenager, full of hope and too much self-confidence. At that stage, it had been my life. Everything had been about the game. I was going to be the star man for my team, Hull Kingston Rovers. What I hadn't seen coming was the injury after a handful of first team games. It set me on a downward spiral, and in truth, it had taken me a long time to get over it. I watched the shoppers shuffling by, like they had no wish to be here, either. We'd all wanted something better from life, I thought.

Julia called me. A rival newspaper had printed a story about the rehearsal room fight between Tasker and Priestley. Shit. I thought it had been kept in-house. She'd set up a meeting with the guy who owned the rehearsal room. She wasn't getting the exclusive, but he still might have something useful for us. I didn't mention that Priestley had already told me about the incident when I'd met him at Paull. I drove away from the estate. Bilton wasn't going to be any further help. He'd made his decision.

I drove down Ferensway and collected Julia from the theatre, headed to Bankside. We walked into the reception area and found the man we wanted stood at the photocopier.

Julia introduced me to David Brabin, the owner. He hadn't been present when I'd initially spoken to Priestley here. It seemed so long ago now. He stared at my face before taking us into the office. There was only one chair free once he'd sat down. I stayed on my feet.

'This is my kingdom' he said, smiling at us. 'It's not much, but I like it.'

I looked around. 'It's intimate' I said.

'There's only two rooms and it's basic, but what more do bands need? It keeps my hand in. I use it for my own band. We play covers, The Jam, The Clash, that kind of thing. It's good fun and keeps me from getting under the wife's feet.' He laughed. 'I'm one of those who never made it, I'm afraid. I've been in plenty of bands, but never a sniff of a deal. It's the way it goes sometimes, but I'm happy.'

'You said you knew New Holland' I said, cutting him off.

'That's why they've been using my place' he said. 'They needed somewhere discreet where they wouldn't be bothered, and seeing as we go back years, they gave me a call.'

'Who called you?' I asked.

'Kane Major.'

There was something in his voice. 'You don't like him?'

'He said he'd pay me cash up front for the room, but I never saw it.' He shrugged. 'It doesn't matter now, obviously. I was just pleased to hear from them. I did loads of gigs with them around the city when they first started. I got my band together around the same time, so we sort of hung around together, playing gigs at the Adelphi and Blue Lamp, all the usual places. We even borrowed their drummer to help us record a demo tape once.' He smiled at us, enjoying the chance to reminisce. 'I couldn't believe it when I heard they were making a comeback. I keep telling my girls I know them, but they don't believe me. One's ten, the other's twelve, so they probably don't care. It's hardly cool stuff to them, I suppose.'

I interrupted. 'You rang the newspaper?' Julia shot me a look. I didn't care. I needed to move things on.

He held his hands up. 'I have no loyalties either way. I want to say that before I say anything else. Having New Holland here was great. It reminded me of my younger days, but ultimately it's a business I'm running.' He shuffled forward in his seat, clasped his hands together. 'I've obviously been following the news and frankly I don't like the way Steve's being portrayed by you lot. The media are painting him as the bad boy of the group and I wanted to tell you that's not how it was. Steve was never unpleasant or rude, or anything like that. Not back then and certainly not now. That's just not Steve's way with people.'

I walked around the room so I didn't stiffen up. It was small and there was no natural light. There was something he wasn't saying. I wanted him to spit it out. 'Why did you call, Mr Brabin?'

I watched him as he weighed the question up.

'Like I said, I have no loyalties here, right?'

'Right.'

'I read about the fight in the newspaper. I saw it and it wasn't how it happened.'

I could see Julia reaching for her notepad. It wasn't how we should play it. I touched her on the shoulder, letting her know she should stop. She understood. I asked him what he knew.

'Steve isn't an aggressive man. He never has been. I know the newspaper said he started the fight, but it isn't true. I was watching them from the doorway. I wanted to hear them play, you know? I'm just a fan at the end of the day.'

I leaned in closer to him. 'What did you see?'

'It wasn't Steve who started the fight. Not at all. It was Greg who had the problem, not Steve. Greg was the one being aggressive.'

We drove back into the city and headed into the bar of Julia's hotel. I slumped into a comfy chair. Julia ordered us coffee.

'Major sold the newspaper the story' I said. It was the only explanation.

'I'll ask around.'

I nodded. 'Good idea' I said, although I was in no doubt it was Major who'd pulled the strings on the story.

'Why would he lie?' she said. 'Why would he want to make out Priestley was the aggressor?'

'Loyalty to Greg?' It was the best theory I had, but it didn't really explain it. Or what the argument had been about, though I had a good idea. 'I spoke to Trevor Bilton earlier' I said.

'How did you track him down?'

'He's a man of habit. He wasn't best pleased to see me.'

'What did he say?'

'He's going it alone. He doesn't want my help.'

Julia considered it. 'He might have the brawn, but he hasn't got the brain.'

'His attitude is that if he keeps telling Fitzjohn he hasn't got the money, he'll eventually get the message.' I paused and shook my head. 'But people like Fitzjohn don't get the message, do they?'

'It's daft, but I can't help worrying about him.' She stood up and walked to the window. 'Despite what he and Gary did to me.'

It was irrational, but it also made sense to me. 'I understand' I said. Sometimes your head says one thing, but your heart another, however stupid it seems.

'Do you believe him?' she asked me.

I grunted a non-committal reply. I found it hard to believe he was telling me the truth about anything. Anyone could have thrown the punch which killed Tasker. Julia's mobile sounded again. She said she needed to go to her room and file a story. I waved her off, sat there and rubbed my face. Things were getting worse. But the clock was ticking.

The door to the office was unlocked. This was the last thing I needed. I stopped and tried to recall. I'd definitely locked it this time. There was no sign of anyone hanging around outside. I pushed the door open quietly and took my time walking up the stairs. The office door was also open. If it was Fitzjohn, I wasn't going to tip-toe in. I needed the element of surprise on my side. I picked up speed and walked in.

Don sat in his usual position. 'You should change the locks' he said to me.

My heartbeat started to slow down. 'Why didn't you say you were coming back?'

'It's a surprise.'

'You should have called. I'd have picked you up from the airport.'

'I'm sure you're far too busy for that.' He pointed to my face. 'Want to tell me what happened?'

I sat down at my desk and shook my head. 'Shouldn't you be enjoying the sun in Spain?'

'I think I've got more important things to sort here.' He put the file he was looking at back down. 'Why haven't you changed the locks?' he asked me.

'Not had the time.'

Don nodded. 'So I hear.'

'How's Sarah?'

'Enjoying the break.'

'Lauren?'

'Loves it. Swimming and the beach. What's not to like?'

'Pleased to hear it.'

We lapsed into silence. I wondered how much he really knew about Max Fitzjohn and what had been going on. So long as Sarah was in Spain, I wasn't going to enlighten him. There was nothing to be gained by it.

'Sorted things out yet?' Don said to me.

'Getting there.'

Don said nothing.

I sat up. 'What do you expect? I'm here by myself, doing my best. It's just me. There's no one else.'

Don stared at me. 'Are you saying Sarah should be here helping you sort this mess out?'

'She's a grown woman, Don. She can make her own decisions.' I don't know why I was being argumentative. I didn't mean it. I didn't want her in danger any more than he did.

'She's not stupid' Don said. 'And you were given fair warning. This wasn't what I wanted for us all.'

I knew he'd always harboured thoughts about me and Sarah getting together, making a go of things. I doubted he was so keen now. 'I need your help to finish things' I said.

Don held my stare. Nodded. 'All I've ever wanted is the best for her. It was tough losing her mother, but I made her a promise, and I'm going to keep it.'

I understood, knew Don had always been protective. I didn't blame him.

'There's a price attached' he said.

You meet a new girl and decide to move back to Hull. You need to get away from London and all its distractions. There's absolutely nothing to stay there for. Kane's too busy with new projects. You need to live a cleaner life. You decide to open a studio. Music is all you know. When it's not in use, you record a solo album. You know it's your best work. You're proud of it. The music press dismiss it. You're nobody to them. You pretend their response means nothing to you. But it does. You tour the record. It's back to the towns and cities you've been to countless times before. The same old tired circuit. Except this time the venues and crowds are smaller. You feel naked on stage. There's nothing to hide behind. You don't enjoy it. It's not you anymore. You decide to quit making music and concentrate on the studio. At first, you find it a distraction, but it quickly becomes monotonous. You take a back seat and let your engineers take charge. You brood. What hurts you the most is that Priestley never called. Not once.

CHAPTER TWENTY-TWO

I didn't want to sit still and reflect on what Don had said. It wouldn't do me any good. I drove out of Hull, heading towards Priestley's farm. It was quiet. I couldn't see his wife's car. Certainly no sign of the media. They must have had their pound of flesh from him for now. Closing the car door behind me, I heard a dog bark. I knocked on the front door. Nobody answered. I tried the door. Unlocked. I walked in. Technically, I was probably breaking the law, but I'd done worse. Much worse. I walked into the front room. Priestley was lying on the settee. I crouched down, ready to check for a pulse.

'I'm awake' he said. 'I can see you.'

I stood back up. 'Do you always leave your front door open?'

'Carly's gone to the shops. She'll be back soon.'

'Do you want anything?' I said.

He struggled to sit up. 'I'm alright' he said, looking at my face. 'What happened to you?'

I sat down opposite him and told him it was nothing. 'Why didn't you tell me the truth about the argument in the rehearsal room?' He'd told me he'd argued with Tasker over song choice for the secret warm-up gig.

'What good would it have done?' he said.

'It would have been the truth.'

Priestley laughed. 'Wouldn't have made any difference, would it?'

I didn't have an answer for him. I'd thought about it as I'd headed to his farm, but I hadn't made any progress. It struck me New Holland had given him both the best and the worst times in his life. And I'd played my part in bringing back the worst times.

'I didn't expect Major to put the story out there, certainly not like that' he said. 'Don't they say in football circles that what goes on in the changing room stays in the changing room? He should learn the lesson.'

'Why didn't you say something?'

'Because it's my business. Not yours.'

'You were arguing about Lorraine?' I said.

He nodded. 'Greg had been baiting me about her, right from the first rehearsal. I don't know why. I wasn't going to say anything. I wasn't going to rock the boat. The plan was to put the past behind us and be professional about things. All the other stuff was years ago. I just wanted to get the band up and running again with the minimum of fuss.'

'Why did Greg do it?' I asked.

'I don't know, I really don't. He was in my face from the start, telling me he was going to get her back and nobody was going to stop him this time. I tried to tell him I didn't have a problem with that. Why would I? I've made my decision. This is what I am now.'

He was talking about Carly. His sense of loyalty was admirable. Looking at him lying there, I remembered her telling me how he'd turned his life around. Yet he remained so fragile. I wondered if the reunion would have been worth it for him. Or for Tasker. I assumed not. 'It was a bit extreme, wasn't it?' I said. I didn't know how to phrase it any more tactfully. 'Slashing your wrists.'

Priestley smiled. 'I was being stupid. I don't know, put it down to having a bad day, maybe. A cry for help. I felt like I'd had enough, you know? It was just too easy to do. I was lucky Carly found me when she did. Could have been a lot worse.'

'That's an understatement.' History repeating itself. First Tasker, then Priestley.

'I know about Jay' he said. 'Greg told me. It wasn't a massive surprise.'

'Why didn't you say anything?'

'It's none of my business.' He took a moment before continuing. 'It wouldn't be fair on Lorraine.' He asked me to make him a drink.

I found the kettle and made the coffee. It was better stuff than I was used to in the office. I passed him his mug and sat back down. 'What does Carly have to say?'

'She wasn't best impressed.'

'Stands to reason.'

'Tore a strip off me earlier.'

'At least she cares.'

'She'd be better off without me.'

'I'm hardly the person you should be talking to about it, but for what's worth, she'd let you know if it was the case.' I was thinking about Julia, and how she'd cooled towards me. Had I been a port in a storm while she was back in the city? It was probably for the best, but it seemed I was as clueless as Priestley when it came to this sort of thing. 'What are you going to do next?' I asked him.

'I've no idea. I've made my bed. I've got to lie in it now.'

I nodded. 'Siobhan told me Greg felt guilty over the way the band finished. I don't think he hated you. Not at all.'

'I didn't kill him' he said to me. 'I wish I could make you and the police believe me.'

DI Robinson had been in touch. Priestley was still a suspect, despite everything. 'Why don't you give us an alibi?'

He laughed again. 'I can't give you what I don't have. I was out walking, like I do pretty much every other night. It's what I do to get away from people. That's the point of it.' He looked at me and shook his head. 'Close the door on your way out, please.'

I drove back towards Hull, stopping once I had the signal back on my mobile. I rang Julia. 'I really don't understand why Priestley got involved in the reunion' I said.

Julia considered the question. 'He was always the serious one. One last chance to right some wrongs, maybe?'

'Maybe.' He'd willingly reopened old wounds. New Holland's reunion had brought him back into contact with Lorraine Harrison, and that was before Tasker and Major were factored into the equation. 'He must really want to set the record straight' I said.

'That's Steve for you.'

I told her Don was back in Hull. Especially to see me.

'You must be honoured.'

'He's not best pleased I've put his daughter in danger.'

'She's a big girl.'

'I don't think he quite sees it that way.'

'I suppose not.'

'Do you miss her?' Julia asked me.

'Sarah?'

'Who else?'

I thought about it for a moment. 'More than I thought I would.' It was the truth.

'Sounds like you've got some thinking to do.'

I knew where to go next. I wanted to speak to Tasker's studio engineer again. I tried the number Julia had for him.

242

No answer. I took a chance and drove to Tasker's studio. The door was open, so I walked straight in. Like the last time, he was hunched over the vast mixing desk, headphones on. His face was a mess, too. This time I decided not to startle him. I moved slowly around the room, so he would eventually see me out of the corner of his eye. I still made him jump.

'You've had a visit?' I said.

'What do you want?' he said to me.

'I need to talk to you.'

'Doesn't mean I want to talk to you. I've got work to do. Nobody else is going to do it now, are they?'

I pointed to his face. 'Who did that to you?' He said nothing. I spoke again. 'Is that why you were so reluctant to speak to us before?'

'I'm not a grass.'

'Nobody's saying you are.'

'I wish I'd kept my mouth shut now.'

But the money helped, I thought. 'I can help you' I said. I told him I'd seen Greg Tasker's dead body, too.

He nodded. He got the point. 'They told me to keep my mouth shut' he said. 'They said if I spoke to anyone, they'd come back.'

He was clearly scared. I moved closer to him. Cranked up the pressure. 'You saw more than you told us, didn't you?'

'So what?'

'If you don't help me, they'll come back' I said to him. 'These people never stop. If you speak to me, I can help you.'

Rusting stood up and paced the room. I said nothing, letting him figure it out for himself.

'What did they say to you?' he asked me.

'Not a lot' I said. I didn't want to give him too much. I wanted him to tell me what he knew.

He stopped and turned to face me. 'What do you expect me to do? I'm not taking another kicking. It's not my problem.' I watched him fumble in his pockets for a cigarette. He lit up before offering me one.

I shook my head. 'You're alright.'

He took a drag and turned back to the window. 'Fuck's sake. You try and do the right thing and look what happens.'

'You can't always control these things' I said.

'You're telling me.' He walked back towards me and sat down. 'I suppose it comes with the territory for you, but I was scared. They didn't hold back.'

I took a photograph out of my pocket. He'd seen the men. He'd told me that much during my visit with Julia. 'Was this one of the men?'

Rusting looked, nodded and turned away from me again.

I left the studio feeling more certain of what I knew. It was time to start bringing things to a head. Julia had called me, but I ignored her message, instead heading back to the city centre, parking my car and walking to Major's office. The receptionist was busy taking a call as I walked into the building. I didn't give her the chance to stop me. I headed straight for the stairs and walked into Major's office. He was on the phone, laughing. Taking him by surprise, I took the phone out of his hand, disconnected the call.

'What the fuck are you doing, PI?'

'We're going to talk' I said.

He looked me up and down and smiled. 'Someone's given you a good kicking, haven't they?'

I wanted to wipe the smile off his face. I thought I'd gotten a glimpse of the real man during our last conversation. That was a distant memory already. 'It was your friends from London. And you're next on their list.' That quietened him down. He knew as well as I did what they were capable of.

He took the hint and gave me his full attention. 'What do you know?'

'Plenty.' I sat down on the sofa.

'Have you sorted it out?' he asked.

I ignored him. 'I'm going first with the questions.'

He nodded. 'Fair enough. I hope you treat Julia better than that, you know what I mean?'

He knew how to push my buttons. I felt my hands bunch into fists. I took a deep breath and relaxed. 'I spoke to Lorraine Harrison earlier.'

'Like a bad fucking smell, isn't she? Did she want you to indulge more of her fantasies?'

'You made Greg dump her when the band first went down to London.'

Major looked at me, a little surprised. He definitely wasn't expecting that. He stood up, collected his mobile off his desk. 'Shall we go for a drink, PI?'

I shook my head. 'Sit down and tell me about Greg and Lorraine.'

'What's there to tell?' He shrugged. 'She used to hang around at the band's gigs. I could never get rid of her. And then Greg started to fuck her, which made it a thousand times worse. After that, we definitely couldn't get rid of her.'

'Why did it bother you so much? Surely it was Greg's business?'

'Not if it affected the band.'

'Did it affect them?'

'What you've got to understand, PI, is that image is everything in this game. Once the band started to get somewhere, the last thing we needed was girlfriends leeching along for the ride. I wanted them to be young, free and fucking anything that moved.' He smiled. 'Better for business that way.'

'But what did Greg want?' I said.

'He wanted what was best for the band.'

'I don't think he did.'

Major laughed. 'What the fuck do you think he wanted?'

'Lorraine was pregnant when you left the city.'

He nodded. 'You're good at maths, PI.'

'It's what Greg and Priestley were fighting over in the rehearsal room, wasn't it? Why did you leak the story to the newspaper?'

'Why do you think I sold the story? I needed some quick money. Besides, it's all good for the band. It gets people talking about them again, which is what we all wanted. I kept it vague. No one cares.'

I wasn't having it. 'But they were really arguing about Lorraine.'

'She was carrying Greg's baby when he left Hull. I told her to get rid of it.'

That stopped me. I didn't think he could surprise me, but he really was one heartless bastard. 'What did she say when you told her that?'

'She wouldn't take the money, but she agreed to stay away from Greg. It was for the best.'

'But she couldn't stay away, could she?'

'Seemingly not. '

'And Priestley had always carried a torch for her?'

'Fuck knows why.' He shrugged. 'Always wanted what Greg had.'

'Greg was pushing him in the rehearsal room, reminding him of the fact.'

'Priestley was sticking his nose in, telling Greg he should do the decent thing and leave Lorraine alone, let her get on with her life.'

'Only Greg wanted her back, didn't he? He wanted to leave Siobhan and start again.'

'He wasn't thinking straight. She had nothing to offer him.'

'Apart from his son.'

Major went quiet, opened his drawer and produced a bottle of whiskey. He waved it at me. I shook my head. I wasn't drinking with him again. He poured a drink, saluted me with his glass.

'Did you force Greg back into drugs?' I asked.

Major laughed. 'Do you seriously think I had to force him to do anything? He was looking for an escape from the drab fucking existence he'd made for himself back up here.'

'He was clean until you showed up.'

'People like Greg are never clean. He was waiting for the trigger, that's all. If it wasn't me, it would have been something else. It's in his blood, PI.'

'I don't think so.'

'Believe what you like.'

'And you made him pick up your debts?' I leaned towards him. 'How low is that?' Major looked like he wanted to punch me. I was hoping he might try his luck.

'He wanted to help me. It's what mates do' he said.

'You made him take the money from the boutique?'

Major laughed. 'What's your problem with that? It was his money anyway. He was entitled to it.'

'Doesn't really work like that, does it?'

'Fuck you, PI. Who do you think you're talking to?'

'Someone who'd rip his mate off for a quick fix' I said. I stood up and walked across to the window. He'd gone silent. I'd scored a hit at last.

'What you've got to understand, PI, is people like Greg want you to make decisions for them' he eventually said. 'They're not capable of doing it. They need people like me to take care of this stuff for them.'

I watched him pour himself another generous measure. 'It's what I'm good at doing' he said.

'What about Priestley?' I said.

Major slugged the whiskey back and looked at me. 'What about him?'

'He needed your help. What did you do for him? What did you ever do for him?'

He said nothing to that, reached for the bottle again.

'He's out of hospital.'

'Pleased to hear it.' He threw another drink back.

I pointed at his glass. 'You should ease off that stuff.'

'Are you my fucking mother?'

'You can have that advice for free.'

'Fuck you.'

He stood up and walked towards the door. I was too quick for him and blocked his escape route. 'Sit down. We're not done yet.'

He was eyeballing me again. 'Try it' I said. 'Please.' I could smell the alcohol on his breath. He walked back to his desk. Not so brave.

'What was it with you and Greg?' I said. I saw him looking at the bottle of whiskey. I was too quick for him again. Grabbed it and held it away from him. 'You was jealous of Priestley.'

He laughed. 'Why would I be jealous of him?'

I wasn't drinking. I could see things more clearly then he could. 'Because they were the band. They were the ones with the special bond. I'm sure you're very good at what you do, but you're not the talent, are you? They were the ones writing the songs and going out on stage in front of the fans. That's where the special bond was.' I'd silenced him. I felt a twinge of pity, but chased it quickly away. I'd hit the nail on the head. He looked beaten. He shrugged and asked for the whiskey back. I gave it to him and walked back to the sofa and sat down. I watched him slug down another generous measure. 'Why did you really hire me?' I asked. 'You knew people were going to be looking for you up here, didn't you?'

He saluted me with the glass. 'I needed back-up, not that you've gone out of your way to look after me. I thought your lot liked to look after their clients.'

'It wasn't in the job description.'

'You'll do as I tell you. I'm paying.'

I laughed. 'We're well past that stage.' I had to play the cards I held carefully. I didn't want to show my hand just yet. 'I can sort this for you' I said.

He looked up at me. Put his glass down. 'You can sort it?'

'I can make it all go away.'

'How?'

I said I'd collect him at eight o'clock the following morning. I was going to need help. I didn't add that he'd be feeling some pain in the final reckoning. And that was just from me. He wasn't walking away from this. I looked at Don's number in my mobile. Not yet. But the time was coming. 'I'll put a deal together' I said to Major. I stood up and left him to his drinking.

CHAPTER TWENTY-THREE

I walked back across the city centre. It was emptying rapidly as the office workers hurried away back to their homes. Hands in my pockets, I increased my pace. I was now more than certain I was right. I knew who had killed Greg Tasker. I had one more visit to make and then I'd go back to my flat and make some calls. Beg if I needed to. I joined the rush hour traffic heading west out of the city centre, patiently waiting my turn. I parked up outside Tasker's parent's house. Keith let me in. I followed him through the house and into the kitchen.

'I'm on cooking duty tonight' he said. 'Kath's decided to go out and see a friend, have a chat, but I can get her to come back.' I watched him pick up a spoon and stir whatever was in the saucepan. 'Rather basic, I'm afraid.'

I nodded. 'Probably better at it than me.'

He turned the heat down and offered me a drink. I asked for a glass of water, drank it back quickly and returned it for a refill.

'I heard about Steve on the news. Terrible business' he said. 'Do you know how he is?'

'He's out of hospital.'

'That's good news, at least.'

I hoped it was.

'He was always the quiet one. The one who took things to heart. Will you be seeing him?'

I nodded. 'Definitely.'

'Pass on my best wishes to him, please.'

I told him I would. 'I spoke to Siobhan' I said. 'She's decided to leave Hull.'

He took the information in. 'Right.'

'I think she's made her mind up.'

He looked genuinely taken aback by the news. For all his wife's dislike of Siobhan, she was still an important link to their son. In some ways, they were also losing a daughter. 'Would you like me to let her know I've spoken to you?'

'No, it's fine. I'll call her before she goes.' He paused. Turned his attention back to the cooking. 'Have you got any other news for us?' he asked.

I told him I'd have some news for him tomorrow. 'I wanted to make sure you were alright first.'

He stopped stirring the food and wiped his hands on a tea-towel. 'We're doing our best.' He offered me a stronger drink. I declined. 'It's hit Kath hard' he said.

'How is she?'

'Getting there. At least I have my work to take my mind off things. That's why I was hoping her decision to see her friend tonight would help. She's known her for years. I think talking to your journalist friend helped her. I'm not sure I agree with it, but it's a release.'

'I understand.' I watched him walk to the patio doors and look out.

'You're a good man, Joe. Your dad would have been proud of you.'

I turned away from him and hoped that was the truth. We sat in silence for a moment.

'I'm ashamed' he said. 'Kath needs me and I haven't been here for her. I've been using work as an excuse to stay away. I didn't think I could cope with it all. I lost sight of what's important, but trust me, I know now. You do what you need to do, but please, just bring some closure to this for us so I can take care of her.'

I was finished for the day. As I turned onto Westbourne Avenue, I drove past my flat, checking for any surprises from Fitzjohn. Satisfied I was alone, I hurried inside, making sure the door was locked behind me. I had work to do, but I showered first. The water was cold. It did its job and I was ready to continue working. I got my notes out and spread them out in front of me. I hadn't eaten since Fitzjohn had interrupted my lunch. Pizza leaflets were pinned to the fridge door. Selecting one, I rang and ordered, put some music on and went back to my notes. I'd flicked through the pile of CDs next to the stereo, settling on 'Exile on Main Street', my favourite by The Stones. I looked at the sleeve and smiled. I'd bought the recent reissue – money for old rope, I thought. Nice work if you can get it. I looked at my notes. I knew who killed Tasker, and why they'd done it. It made sense. My notes were detailed, so I set to work condensing them, double-checking the connections and theories, testing the assumptions I'd made. I lost myself in the task until the buzzer to my flat sounded. My first thought was Fitzjohn, but then I relaxed as I remembered I'd ordered food. I glanced down out of my window, surprised to see Sarah stood outside. I paused, turned the music off, picked up the receiver and let her up. She walked in, moved a pile of my notes and sat down on the sofa.

'This is a surprise' I said. 'How was Spain?'

'Lauren thought it was great. I haven't seen her so happy in ages.'

'Pleased to hear it.'

She wasn't best pleased to be coming home for school.'

I smiled. 'I'm sure she wasn't.' The last time I'd spoken to her, she couldn't wait, loved her teacher. But I doubt it compared to being on holiday.

The door buzzer went again. This time it was the pizza. Sarah made to leave, saying she was getting in the way.

'Stay' I said. 'Please.' I opened the pizza box lid. 'I've ordered too much, anyway.'

She sat back down whilst I found some clean plates and cutlery. There was a bottle of wine on the unit top, next to the toaster. 'Cheers' I said, passing her the food and drink.

'Dad said I should stay away from you' she said.

I nodded. I wasn't surprised. Don had been clear. 'He spoke to me about it.' I'd been thinking things over. 'I've made a mess of everything' I said. 'A total mess.'

She told me it didn't matter. Not now. 'I'm angry with Dad' she said. 'I knew he wouldn't be able to leave it alone. I make my own decisions, but he won't listen.' She shrugged. 'He bought me the plane tickets, so I had to go. I should have stayed. Offered you some help.'

'He only wants the best for you' I said. I couldn't blame him for that. I'd brought trouble to their door on more than one occasion. She didn't need that, especially with Lauren around. 'I tried to call you.'

'My phone was flat. I lost my charger somewhere in the office.'

I smiled. 'I lose mine all the time.'

'Dad mentioned the state of your face' she said.

'I had a spot of bother with the people who broke into the office.'

'He said.'

There wasn't much I could add. I was going to need Don's help to finish this. I would have to accept whatever he threw at me. 'It just spiralled out of control. It's why you couldn't stay around. I don't want you having to deal with these people.'

'I probably wouldn't fare any worse than you.'

I laughed. 'Major stitched me up good and proper, right from the start' I said. 'He knew these people were going to come up here looking for him.' He'd told Fitzjohn that Trevor Bilton had the money. I'd been used all along.

'Did you get any more money off him?'

'No.' I passed her another slice of pizza and refilled her glass. Don had been against me taking the job in the first place and he'd been proved right. The teenager within me had been hugely excited by the scenario laid out by Major. The lure of the road. I'd been stupid enough to fall for it.

Sarah pointed at my mountain of paperwork. 'Old habits die hard?'

'Pretty much.'

'How's Julia?'

'Fine, so far as I know.'

'So far as you know?'

'I mean, she's alright. Working hard. She's been a great help.' I put my food down. I'd said the wrong thing. Again.

'Right.'

'I know she's helping for her own reasons, not just because she wants to.' I paused, seeing the truth. 'I haven't handled things particularly well. I know that.'

She put her food down. 'You're allowed to live, Joe. I don't have a problem with that, I really don't. Nobody expects you to live the rest of your life like a monk. Debbie wouldn't have wanted that for you. You've got to be happy.'

I glanced at my wedding photo. I really wasn't sure what Debbie would be thinking. I knew I would want her to be happy if things had been different, so maybe it worked both ways. I understood what we were talking about. The problem was, I wasn't happy. 'I'm not seeing Julia' I said. 'Call it a holiday romance, if you like. I don't know what it was.' All I knew was it wasn't right for me.

Sarah picked up a slice of pizza and smiled. 'You're not the only one who's had a holiday romance.'

I didn't want to ask for the details. Sarah said no to more wine. I put what was left back in the fridge. I needed to keep a clear head for the morning.

'What else is new?' she asked, once I sat back on the sofa.

I told her what I'd learnt since she'd gone away. I told her about Jay Harrison and what Major had done to keep Tasker apart from his son. It made some sort of sense, now I knew. I understood why Jason Harrison had been so abrasive, but it was all so sad. Nobody was happy with what they had. I told her about how Priestley had always carried a torch for Lorraine Harrison, and how Tasker knew it, took advantage of his friend's feelings. It was about establishing a pecking order for the reunion. Old sores hadn't healed and there was an unpleasant undercurrent within the band, culminating in Priestley's suicide attempt.

'I spoke to Major earlier' I said. 'It's really quite shocking how angry he is. I think he's jealous, certainly of Priestley, maybe even Tasker, despite him being his friend. I don't think he's got any real purpose to his life, so he was going to do his best to make sure Tasker and Priestley suffered for it. If he couldn't find any contentment or purpose, I don't think he wanted them to have it, either.' I shrugged. That was my reading of it. I pointed to the pile of paperwork. 'I've got to get to the bottom of things now.' I realised I was doing it for Jason Harrison, too, after the way I'd almost brought his world crashing down. I didn't need to ask what I should do about Jay Harrison. I decided there and then I couldn't tell Greg's parents about Jay. It wasn't my decision to make and it felt like I'd already done enough damage to the Harrisons.

Sarah stood up. 'I should be going.' She phoned for a taxi. It pulled up outside my flat five minutes later. 'It's been nice to see a friendly face' I said.

'Same here' she said.

We stood together at the window and looked out at the taxi. It sounded its horn. It was dark with little sign of life. I stared at our reflections in the window. I turned and smiled at her. I liked the calmness of the scene.

'Why did you do it?' she asked me.

It was a good question. If people ask for help, you give it. Keith Tasker had told me how he'd helped my family when asked. My parents couldn't repay the favour, so I had to. 'Sometimes you don't have a choice' I said.

'Do you know who killed Greg?' Sarah said.

'I'll let you know' I said. My night wasn't done yet. I still had arrangements to make for tomorrow.

The taxi driver sounded his horn again. She kissed me on the cheek. 'Be safe, Joe.'

CHAPTER TWENTY-FOUR

I looked at myself in the mirror. The cuts and bruises were starting to heal over. I nodded at my reflection. It was early, but I was alert. It was time. I'd spent an hour on the phone after Sarah had left my flat, and I'd had to work hard to convince people I was right. I'd forced some breakfast down, as it promised to be a long day.

I collected Kane Major from his hotel. He complained about the early start, but I zoned him out, telling him the rest of the country coped with it just fine. I wasn't in the mood to pander to him. We drove in silence after that. We watched Julia get out of a taxi. 'What's she doing here?' he said.

We'd parked up in the Humber Bridge car park, right under its watchful eye. We were in the far corner, well away from the trickle of other cars coming and going.

'You said she had full access to the story. Remember?' I said.

'Are you taking the piss?'

'Not at all.'

'She can't be here now.'

I smiled at him. 'I really don't give a shit what you think.'

'Like that is it, PI? Remember, I gave you this job.'

I didn't know whether to laugh or cry. 'Do you think I'd have taken it if I knew what was going to happen?'

'Are you a man or a mouse?'

I took a deep breath. He'd struck a nerve. His attitude was the opposite of Don's. Don wanted me nowhere near danger. But things weren't always that simple.

Julia walked across to us. Smiled. 'Morning, gentlemen.'

She was in a good mood, but she was about to get a big exclusive.

'She'll be writing it all up' I said to Major. I didn't add that she would do that whatever the outcome. I turned away from him and looked at the bridge. The city should do more to promote it. The piss-poor cafe and souvenir shop wasn't enough. Not by some distance. I turned back to Major. 'You're a weak man. Did I tell you that?'

'Fuck off, PI.'

'If things don't go your way, you're like a petulant child. No wonder you've got nobody.'

'Fuck you.'

I turned to Julia and shrugged. We watched as Trevor Bilton walked across the car park towards us. It'd taken me several phone calls to reach him, but I hadn't given in. I couldn't afford to. He stopped ten yards away from us, hands in his pockets, staring at us.

'Drop the gangster shit' I said. 'We're all friends here.'

He pointed at Major. 'My brother took a beating for that cunt.'

'I think you owe the man an apology' I said to Major.

He said nothing, turned away from us. I told Bilton to come closer. 'He's made an idiot out of all of us' I said. 'He's played us all for fools. He drew Greg Tasker back into a world he didn't want to go back to' I said. I made sure I had Major's attention. 'Didn't you?'

'Fuck you.'

'Greg was trying to please you. He felt like he owed you something. Stupid, really. He owed you nothing.'

'He owed me everything, PI.'

I shook my head. We'd been through this before. I didn't want to hear him trying to justify his actions again.

Major laughed. 'You'll be telling me you believe in Father Christmas next.'

'Have you spoken to his parents?' I said to him.

'Why would I?'

'Because you're supposed to be a friend of the family. They're in pieces and you've done nothing.'

Major shrugged. 'What could I do?'

I stepped away from him, so I didn't lose my temper and hit him. He just didn't care that they'd lost their son. He didn't feel it like I did. My thinking was interrupted by another vehicle approaching us. It stopped and Max Fitzjohn got out. I nodded a greeting to him. It was coming together.

'I want my money' he said, looking at each of us in turn. He stood, legs slightly apart, bolt upright. Trying to show us who was in charge.

'I haven't got it' I said.

He pointed at me. 'This is a joke, right? You dragged me all the way out here at this time to tell me you haven't got it? Didn't you hear me before?'

'I've never had your money.'

He looked at Major and Bilton. 'Who's got it, then?'

'I've no idea' I said.

Everyone tensed. Fitzjohn was clearly struggling to control his temper. He started to pace up and down. Short strides. The last car I was waiting for swept into the car park. I'd told people they had to wait until everyone was here. The car parked and the door opened, stopping Fitzjohn in his tracks. Then he lost his temper completely.

'What the fuck is going on?

DI Robinson walked up to join us. 'This is a surprise. How pleasant to see you all in one place.'

I nodded to Don, who'd stepped out of the passenger seat. Robinson introduced himself and showed Fitzjohn his ID. 'Humberside Police.'

Fitzjohn said nothing.

It was now or never. Everyone was here. I spoke.

'I was wrong' I said, getting Robinson's attention. 'Priestley didn't kill Greg Tasker.' He had no reason to. The reunion was purely business to him. I was staking my reputation on it. I had to accept he didn't have an alibi, he was a night walker, but I just couldn't buy into him being a killer. It didn't sit right with me. If I wasn't allowed the courage of my convictions, I was in the wrong job. All he was guilty of was trying to do his best for the band.

'Interesting, Mr Geraghty, but let's stop this messing about, shall we?' Robinson said. 'I'm sure we're all aware Priestley didn't do it.'

'Major's jealous of him' I continued. 'He doesn't like the fact Greg and Steve were the real talent in New Holland. In fact, I'd say he tried to set Steve up for a fall by selling stories to newspapers. Anything for some easy money.'

'You're having a fucking laugh, PI' Major said. 'Have you any idea how stupid you sound? Bringing us all out here to listen to this shit? This isn't an episode of Scooby Doo. I didn't kill him, alright?'

'And nor did Jason Harrison' I said to him. 'You might have caused him a lot of pain, but he's not a killer. In fact, he's twice the man you are.'

Major sneered. 'The man must be a fucking idiot.'

'I'd got it wrong by looking at him. He'd done nothing wrong.'

'This is all very touching, PI' Major said, 'but I've got more important things to be doing.'

'Stay there, Mr Major.' He turned to Fitzjohn. 'You, however, are going to leave my city. You're only minutes from the road out of Hull: I suggest you use it.'

'I want my money' Fitzjohn said. He pointed at Major. 'And he owes me.'

'Face facts, Mr Fitzjohn. You're not getting your money. Frankly, you're lucky I'm allowing you to leave my city of your own free will. I don't care who you think you are, I'd take you down as quick as look at you.' He stepped towards him. 'I won't tell you again.'

For a moment, I thought things were going to spiral out of control. Fitzjohn took a step and met Robinson half way before seeing sense and relenting. There was probably thirty years between them, but Robinson was a tough old bastard. I'd give him that.

'This isn't over' Fitzjohn said. 'I want what I'm owed.'

'Do yourself a favour. Give it up and leave whilst you still can.'

We all watched as Fitzjohn walked back to his car. He got in the back and it pulled away. I nodded to Robinson. One problem sorted.

Major looked genuinely shocked by what was going on. Whether or not it got him off the financial hook, I didn't know or care. He'd have to sort it out for himself when he went back to London. Fun though it was to watch him squirm, I told him I knew he hadn't killed Tasker, either. I told him I knew why we'd broken into Greg's flat. He wanted whatever he could get his hands on, but most importantly, he wanted the CD of songs Greg had demoed. I told him I had a copy. I didn't tell him I'd posted a copy to Sarah, just in case anything happened to me. She'd understand; I wasn't having Major deciding what to do with recordings Greg had left behind.

'If you so much as think about cashing in on them, I'll leak them on the Internet' I said. 'I'll make sure you don't make a penny off them.' It wasn't much of a threat, but I hoped it'd make him think twice. I told him to make his own way back to the city centre. I wasn't interested in helping him any further. I was finished with him. If I ever saw him again, it'd be too soon.

Robinson spoke. 'Which leaves us with you, doesn't it, Mr Bilton?'

He laughed. 'You think I killed Greg Tasker?' he said.

'You or your brother' I said. I took him through it. I told him how he'd wanted my help when he thought I could get Fitzjohn off his back. Once he'd realised I was more interested in Greg Tasker, the shutters had come down. They'd tried to play me, asking for my help. His brother had told me he was skint, yet days after Tasker's death, I'd seen a new plasma screen television in his flat. Just after Greg had disappeared with several days takings from the boutique in his pocket. Money that wasn't in his pocket after he was killed.

'Bullshit' Bilton said. He looked at Robinson. 'Even people like you need proof these days. You can't believe this shit, surely?' He started to walk away.

Robinson blocked his way. 'Mr Geraghty hasn't finished yet' he said.

'The night you killed Greg, somebody saw you' I said. 'They made a statement to the police, but then sold their story to the newspapers. You didn't like someone being so close to the truth, you panicked that you'd been seen, so you tried to frighten him into keeping his mouth shut, handed out a good kicking.' I thought back to Rusting's eagerness to make some money. Robinson had told me he'd make sure Rusting would get any protection he needed. But there was always a price to pay. 'The mistake you made was doing it yourself. If you'd been a bit more professional about it, maybe sent the boys around with an envelope full of money, you might have bought the man's silence. He probably wouldn't have spoken to me.'

'He won't make a statement' Bilton said.

I looked to Robinson.

He produced a sheet of paper. 'Already has, Mr Bilton. Looks like your long run of luck has come to an end.'

Betty Page would be pleased. She'd given me the photograph from which Rusting had identified Bilton.

'You think I killed Tasker?' Bilton laughed. 'You've got no idea, have you?'

I knew what he was talking about. 'Gary was with you, wasn't he?'

'He's my fucking brother. He's always with me. Blood's thicker than water.'

'Why?'

'Why, what?'

'Why was he with you?'

'To earn some coin. Why else? Easy work and he needed the money, so I took care of him.'

'Took care of him?'

'Fuck off, Geraghty.'

'Who threw the punch?' I asked.

Bilton laughed. 'Like I'd fucking tell you.'

'Forensics will sort it out' Robinson said.

I hoped so. The brothers were both guilty in my eyes, though I felt sorry that Gary Bilton wouldn't be continuing his work on the estate. He'd be missed. It was weird, but it made some sort of sense.

Don was still stood with us, saying nothing. Julia said she'd go and wait for me in the car. I smiled, tried to convey that I understood what she was feeling. I waited for her to go. For better or worse, but hopefully for better, this was the end of a chapter in her life. It was never going to work out between us, but I wasn't sure that was what either of us had really wanted. Or needed. Maybe the work situation and Gary Bilton's appearance in the investigation had been a convenient excuse to put the brakes on. It'd helped clarify my thinking. It was time to make an effort and move on. But it didn't mean I had to necessarily forget about the past.

They could co-exist without rubbing up against each other. There was a middle ground to be found and I was getting a clearer picture of what it should involve.

I turned to Don. 'Thanks for that' I said.

He nodded. 'You called it right, Joe. I'll give you that.'

'Still needed your help.'

'You know the price for it.'

That was true. I'd laid it out carefully to Don the previous night, so he could talk to Robinson with confidence. It had to be handled so I could get Fitzjohn chased out of the city at the same time. It needed finishing in one swoop. No loose ends. I was counting on Fitzjohn weighing the odds up and deciding it was best to lose some face. He might be leaving empty-handed, but he wouldn't want to be arrested. This way, he could disappear back to London and spin whatever story he wished to whoever was interested. The wider investigation would continue as before.

I'd explained to Don I wanted Major to leave empty-handed. It was the only way to finish it properly. Major was being chased for a debt and he'd pointed the finger at Trevor Bilton via Tasker. He'd gone for the easy target. Major had acted out of nothing but selfishness, thinking he could hide behind his reputation, so there was no way he was having exclusive access to the unreleased CD. No chance. There wasn't much I could do for Greg's parents, especially as I'd made the decision not to tell them about their grandson, Jay, but I could help them control their son's legacy in a way they were comfortable with. I was grateful Don had been able to persuade Robinson to handle it my way.

'My price, Joe. Remember?' Don repeated.

We looked each other in the eye. I nodded. 'I know.'

I held my hand out for him to shake. He took it. I'd promised I wouldn't involve Sarah in any more of my cases. Things had gone too far and that was my cross to bear. Our partnership was over. I understood that. Times were changing. I said goodbye and started walking towards my car. Julia sat in the passenger seat, waiting for me. She was blowing her nose into a handkerchief. This wasn't what she'd come back to Hull for. We hadn't spoken directly about it, but we didn't need to. I promised I'd take her to the train station once we were done. I looked at my watch. It was still early, but I was willing to bet my brother was up and about. I smiled to myself. Maybe I'd drop in on him when I was done. He'd know what I should do next.

You need more. You don't know how to get it, but your fire for music is returning. Your fire for life is returning. You've made a lot of mistakes. You've denied your son. You need to make amends. You demo countless new songs. Kane calls you. He thinks the time is right for a New Holland comeback. You're not sure how to react. You can see the possibilities, but you're not sure. You're back on an even keel. Sort of. You know what you want now. You have the strength. What's bothering you is what's always bothered you. Priestley. Kane tells you that things have changed. Time has passed. Time is a great healer. It's a fresh start. You're still concerned. But you want your band back. You all meet in an anonymous rehearsal room. It's awkward, but you've taken the first step. You and Priestley circle each other warily. You rehearse. You both agree to give it a go. You try not to argue. You try not to pick at old sores, but you need to assert your authority. You can't help yourself. You know what you're like. You talk to a journalist you used to know about the reunion. You know it might all fall apart as easily as it came together, but you don't tell her that. You're still wary of Priestley, but you don't tell her that. You don't trust yourself, but you don't tell her that. You take a deep breath. You have to do this. You can do this. You smile to yourself.

A new start.

Lightning Source UK Ltd.
Milton Keynes UK
UKOW02f1306070916

282414UK00001B/12/P